The Blue-Eyed Butterfly

a novel inspired by true events

SHARON SUSKIN

Jan-Carol
Publishing, Inc
"every story needs a book"

The Blue-Eyed Butterfly
Sharon Suskin
Published August 2024
Second Printing January 2025
Little Creek Books
Imprint of Jan-Carol Publishing, Inc.

Front cover images:
Painting: Claudette Watson;
Woman © Upslim/Adobe Stock;
Butterfly © Suns07butterfly/Adobe Stock

ISBN: 978-1-962561-32-7
Library of Congress Control Number: 2024943818

You may contact the publisher:
Jan-Carol Publishing, Inc.
PO Box 701
Johnson City, TN 37605
publisher@jancarolpublishing.com
www.jancarolpublishing.com

To Mama,
I am indebted to you for trusting me to share the stories
so that your words will carry to others who have fought "the good fight"—
those who have lived worthy, happy lives, in spite of their circumstances.
I continue to feel your love and presence.

The Blue-Eyed Butterfly

Author's Note

Locked in silence. During the early to mid-1920s, women were forced to keep silent about domestic violence, unwanted pregnancies, or sexual abuse. They were hidden or sent away, but mostly, they stayed with no relief and no way out. As blankets of extreme poverty lay upon the Appalachian Mountains, women's mental and physical survival relied heavily on their will to live.

This book is based on true events of three women living in a time when there were no shelters, no crisis center, no groups to meet with, or counselors to call to help heal their troubled dreams or the scars that took root in their souls. Their circumstances forced each woman on a journey of brutality, resilience, love, and forgiveness, and united them in ways they could not have foreseen.

Callie was strong-willed and determined. Her home was in the hills of East Tennessee, where her mother died with the birth of another sibling. Lillian, a young girl of eighteen, grew up in the western mountains of North Carolina during the Great Influenza Epidemic that took her father's life and left her mother and sisters anguishing in poverty. Lydia, who had been briefly abandoned during the beginning of her life, tried to fit in with her new surroundings, though her appearance was strikingly different from Callie. It was Lillian's love story that brought the three together and led to a blueprint for endurance and survival.

Callie

1917

The flames were fading to embers, and the night laid heavy on my shoulders, carrying a weight of which no child should be asked to bear. Failing to anticipate the shrill sound that pierced my tender ears and eventually my broken heart, I reached for the poker and angrily jabbed at the blackness of the fire, sensing the miseries that were coming. I sat motionless, gripped with fear, until only a flicker remained, and without thought I threw another split of wood on top of the smoldering cinders, daring the flame to die. Dread twisted my gut as her pleading screams exposed her helplessness, causing tears to pool in my eyes and spill down my frantic face.

Before the creak of the door sounded, his voice bellowed, and I shot off the chair.

"You lazy piece of shit!" he shouted. "Git me some water."

Now, I knew I wasn't lazy, because Mama had taught me a lot about managing the household. I cooked and scrubbed the cabin floor on my hands and knees. The garden rows were clean. The weeds were hoed out almost as soon as they broke ground. I looked after the young'uns and pretty near did everything she did.

Papa, with his dark brown, crinkled eyes sunk in a face of weathered skin, scowled. There had never been any attempt to hide his feelings beneath that haystack of burnished beard. Now his roughened hands flailed like a scarecrow in the garden, trying to keep the scavengers away. I knew when to mind my own business and keep myself from his reach if I could. Anger and frustration

3

raged within his soul on this night when the death angel slipped through the cracks of our home, snatching life away from us and stripping Papa of his persistent control.

I grabbed the bucket and flew out the door. My tattered nightgown and bare feet were accustomed to the wind, although it whipped around my legs as cold and calculating as a queen bee's deadly sting. The dry season was upon us, and we started rationing water from the cistern last month. I pumped the handle and prayed there would be enough to lessen Mama's fever, and soon the weighted pot challenged my strength. One last boost, and I hooked the slopping water pot over the fire, spilling so slightly a little on my garment.

As I ladled the boiling water into the bowl, a chill passed through the warming room, and awareness perked every part of my soul. Silence slipped in and stole the air out of my breath, and my eyes glazed over, numbing me to the blistered burn on my hand. But I continued to carry the pan of water toward the still-barred door. It was of dire importance that I delivered the water. I could save her.

Papa stormed out of the room, oblivious to my presence. The smell and sight of the bloodied bed overpowered me, lurching me backward. Her eyes were closed, but the steady rise and fall of her chest offered new hope that she would survive the birth. Her newborn boy lay swaddled beside her. Still! His soul had left him before he could start living. Mama had already born my three older brothers and two younger sisters, who slept soundly in the attic.

Mama slept too, and I gently wiped the beads of droplets from her forehead. They laid like dew, which had settled on tender leaves after a throbbing sun had scorched them. I tried to absorb every part of her face as I remoistened the thread-bare rag, then wiped down her arms and legs so I could remember her and her teaching us how to be good to each other. My finger traced every line in her face, as though following a map, showing a person direction on which way to go next. Then I followed the edge of her hair, down her cheeks, toward her lips, which uttered no message.

Whispering to her, I touched her so gently, "Mama, tell me. Tell me what

I'm supposed to do next." But she lay there, unmoving.

The door snapped open suddenly and forcefully like branches loaded with ice and snow, causing me to catch my breath in a hold. Papa staggered back into the room, smelling of stale whiskey, and blabbering words of ill-temper.

"What are you doing in here, you sorry…Git out! Are you trying to kill her?"

"No, Papa!" I shrieked. And I ran, leaving Mama alone with him. I stumbled to the attic, where the others slept, and huddled in the darkest corner, unable to suppress my sobs of hopelessness. Somehow, I knew she would be gone before the rooster's crow.

Earlier in the night, Hazel had awakened from her fitful sleep. She was seven years old and almost as tall as me, but skinnier than bird legs.

"Why didn't you call me?" she asked. "You're always trying to do everything by yourself." Hazel was soft-spoken, but the tenseness of the night enveloped an urgency and impatience that we all felt. She begged to see Mama and promised not to cry. So, I relented and allowed her to do so. We crept into the room where she lay quietly. Papa was pacing on the porch like a mountain cat cornered in a cave.

He had never been a compassionate man. Whether he loved Mama, I couldn't say for sure. His needs were unimportant now. As Hazel reached out to touch Mama's trembling hand, she fell into a heap on the floor. I carried her limp body up the steps to her waiting bed, tucking her next to Rachel. A mop head of black curls lay tousled around her four-year-old chubby face. Our older brothers Peter, Baxter, and Stanley lay asleep in a bed on the other side of the room. The only privacy we all had was a quilt thrown over a line, dividing the space. The attic showed no mercy for any human.

I then slipped back to Mama's bedside. Her eyes fell away as I warmed my cold hand against her feverish brow. She slept for a while, and when she awakened, she tried to speak, but no sound came. Her eyes were covered with sadness, and I was afraid. The sips of cool water I offered, quenched her parched mouth, but the quiver on her lips forced me to turn my head away, for fear that she would see my desperation and longing for her. She must have known her fate as she drifted into a restless sleep again. I pulled my chair closer, watching her chest rise and fall. I willed my breath to the same rhythm, praying that I could breathe more life into her frail body.

There was no doctor. No midwife. No money. I kissed her cheek and said, "Mama, don't leave me. I need you."

But this morning, sadness and despair ruled over the cold. My own will was broken, ladened with grief. They had taken her now soulless body before daybreak. All that was left of her and her baby were the blood-stained bed sheets that were witness to a ravage of pain that bound them together.

* * *

The wildflowers lay heavy against one another, sprouting among cracks and crevices, undeterred by a passel of rocks that had owned the land before Papa. I drank in their fragrance as I carefully gathered each one. There was still a crispness in the air; spring was nearby, waiting, teasing us into believing winter storms had passed. I gathered my shawl around me to fend off the bite and walked on toward Mama's grave. It had been a long, unforgiving year, but we had pulled together. Life in the country was hard and brutal, drudging out a living, with few farming tools and little money. A meager existence was eked out of the unrelenting ground. Now, Mama didn't have to worry about harvesting the field, canning, and the daily care of the children.

I brushed off the dust that had clung to her tombstone and placed the flowers at the base. That had become my responsibility, along with pacifying Papa, impossible as it was. I sighed, told Mama goodbye again, and headed toward home.

At first, the neighbors came by, bringing freshly made meals and sugar cakes, but no one came now, because of Papa. He ran them off, saying he didn't need their charity. However, at the supper table, there were only biscuits or cornbread to eat and milk from our cow, to drink. Sometimes, Rachel would get the sniffles at night from the hunger in her belly. We never talked about Mama when Papa was around. He wouldn't allow it. I followed his command when, in the solitude of our bed, Hazel and Rachel would cry out, longing for her.

"Hush," I ordered. "It doesn't do you any good to talk about her. That won't bring her back." Whimpering, they would fall into a tumble of nightmares, cradled in my arms, while my thoughts of her holding me the way she used to gave way to exhaustion from the chores of the day.

Rising before the morning sun dried the dewed windows, I gathered wood from the porch as I had on every morning. Hazel and Rachel, blanket wrapped tightly around them before the warmth came from the fire, screamed with both fear and delight when the wood popped and sparked, tossing an ember at their feet. While I went to the smokehouse to cut off a slab of bacon from the quarter of a pig Uncle Haynes had given us, the boys scuttled off to gather some eggs. Outside, I could hear the roughhousing between the three of them, but as soon as they reached the back steps, I could almost feel their backs straightening, and quiet composure ensue. Papa didn't tolerate any nonsense. His critical tongue and well-worn belt often flailed to the boys and occasionally us girls. Mama had always been our safety net from his ire. Now, there was no one.

Once a month, he hitched Jack, our old mule, to the wagon and rode into town to buy flour and feed. When he was away for the day, I would make sugar cookies and treat Hazel and Rachel to them. They giggled with delight, and after they finished, they chugged down a tin cup of milk. On one occasion, I cut a piece of sackcloth that I had saved, tucked a ball of twine underneath, snipped a small length, and fashioned it to appear as a head. Then I sewed buttons on for the eyes and nose. I hid those makeshift dolls behind my back, taunting them to guess what mystery I held. They squealed and sprung to their feet, grabbing at my arms to see the surprise.

"Git back," I said, "and I'll show you." They snapped back to attention. Then, I thrust the ragged dolls toward them, and they clasped their hands to their cheeks, astonished that they had a treasure to cherish.

"Now," I told them, "you must tuck them away, upstairs under your pillow. Papa mustn't know." They nodded their heads, still in disbelief. We loved each other and they respected me. That brevity of happiness would be my last, for years to come, with no thought in mind that anyone would need to care for me.

Our ramshackle home had provided one room of privacy, with a sleeping space for Mama and Papa. Not counting the open loft, which we referred to as an attic, the main room below served as our gathering place. It was filled with a faded couch, the arms well-worn from previous families, which had been given to us by Uncle Haynes. A rough-hewn table and chairs sat near the makeshift kitchen where shelves were nailed to the wall, holding a few chipped dishes, alongside a cast iron skillet and one pot. The boys often played marbles on the floor at night with Rachel and Hazel horning their way in, and Papa eventually swatting their be-hind. I sat, mending a sock in front of the fireplace, in Mama's rocking chair, longing for her presence. Those were ordinary nights since Mama left us. But tonight was no ordinary night.

The boys lay snoring in their beds, their heads stuffy from colds as I offered Rachel one last sip of water. I tucked her in again and returned the glass to the kitchen. Papa had retired earlier, but now I saw a glimmer of flickering light between the cracks under the door.

"Papa, are you alright?" I asked, leaning closer, putting my ear close but not willing to knock.

"Come in here," he replied calmly. It was unlike him. He was sitting on the side of the bed in his dingy nightshirt, which I had washed so many times with lye soap and was shed of any whiteness which remained in the cloth. His hair and beard, left unattended since Mama had died, lay intermingled as one tousled mess.

I learned never to show fear to Papa, because when he raged at the boys, they tried to show courage. But their eyes failed them in their weakness. Now I stood alone before him, in my nightshirt, too. Vulnerable. Did I let it show? My eyes didn't waver, but my heart pounded while I, standing there, scolded my heart for betraying me. Surely, he could hear!

"You're staying with me tonight," he commanded.

"No, Papa, no!" I began to scream before he could clasp his tobacco-fumed hand to my lips. Everything I had taught my heart and mind vanished.

"Shut up," he whispered in my ear as his burly hands lifted me onto his and Mama's bed. "You're going to do as you're told."

I tried to leave. Truly, I did! But I didn't cry. I wouldn't let myself. It was the only control I had. I lay there that night, defeated. When I was certain he had fallen asleep, I slipped out of his bed, hating him, and climbed to the sanctuary where Rachel and Hazel, still innocent, lay.

I held them closer than ever before, weeping, knowing that I had relented unwillingly to Mama's place in Papa's bed. At morning's light, I still lay awake, dreading the sight and sour smell of him again. But there was no hiding place. To everyone else at the breakfast table, it was just another day, but my heart was hardened, and silence and anger brewed inside. Darkness would come too soon and snatch my sanity once more.

The nights were his, and the walls within held a secret. A secret my feet were unable to run away from. A secret that ripped my soul. Now, he had also taken Mama from me, for I could no longer bear a visit to her grave. I was ashamed because she knew.

Lillian

The stench of death permeated homes and graveyards. It was 1917, and I was barely eighteen, living with Papa, Mama, and my sisters.

Hopelessness, an unwelcome intruder, lived in towns, as well as the countryside. It affected both the rich and the poor. My papa and five-year-old sister lay gravely ill for days, with consciousness ebbing and eventually claiming another two victims. Trees were cut, planed, and nailed, shaping the wood into a coffin, one for Papa and one for Lila. Neighbors and family members often bartered to pay. We, on the other hand, had nothing to barter. All we had to offer were our hands and feet, to work off the debt, clean homes, or sell baked goods. Papa and Lila had been buried on the cemetery hill. With snow brushing our chapped faces, Mama, my sisters, and I mourned our loss. Few family and friends came, distancing themselves for fear of the same fate. Now, we had to set aside our grief and survive and make a living any way we could.

Word traveled through the hills and hollers, of gossip and tragedies, but good news also trickled through as well. We heard that the Youngren family, who lived a good day and a half night's walk away, needed a housekeeper and a keeper of the children. Without hesitation, the day after we heard, I quickly pressed the best of my two dresses, twirled my long black hair neatly into a bun, pinched my cheeks until the skin flowed pink, and headed down the dusty road.

I left by the light of the full moon, as it was still ordering the stars about. It lit my way. By the time I arrived at mid-noon, two other older women of ages whose wisps of hair had started graying around the curve of a woman's face were standing just inside the foyer, waiting their turn. Their hands were empty, but I had taken the time to make a caramel pie, knowing my young age would be held against me for lack of experience. I hoped to show Mrs. Youngren that I could cook. When they saw my basket, I quickly thrust it behind my back. Their wistful faces frowned, realizing they had not taken advantage of the moment. I turned my head away, pretending not to notice their displeasure.

Each one, in turn, was questioned and left without satisfaction. I dared not meet their stare as they left, keeping my eyes downward toward a loose thread on the sleeve of my dress that I fiddled with. Now I had to step forward and prove myself to be more efficient than the others. But leaving that early without breakfast caused my stomach to churn and growl like a starving animal. With the pie still in hand, I thrust my elbows toward that noisy beast. So hard that it stopped complaining, just as Mrs. Youngren approached me.

Graciously, she invited me into the parlor and offered me a seat.

"And what is your name, young lady?" she asked.

"L-Lillian," I stuttered. The hairs on my arms began stiffening, and my hands started to shake, losing my self-confidence.

"May I offer you a drink of water?" She must have noticed the color leaving my face. A brief nod was all I could offer. She returned with a glass of sweet tea instead.

"I thought you might need a little sugar. Did you have food today?"

I sipped on the tea. "Yes, ma'am. I had a full breakfast."

I had no habit of lying, but before my tongue could be tied, that lie just slipped out. She didn't challenge me, and I wasn't about to admit I had used near the last bit of flour and sugar for her. Now, I wondered if she thought me such a weakling that I wouldn't be able to do the job required of me in her household.

"What do you have there?" She looked down at my hands clinging to the baked good, wrapped in cloth. I had forgotten it was still in my possession.

"A caramel pie for you," I said.

"Did you make this?" she asked, taking it from me.

"Yes, ma'am," I answered. She smiled and thanked me.

"How thoughtful. It smells delicious. We will serve it at supper tonight. Come with me, and I'll put the pie away while I show you the house."

Although she had born eight children, which was not uncommon in the hills, her porcelain skin had been spared the sun and wind of the harsh winters. Mr. Youngren had been able to provide for her and his family, more comfortably than most. We, along with all our other neighbors, had heard of him and the log mill, which he owned. It was thriving in a destitute community. And so far, they had been spared the fever and death that surrounded the rest of us.

The two-story home, a white clapboard, resided on a knoll a distance from the town. The wrap-around porch beckoned to summers of rocking chairs and lemonade and ladies with handheld fans cooling the sweat on their brows. With eight children, every inch of space was used, both upstairs and down, as I noted when Mrs. Youngren showed me their home. It was clean as a whistle, with finely carved furniture gracing each room. She took me upstairs where large rooms were fitted with beds, three beds to a room. The youngest, she said, was still being held in a crib in her and the mister's bedroom.

"But our oldest boy, Hugh, sleeps when he's here on the third floor. Says it's nice and quiet. He works hard and deserves it. Won't take you up there now. He's sleeping. Getting ready to go on a big trip for his papa. He'll leave at daybreak tomorrow and won't be back for a while."

Before I could ponder on the steps to the third floor, Mrs. Youngren turned purposely, asking, "And what experience have you with children?"

I responded easily, "My younger sister, who recently passed...I helped Mama care for her since birth, and I cared for her when she fell ill with a fever. I know when a child is starting an earache or the stomach is swollen with waste. I know how to get rid of both. We never had a doctor, so we learned to heal ourselves with the herbs we grew. The fever was too much, though. I understand that the fever was too much, even if we'd had the doctor's medicine."

I wondered in that moment if I had said enough, or too much. But she nodded, and we walked on, ending up in the kitchen.

"Five of our older children go to school," she continued. "They are responsible for their care. But pack lunches, only for the three youngest. After the older children have left, the younger ones, even though one is four, need attending. I will be taking them out during the day to visit relatives, and while I'm gone, you will have time for household chores. As you can see, there are always things to do. Sundays are for church. So that would be your day off. You can either stay here," she pointed to a room off the kitchen, "or go home to your family. Oh, but please prepare something that I can heat quickly. Do you have any questions?"

"No, ma'am," I replied, suddenly realizing she was offering me a place in her family.

Mr. Youngren had fetched a driver to return me to my home, where I collected some belongings and returned the following day. It was the uproarious and chaotic environment that unsettled my former solitude.

I eventually was able to put a name to a face, except for one, the oldest, who was away from home. Four girls and three boys, not including the one I hadn't met. I savored the early morning's stillness, kneading dough for biscuits, popping them in the oven, and then sipping strong black coffee, while they baked—a reprieve from the rest of the hectic day.

There was never a doubt when they woke, for the shuffling footsteps and creaks from the ceiling gave them away. They ran and stomped and rattled the stairway, trying to beat the others to the kitchen.

"Hmm, something smells good," they said as they clamored for a seat that they knew wasn't their own. The mister and missus followed closely behind them, correcting the bad behavior.

"Children!" the mister said. "Stop with your rowdiness this minute." That's all it took for them to straighten their backs and stiffen their lips.

Two weeks passed quickly, and the family's kindness and patience, while learning their ways, had been comforting. Tickled toes and smudged cookie faces rewarded me with giggles and grins, momentarily forgetting the impoverishment and sadness that I left behind. My relief, not without guilt, came from knowing that my sisters and mother were fed from the money I was able to send. Work was so sparse that neither had found an offer to help provide.

Mr. Youngren, in his graciousness, demanded the children respect me, and when necessary, obey me. He left soon after breakfast, his back a little stooped, pulling on the same black hat that hung on the hall tree. Shades of sandy blond hair protruded from underneath, still giving him a youthful glance of his earlier years, though the brutal seasons of sweltering heat and the blighting cold had gnarled his fingers. His pointing finger was missing on the right hand, caused from a moment of distraction while feeding a piece of wood through the saw's blade at the mill. At least, that's what the oldest girl, Evelyn, whispered to me when he left one morning. I often saw him wince in pain, and in the evening, Mrs. Youngren would prepare a liniment for his comfort. And yet, the mill was all he knew. What he wanted. Even though he was the owner, it owned him, and the toll on his health was evident.

While serving supper, I couldn't help but overhear the comings and goings of their lives. A confrontation at school, and an ensuing fight with another boy, had left the middle boy, Aaron, with a black eye. A light reprimand came from Mrs. Youngren to avoid such childishness, but a stronger response came from Mr. Youngren on how to defend oneself. The children "eyed" each other with a smile or a nod, depending on whose side they were taking.

But there was also news of illness and death from other families. The flu had not claimed a death in this family, but it had ravaged two of the younger children, Mae and Shirley. Fortunately, they had survived.

March held an aloofness, tempting us into believing it was spring. I cherished the nights in my room, squirreled away, hearing only my voice, reading from a borrowed book in their library. A welcome escape to lands I would never visit. Stories that were unimaginably told. Although I had little education, reading would be my gateway to learning. My dreams lay within each page. On this particular day, the sun streamed through the windows, spilling onto the floor and warming my cold, soap-drenched hands. After each meal, another meal lay discarded in bits and pieces on the floor. The remnants of sticky molasses dissolved as I scrubbed on my hands and knees. I hummed a song that Mama had taught me, although I couldn't recall the name of it. Engrossed in my daily task, I brushed a wisp of hair from my face, all the while suddenly aware that I wasn't alone. I looked up and was so startled that I knocked the pail of water over, flooding the floor, and trying to stand slipped in the soapy mess. I knew instantly who it was.

Mr. Youngren usually left talk of work on the front doorstep, casting the ill temper of the men aside. One night, though, I overheard him comforting the missus about their oldest boy, who had taken an order of lumber up north. She expressed concern that the trip was too long and dangerous for an eighteen-year-old, but he put his arm around her and reassured her that he had proven to be responsible and dependable, showing leadership at the mill.

Now, in the doorway, stood a tall spit of a boy, casually leaning against it, with legs and arms crossed. His tousled sandy hair was slicked back, head lowered, peering through blue eyes that pierced me like a paring knife. Not only his presence but his self-assured posture rattled me into an undignified rag doll, my flopping arms and disjointed legs grasping for a table, a chair. Anything of substance. But instead, he had eloquently as a shooting star at midnight caught my flailing body. As quickly as he had caught me, I pushed him away, flushed and disheveled, my heart pounding. But he stood smugly, as though he had captured and rescued a fallen bird. Anger and embarrassment stewed in me like a boiling pot on the stove.

"You must be Lillian," he said, taking the bucket from my hand. "I didn't mean to startle you. What was the song you were humming? I didn't recognize it."

I had already grabbed the mop, attempting to regain what pride I had left, but he had taken it from me and started mopping up the mess that was his causing.

"It was nothing," I said, reluctant to share anything personal about myself.

"Well," he said, "maybe sometime you could sing it for me. I'd like to hear it. You have a pretty voice."

"Thank you," I replied as I straightened the table and chairs, putting everything in order once again. My face was still flushed with heat. I hoped he would leave.

"I'm Hugh," he continued, grabbing a leftover biscuit and a cup of black coffee.

"I gathered," I said with my back turned away, washing the remaining dishes, not taking a backward glance. I scrubbed harder on the skillet where I'd almost scorched the morning gravy. He sat at the table and talked endlessly, as though taking the presumption that he had known me for my lifetime.

"I'm the oldest, you know."

I looked at him, annoyed. "I know."

It was of no importance to him as he continued, "Papa's turning the mill over to me. Well, eventually. He said he trusted me. That's important, isn't it?"

He waited for me to answer. I rinsed out the skillet and began to dry it, turning to him. "It's one of the most important things you can give to a person."

He put the cup down and looked up at me, laying his arm over the back of the chair. "Not only with people," he began, "but also with animals and things."

My curiosity was raised. "What things?" I asked.

"Well, things like the rain will come, and the sun will follow. Sometimes a rainbow, if we're lucky. And trust in hope and love." His words were as warm as mittens on a cold day. His ability to put me at ease unnerved me even more, and when he left, he took the morning with him, empty as a ghost who no longer felt the need to linger. His touch was a memory now, and when he caught me, it ran a fervency through my soul.

Breakfasts and suppers now gave new meaning to casual greetings and stolen glances. He began arriving in the kitchen early before the others awakened. It was there that we talked, and I began to become at ease with our conversations. They conflicted with both joy and fear, and I dared my longing heart to betray me, to any improprieties. He continued to work in the mill, not returning until long after supper. Every night, I left his dinner in the warming drawer and usually was retired to my room before he came home. But when that happened, a knock came to my door, and a whisper traveled through it.

"Thank you, Lillian, for keeping my supper warm."

At first, I never answered, hoping he would think I had fallen asleep. But I'm sure my light slipped under the doorway, and he knew. After a time, I laid against the door when he knocked and answered him. "You're welcome."

He stood there for a moment before his steps faded away.

Ever since the first time I saw him, I could feel him watching me, even when I couldn't see him. He would come home for lunch now, instead of eating in town. And he lingered at his papa's desk, writing proposals and figuring costs for the mill. He sometimes labored over that the entire afternoon. But when Mrs. Youngren left with the younger children in tow, he put aside the business at hand and returned to his mischievous ways. I had become accustomed to his shenanigans and was unable to suppress a squirrelly smile when one was loosed.

It was when he stood straight above me in the barn's loft that I let out a squeal worthy of a piglet's voice, grabbing the milk bucket before Josie the cow kicked it over. Hands on my hips and scolding words on my lips didn't faze him as he jumped down. He belted out a laugh and took the bucket from my hands. My legs weakened and my arms fell to their sides when he placed his hands on my shoulders, taking a moment to feel the tremble in my arms. Then, cupping his hands to my face, he leaned toward me, his lips soft as newborn skin. They touched mine, and I lost all sense of reason, my mind spinning, blurring reality. He pulled me to him, and I wrapped my arms around him, my longing for him undenied. Lost in the moment of loving him, wanting him. I stepped back, breathless, my body weighted with his touch, not knowing what to say. Fear paralyzed me as my head snapped toward the open barn door that someone saw us. But no one was there. Only a wayward chicken in search of her brood.

"Wait, Lillian," I heard him say as I ran toward the house. But I didn't dare look back, my heart in a twitch of confusion.

If I wasn't in the house or barn, he knew where to find me—on the knoll, under a sprawling oak tree yet bloomed, not caring if the sun had warmed the earth. Book in hand. Or the time when I snuggled my face between freshly washed sheets, smelling the sunshine within them, when he, in a moment of surprise, crept behind me, seeing only my feet between the hangings, and pulled the sheet off the line, wrapping me in it, and with a swoop, bound me, helpless, covering my mouth with his hand, so the tortured sound would not arouse any suspicion. And times when he took his fingers and closed my eyes, allowing his hand to glide down my face and lips. I would bite him playfully until he released me, us tumbling to the ground. He tickled me unmercifully.

His intrusions became welcome, and I often lay my book aside during my reading time and listened to his dreams and ambitions. Touch became painful as our hearts longed for each other. His kisses burned when my tears became salt, knowing he would soon be leaving. I wondered, lying in bed at night, two floors above me, if he was awake as well in a rumble of thoughts fighting against each other. I wondered if I should leave.

* * *

As early spring warmed the hillsides and fresh blooms fragranced the meadow like fresh linens on the beds, the new earth left me with a thirst unquenched. Blackberry winter had lavished the briar patch with fat, plumped-up berries, and my bucket was brimming over. Jam would adorn slices of homemade bread.

Now, he had been gone for some time, but the missing of him was no easier. The night before he left, he beckoned me to join him at the porch steps to say goodbye. By now, we had stolen moments of conversation in the barn, when I gathered eggs in the morning. He had searched me out on the hillside, gathering berries, and came to also gather and talk. His laugh flowed like a cool mountain stream, and one time, I pricked my finger on a briar. He took it in his hand and wiped the blood away, then kissed it. I drew back, frightened and unsure of his touch, and ran for fear my strength would betray me.

So, I joined him that night on the porch steps, one last time, my shawl wrapped tightly around me. "I'm going to miss you, Lillian," he said, simply at first. "But I'll be thinking about you every day and every night." He took my hand in his, and I let it lay within each finger, wrapping them together.

"I-I..." I began, but before I could reply, a light came on from the second floor. I jerked away and ran to the safety of my room. It was when I heard his footsteps and the screech of the stairs that I knew I would not see him again for a spell.

Life became simpler when Mr. Youngren sent Hugh up north to open a new logging mill. He had been gone for some time now, and I had mostly tried to put aside thoughts of him and delve into matters of the house. Spring cleaning was upon me, demanding extra attention. And of course, gardening. I loved the beauty of the outdoors, especially after a brutal, unrelenting winter.

May turned the children free of school, like bear cubs from a den. Wails of skinned knees from skinned cats on a hefty tree branch shrilled daily. The hayloft became a fort, defendable by both girls and boys. And screams chilled our bones with the arrival of a snake or two, spotted by the children. But the summer was not wasted on frivolous play for the entirety of the day. Mrs. Youngren placed responsibilities in their care. On laundry days, most of the girls, depending on their age, helped me tote the sheets and hang them on the line. She sent them to the kitchen so that I could teach the girls to bake.

I liked having them with me, all floured-faced and sticky, with doughy fingers. It was certainly more of a mess to clean up, but they pitched in, uncomplaining, and helped me. My love for them was, in turn, rewarded back to my waiting heart. The boys cleaned the stalls in the barn and weeded the garden, approaching both with more than an ounce of grumbling. But after the work was finished, afternoons were quiet, with naps for the younger children, and in the parlor, the older girls and Mrs. Youngren read a book that had been pulled from the shelf.

The older boys rambunctiously sought out other boys from neighboring farms to wile the hours away. Mrs. Youngren occasionally dismissed me for a few hours of personal reprieve, on those days. So, I often took a basket of fruit, usually a hand-picked apple from one of their trees, a slice of ham left over from breakfast, and a smidgin of bread for my lunch, and walked to the top of the hill. Spreading a blanket under the tree I now claimed as my own, the lopping hills lay before me with soft meadows that stretched out like a young woman's hair until the distant earth blended with the sky. The gentle breeze caressed my face as I closed my eyes and permitted myself, for a moment, to feel the touch of Hugh's hand on mine. To allow myself to miss the discomfort of his eyes following me across a room.

The last time we had spoken, the morning he left, I was upstairs smoothing linens and tucking quilts over feathered pillows, when he quietly slipped beside me.

"Lillian," his voice was but a whisper. I turned to face him. "I must go help Papa, and the time of my return is uncertain. But I can't leave without telling you how I feel. I have fallen in love with you."

I stepped away but held his gaze, unabashedly invading the depth of his eyes, searching for the trust we had spoken of, afraid to let him know that I loved him. When his declaration went unanswered, he turned, and at the door's edge, I whispered, "I love you, too."

But he had not heard me.

* * *

The commencement of summer offered remembrances of summers past. And the children pleaded with Mrs. Youngren to take them down to the brook. She would not oblige but was willing to entrust them to my care if I was willing. Gladly, I accepted, bare feet racing to the stream, I took the children among the tall oak trees, where the water flowed over velvet pebbles and rocks snatched rays of sunlight.

Mary and Hank, the eight and nine-year-olds squealing at the first touch of the frigid stream, didn't let that dissuade them from attempting to catch polliwogs. As I waded in with them, the cool fresh water soothed my weary feet. And I too chuckled when the polliwogs brushed past me, in an attempt to escape a young child's grasp. It was on this day that, with dress hiked up and feet balancing on unsteady rocks, I looked up to see Hugh, with a broad smile and a swayed step, walking toward us. My heart leaped, and if the children weren't there, I would surely have fallen into his arms.

They instead rushed to him, him teasing and throwing them like a sack of feed over his shoulder. We were all delighted that Hugh was home. "Come," they beckoned, "we want to show you what we've found."

But he, instead, walked toward me, steel blue eyes engulfing my thoughts and fears. "Lillian, it's good to be home."

I smiled and said, "Yes, Hugh, it's good that you're home."

The warmth of his smile was like hot chocolate on a cold day, soothing and inviting. I spread the quilt on the edge of the bank and sliced the watermelon that I had tucked in my basket. Mary and Hank were ravenous, and with sweet juice running down their chins, they mischievously spit seeds at each other, and us. We ducked, bobbing with near misses. Laughter splitting our sides was as sweet as the melon. It was a perfect afternoon. But it was fleeting, and the children begged to walk farther upstream, hoping to capture some elusive, slimy lizards.

"Just a little ways," they pleaded.

"Alright," I replied. "Just ten more minutes." Their enthusiasm led to a competing hare race, and off they ran.

Hugh and I sat on the bank, dangling our feet in the frigid mountain stream. He was quick to speak of wheeling and dealing, to acquire more logs and transfer them to the mill. One night, he said, two drunk men got into a fight. Money was missing from a satchel, and before he knew it, fists were hitting both air and jaws. One had barely missed him as he jumped out of the way. Not realizing I was holding my breath on every word, he reached down, cupped a hand of water, and flipped it in my face. I gasped, him bursting out with laughter.

It had been a tall tale, and he was pleased with himself that I had succumbed to his wicked humor. And I, on the other hand, feigned anger until he slipped his hand in mine, brushing each fingertip with his, warming my quickened breath, wanting him, knowing that he wanted me.

"Lillian, each day I was gone, I couldn't stop thinking about you. When the days were cold, the memory of the kindness in your heart warmed my nights. When I felt discouraged, I was heartened by the remembrance of your smile." He leaned closer, pulling me to him. Our lips parted, and I could smell the sweet scent of his breath.

"Look what we found!" the children shrieked in unison. I leaped to my feet, flushed and embarrassed that I had lost sight of the children. They, in their adventure, had not seen us.

Hugh left again the next day, but not before making a point to slip down the back steps, into the kitchen, before the rest had awakened. He told me, laughingly, that the kids had scared the wits out of him yesterday. I giggled, "Me too," putting my hands to my flushed face.

"I have to go back up north, but I'll be back in two weeks," he said. "There have been some problems with the new foreman I hired. I heard he doesn't show up regularly, and when he does, his breath of alcohol could light a torch in the entire encampment. Will you be here when I get back?" he questioned, searching my face.

"I'm not sure," I replied. "As you know, your mama and papa are taking the children to visit your aunt this week, and I'll go back home. I may stay a little longer if I'm needed there."

"Well…" Hugh stopped, unfinished, creaking steps acknowledging the near presence of one of the Youngrens. And with a quick brush of his hand on mine, he was as a wind before a summer storm. Gone. Words left hanging in the air, unspoken and unknown.

* * *

I lifted the last child to Mrs. Youngren, as she tucked the hem on her coral blue dress inside the rim of Mr. Youngren's apple-red touring car. He, in his pinstriped suit barely constraining his robust belly, was impatiently adjusting his frame to the slick black seat on his newly acquired transportation.

"Hurry up," he proclaimed. "We're going to be late."

He wasn't usually an anxious man, but the trip was meandering up the mountain and the new automobile was a proud possession to be presented upon arrival to Aunt Millie in Hot Springs. Mr. Youngren made several pilgrimages to the town throughout the year, bathing in the mineral waters to soothe his knotted feet and hands.

"Here you go," I said as I handed the child to her. I waved goodbye and sauntered back up the steps.

The house was as quiet as the absent breath of Papa and Sis. A chill left me shivering, although the air was stagnant, and beads of sweat trickled down my back. Mrs. Youngren had asked me to stay, knowing Hugh wouldn't be back for another two weeks, way beyond the time they would return. Sometimes, people would wander up the winding driveway lost, asking for directions. She curtly supplied them with the information they needed, turned heel, and left them standing. She didn't put up with any nonsense if she thought there might be suspicious characters nosing around. I assured her that I was not uncomfortable staying by myself, squaring my shoulders back to further assert my confidence.

She eyed me wryly but said, "Alright, but if you need me, here is Aunt

Millie's telephone number to ring me up. And you know where Mr. Youngren's shotgun is." We laughed, knowing I would never touch a gun.

It was only a few hours after breakfast, dishes washed, dried, and put away, when I scooped up gathering baskets. The garden was busting with pole beans and corn for canning, and cucumbers for pickling. I was able to convince Mrs. Youngren to use a small portion of my mama's secret pickling recipe, along with hers. My grandmother had long ago taught me and told me of her secret. Just the name itself was wrought with curiosity: Plastic Pickles. Sweet and crispy. Transparent.

I thought of Hugh. Could he see through layers of my aching heart, unable to hide the transparency of the love I felt for him? I suddenly rolled from my knees to the bed of dirt, blaring a most unladylike roar of laughter. I had just compared my love for Hugh to a pickle, and most certainly a pickled situation.

My fingers played over the keys of each book's bindings as I walked freely along the library wall. Each book was there for the taking, waiting for me to pluck the knowledge that lay within. I was giddy playing games with them, as though they were alive—yes, alive, and taking me with them, drawing me to their truth. I closed my eyes, twirling, pointing, and walking slowly to the one who was willing to move out beyond the others.

Ah. History! My love of history would carry me throughout my life. If only my dreams could be realized in a classroom. For now, though, I settled with my book into the armless rocker on the back porch until the streaks of sunset, hanging like hair ribbons, dulled my sight. Dusk had come. I checked each already locked door twice, as I had every night. The lingering heat lay stubbornly in my bed, tossing me from side to side until I relented and opened the window. Years of rain had warped the frame, and with multiple tugs I took the stick lying on the sill to prop it open. The lace curtains welcomed the breeze, waltzing them in and out while the choir of field crickets sang. Their harmony lulled me to sleep, my companion book opened beside me.

In my dream, I felt a glimmer of light washing over my face, flooding the room, then quickly vanishing. My grogginess was unable to determine if the light or the absence of light had awakened me. But, with a rattle of the front doorknob, I sat up straight as a stick, as though implanted ferociously and as abruptly as a tornado marking its territory. The light wasn't from my dream but from the lights on a car, which had driven up the driveway. Now, the shotgun that I knew I wouldn't shoot lay ceremoniously propped in the back of Mr. Youngren's closet, a milestone away from my racing heart.

I grasped the covers, mind unfocused, ears straining for guidance to stay or gather the courage to slip down the hallway to retrieve the weapon. I could hear the intruder outside, walking cautiously, deliberately, grunting as though he were demanding the window to rise. I bolted, silently creeping between doorways, stopping to see a shadowed figure unflinchingly jimmying the window frame. I crawled down the hallway and grabbed the gun. The barrel was cold and clammy, not unlike my hands that gripped it. Trembling like a rain-soaked dog, I braced myself against a corner wall, my chest heaving, trying to push away the faintness in my head.

Then, the release of the window, which had separated me from the intruder, slid upward. I swiveled, shotgun raised, pointing directly at him. Caught! One leg straddling, like a rider on a horse, between freedom and his fate.

"Stop!" I yelled, figuring if I scared him, he would, in a panic, run. "Or I'll shoot you right where you are!"

Startled, he jumped, hitting his head on the raised window, and howled from the pain. "Lillian," he groaned, "It's me, Hugh!"

It was a miracle the gun didn't fire, because I dropped it, darting to Hugh's aching head. I was confounded with anger and fear.

"What in the Sam Hill do you mean scaring me like that?"

He could only moan again, and I relented to sympathy. "I'm so sorry, Hugh. I thought you were a burglar." I returned with a cool, wet cloth, caressingly placing it on the back of his head. "But you scared the moth out of the wool, and me as well!"

"I'm sorry, Lillian," he offered, apologetically. "But I didn't think anyone would be here. Somewhere along the way, I lost the key to the house."

I helped him to the kitchen chair. He continued, "I know I wasn't supposed to return until at least another week, but I need to get some of the men from the mill and take them back. They have the experience I need to train the other men, so I'll only be here a few days."

I listened intently, and I fell into the realization that I was alone with him for the first time, standing uncomfortably in my nightgown. I stammered, "Well, I…I'll leave in the morning, since you're going to be here, until your family returns."

He protested that I could stay, but I insisted, knowing that although the house was hidden from the rest of the community, I would be putting myself in a compromising situation if word got out that he was here. We said goodnight, and behind my closed door, sleepless, I sat on the window-sill, watching fields of stars, flickering like lightning bugs, directing lovers to find their way into each other's arms.

The cool night air gently lifted the sheerness in the curtains and wrapped themselves around me, and I breathed in the fruit of the dew. I had started back to bed when a faint, hesitant knock sounded at my door. There was no need to answer, and I stood waiting in the middle of the room as Hugh opened the door, then swiftly walked toward me, a robe pulled around him, his body still moist from bathing.

His hands cupped my face, and he lowered his lips to mine, brushing lightly, then hungrily. I returned his wanting. His fingers were lost in a maze of my tangled hair as he kissed the nape of my neck and then lifted me to the suppleness of our waiting nest. The tenderness of his touch swept me to a passionate love I had never felt and the security of his body to mine. We fell into oblivion, then slept peacefully entwined in each other's arms until the first beams of light filtered through the window.

He rolled lazily toward me, brushing a strand of hair from my cheek, kissing my forehead and each closed eye. I breathed deeply, eyes fluttering, then focused on his smiling face.

"Good morning," he whispered in my ear. "I'm as hungry as an unfed man after working the harvest."

I suppressed a peal of laughter, thinking that the hunger he had last night was not of food.

I made his favorite, pancakes drizzled with honey instead of maple syrup. We sat in the kitchen that morning, him teasing me, taking swipes of honey from the bowl and precisely planting it on my nose, then pulling me to his lap and playfully removing it with his kisses. I shrieked as the children had done in the water, on another day. Our passion became unbridled, and we acknowledged it in our comfort with each other as he carried me, once again, to bed.

"You must let me go," he whined a little as he lay beside me.

I propped myself up on one arm, nuzzling the center of his throat, laughing, "Sir, you are not bound as the thief that I thought you were."

He grabbed me, tickling every vulnerable prickled nerve. I had no right to and would not ask him to stay. His business matters had to be taken care of.

But he, for some reason, took Chestnut that morning instead of his motor car. Mr. Youngren kept one horse, as brown as brown can be without calling him black. He stood muscular and tall, and far-reaching as midnight. They used him to haul wood for the winter and plowing in the spring. The older children often rode him bareback in the summer, bringing him back wet. Most often I brushed him down, double stacking wood crates to reach the upper limits of his back, rewarding him with an apple for not high-tailing away in a gallop. Though he carried himself proud, his temperament suited the children's unrestraint.

I had not actually seen the path Hugh took to town after he kissed me goodbye. I started the dough for the bread but added extra salt in a moment of misplaced reality and had to start over again. Now, there was no place in my thoughts to question his reasoning, riding a horse instead of taking the motor car, for I drifted back to our morning of love and the bliss of peace it had given me. It was midmorning when he returned, sheepishly sauntering into the kitchen, closing his eyes, whiffing in the smell of my freshly made bread.

"Hmmm, that smells so good," Hugh said as he enclosed his hands around my waist, turning me around and lightly kissing my dusty cheek. I smiled with unmasked eyes, drinking in each touch.

"Were you able to line up the men you needed to take back with you?" I questioned.

He took my chin and tilted it up toward the devilish twinkle in his squinted blue eyes. "No, I didn't," he teased. "I didn't go into town. No one is going to know that we're here together. No one knows I'm here."

I searched his face. He continued, "Pack the bread, some fruit and jelly as well. I'll cut some slices of meat from the smokehouse. Pull some rough clothes together. Enough for two nights away. Pack a blanket."

"Why?" I asked as he put a hushed finger to my lips, silencing my quizzical stare. Obediently and excitedly, I complied. Chestnut was waiting in the barn, saddle dressed and saddle bagged, hoof scratching the scattered hay, unusually restless, as though he knew the opportunity before him.

I, with no presumption, left with Hugh mid-afternoon. The wheat fields gracefully swayed, pulling us to the retreat, past the meadow, to the knoll far back where the birds sang, and a flip of a quilt gave solace to the day. I sat, cross-legged, book in hand, under the giant acorn-laden oak tree. Hugh stained my lips with wild berries we had stopped to pick along the way. Unable to withstand a book that competed with his affection, he took the book and lay me back, and our bodies melted as one. The lull of sleep washed over us, my head laying on his chest until the dew began to gather.

"We must go, Hugh," I cautioned. "It's getting late."

"No," he smiled, gathering our belongings and packing them on Chestnut. "We're not going back tonight. Papa has a cabin two miles yonder among the forest, long deserted by his father before him. We're going there."

He rode Chestnut hard, with me, arms anchored around him, my hair now loosened and whipping around my face, leaning into him with both fear and exhilaration as my companions. It was dusk when we arrived. The surrounding towering oaks shadowed the cabin, becoming a silent partner in our quest for solitude. I now knew where Hugh had gone in the morning. The splintered wood now lay, waiting for a burst of light from the fireplace. He had swept the dust-filled floors and tidied the wrought iron bed with a long-forgotten, tattered quilt. Wild black-eyed Susans adorned the creviced wooden table. And he lit the wood before he took my hand, as I stood speechless before him.

"I love you, Lillian," he uttered softly, the flickering light reflecting off his face. "The first time I saw you, you reminded me of a songbird with a broken wing, haunting me day and night, resonating in my head, confirming each day that the sound of your voice had captured me, wanting to come to you." He bent down and kissed me passionately.

I whispered, as he laid me down in front of the bustling fire, "I, too, have loved you from the moment I saw you. I saw you in the shadows of night, and the pools of water during the day. I knew, surely, as you brushed beside me in the mornings that you could hear my heart speaking to you."

Arms interlaced, we fell asleep. No want of hunger could fill the satisfaction of our professed love for each other.

My last conscious sound was the hoot owl, announcing to the night creatures it was safe to frolic in their forest home before I nudged closer to Hugh. Now, a trickle of light showed through the glass of two tiny, rippled windows, and I tucked the covers over my shoulders and reached out to Hugh, only to find him gone.

The withering fire left a chill during the night, but now the fire had fresh logs and a roaring blaze. I had not felt him leave our bed, but I knew he would be back soon, so I hurriedly grabbed the dented, rusty-handled bucket and gathered water from the nearby spring, the same one Hugh had led Chestnut to yesterday. The squirrels scampered from tree to tree, squawking at each other in disapproval of stealing each other's acorns. Yet the stillness drowned out their grumpy nature and the air felt cleansed of the laboring heat back home.

I turned, with a water bucket in hand, straining to hear the unnatural shrill sound that whipped around trees, bouncing from bark to bark as though each one offended and unwilling to accept the intrusion. I tried to harness that intrusion, without success, until I saw far beyond the trees, at the edge of the forest, Hugh with a shotgun slung over his shoulder with a floppy object tied to the end. As he walked closer, I could see that he was holding a dead rabbit over his head, as proud as a preacher winning a lost soul on a Sunday morn.

"Breakfast!" he shouted.

I laughed uncomfortably, "I've never eaten rabbit before."

"Well, today the adventures are just starting," he roared.

We licked our fingers, having devoured the roasted meat Hugh had prepared.

"More," I said, running my tongue over my lips.

"Of me," he laughed, "or the rabbit?"

"Of course, the rabbit," I teased, as he lunged forward, me anticipating his every move as he tried to catch me. I clung to the table's edge, moving my body from side to side, wickedly taunting him until I pretended he had captured me. Playfully, he backed me onto the bed, hovering over me.

"I would love to keep you here just as you are all day, but I have other plans for you," Hugh said as he kissed each word onto my face.

When Chestnut heard the creak of the cabin door, he whinnied in anticipation of our newfound freedom, prancing in place, unable to stand still. Hugh lifted me, leaning over and, with one hand as I cowered and jumped, planted my fanny in one swoop to the back of the saddle. We rode languorously until we reached a steep hill, and Hugh dug his heels into Chestnut's sides.

"Hold on and lean forward," he ordered, as Chestnut labored to reach the top.

My fingertips clenched Hugh's taut belly, trying to find some softness to hold onto. As we reached the top of the knoll, I was wonderstruck at the sight of the meadow below, bursting with yellow goldenrod and orange milkweed, swirling with pinks and blues of which I had no name for. When God took His hand and made earth, after he formed the animals and the humans, when He created the flora and fauna, He must have dropped His pallet and brush in this spot, creating a plethora of woven colors, swirled and dipped with glints of gold in-between.

The billowing wind lifted the sweet aroma to us, around us, bathing us, as Hugh urged Chestnut along the winding slope. We strolled through the meadow, Monarchs and eastern tiger swallowtails feeding in abundance, while honeybees controlled the frenzy. We lay among the tall grasses, near a rock bed that cradled phlox and butterfly weed. We leisurely pulled off hunks of bread and dried meat, feeding each other until food no longer satisfied our hunger for each other. The warm afternoon sun and the intermingling whiff of sweet scents cast a spell, eyelids heavy, and we relented, drifting as an empty boat on a windless lake.

I recall, as a child, seeing the clutch of a rattle in my baby sister's hand, and I knew, in my aroused sleep, the sound of the seeds in the rattle. I squinted my eyelids tighter, not knowing if I was dreaming or on the throes of reality.

"Don't move," Hugh whispered in an attempt not to startle me, "and don't open your eyes."

My heart quickened, and I spontaneously opened my eyes. The Timber Rattler was poised on the lowest rock near me, head high, body coiled, proudly shaking his tail in warning. Hugh had slipped behind him, unnoticed.

I jerked backward, as his venom-filled fangs lurched at me. Hugh grasped the back of its head, paralyzing any attempt to snag me. I can't remember if I uttered a terrified scream before blackness lowered its curtain. But I recall trembling uncontrollably, and Hugh holding me, telling me I was safe as my senses aroused and the spinning in my head slowed.

I tried to shake off the discomfort that had crept into our perfect day as we headed back to the cabin. But the terror I felt had robbed me, holding me captive as my body lay listless on Hugh's back. Chestnut planted each step nimbly as we retreated from the field, now hushed by the fading sun. We rode in silence, winding back up the mountain, the gentle wind caressing us as a mother lovingly rocking her baby. But it was the distant grumbling of thunder that perked our ears, and simultaneously the clap of wind rushing past us, warning us, snapping crackling tree limbs as though they were bones, that caused Hugh to turn Chestnut.

He reared at the sight of the roils of churning clouds, dark as a closed grave, looming menacingly, charging as though whipped by a fiendish tail. The thunder within bellowed like a wounded bear, lashed by another's claws, while golden branches splintered and threw themselves at the outcast, spilling across the sky. The lightning struck without care, charging a tall oak we had passed moments before. The ferocity shook the ground, smoldering the tree with the stink of burnt wood. Chestnut reared again, frightened.

"Go, go," I said, pushing Hugh urgently. With no further encouragement, Hugh commanded Chestnut to run, unbridled, until the storm turned, seeking another victim. I clung to Hugh, revived and grateful.

The last snippet of light guided our arrival at the cabin, and he lifted me, taking me in his arms.

"Hugh, you saved my life today. Thank you."

"Don't you know that I was as frightened as you, knowing that I might lose you?" he gently scolded. "Now, go wash up. I'm fixing supper tonight."

I obliged and walked down to the stream, a spit bath cleansing the salty mixture from my body. The stare of death I had faced, and thanks to Hugh, I had overcome. My heart filled with love, and I longed for the night to come when I lay by the firelight in his arms once again.

By the time I returned, Hugh had found an old iron pot and was tossing wild oyster mushrooms we had harvested the day before, along with some chopped-up meat, over the open flame. I wasn't familiar with the enticing aroma, but I was ravished and ate accordingly.

"Be careful," Hugh warned as I bit down on a tough, sinewy piece. "There might be a few bones I missed."

I nodded, not stopping until I skewered the last piece of meat. "By the way," I questioned nonchalantly, "what kind of meat is this anyway?"

With a sly smirk and one eyebrow raised, Hugh proclaimed, "Why, that's rattlesnake!"

* * *

My face scrunched up into a grimace, as the twitch on my nose became more annoying. The night before, a fly had slipped through the doorway, and I swatted the varmint with the tail end of a rag. Evidently, he had escaped death and was now determined to torment me. With a deep sigh, I reluctantly opened my eyes.

Hugh lay, one arm propped up, twirling a stray feather, wickedly amused at my discomfort. I wailed, grabbing the pillow beneath my head, and pounded him into a fetal clump, with him begging me to stop.

"Uncle," he lamented. "You're trying to kill me."

"And you, sir, are trying to drive me insane," I defended.

He rolled over, entrapping my hands above my head, pleased that his strength had overpowered me. My body lay limp in submission, urging him to kiss me, and he lowered his body to mine. Swiftly, I reached low to the groin and tickled him. Bravely and unexpectedly, he fell like a stag crippled from a hunter's bullet, onto the bed, releasing me from his snare. Retreating, I swung the door open and ran, nightgown gathered, searching for a hiding place, only to be caught unmercifully in his arms. I screeched with laughter, scampering squirrels to the safety of skyward branches and field mice into a panicked flurry under rotten tree trunks. The reprieve gave us a moment to forget that this was our last day together. Tomorrow, the family returned. It was unspoken among us but hanging as stale, musty air too obvious to ignore.

Hugh saddled Chestnut after breakfast and directed him toward the steeper mountains. As Chestnut steadily ascended the narrow, winding trail, the smell of pine mixed with decayed leaves and a floor of moss latching to helpless trees, wafted our senses as a labyrinth of foliage lay heavy with moisture, clinging to hair and skin, bathing us in its humidity. Along the narrow path, Hugh dismantled a spider's intricate web with a sword-like stick as the low-hanging branches lay in wait to dismount us.

I didn't care where he took me as long as I could share my life with him. Our time, in its brevity, would carry remembrances of him, in his absence.

"We're almost there," Hugh assured. The mountain had suddenly flattened into a sublime, grassy knoll, brimming with pink and white, bell-shaped clusters of rhododendron blooms, mystically titillating our every sense. I breathed deeply, drinking in the enchanted aroma, which reminded me of sun-kissed linens draped over our freshly made beds. We were encapsulated in the forest, cocooned in our fantasy of love. Now, I knew where the summer birds went to cleanse the dust from their wings.

Hugh lifted me from Chestnut's weary back. "We're going to need to walk the rest of the way," he said, kissing the salt off my drenched forehead.

The terrain had changed, and now huge, menacing boulders loomed above us, and weather-beaten faces seemed carved into the stones, their searing eyes following. The clop of Chestnut's hooves broke the deadpan silence around us as we wound around the cave-like enclosure. I edged closer to Hugh. Suddenly, Hugh stopped.

"Listen," he said. The nearing roar, like the tumultuous grumblings of nature's forces, spread mists of steam along our path. As we turned the corner, a cascade of plummeting water, rainbows dancing within, was framed with jagged rocks, and wildflowers straining between carpets of vibrant green moss. It erupted, like a fluid curtain of unpossessed anger, only to fall into the tranquility of a sleepy pristine pool, which reflected stars of glinted sunshine. Guards of rocks corralled the elongated pool spilling into a gradual decline below. Unspoiled and untamed, the waterfall left my heart racing.

I whirled around, and Hugh had already stripped off his clothes and, butt-naked, made his way into the water. "Come on!" he shouted, and I, too, freed myself from the intrusive clothing and dove into the lukewarm water, coming up alongside Hugh.

"How did you find this place?" I questioned, giddy with the intoxication of this serene paradise.

"Papa took me hunting years ago," he said. "I was just learning to shoot, and I wounded a deer. We couldn't let the deer die alone. So, we tracked him and found him here. His body was still warm. We dressed the meat and laid the carcass among the trees so other animals could eat and survive."

For a moment, I was sad knowing that an animal had been sacrificed in my Eden, but the swift splash of water in my face and Hugh hungrily wrapping his arms around me snapped me out of it. "Let's catch some fish," he laughed.

"How?" I replied. "We don't have any fishing poles."

"We're going to catch them with our hands," he assured. Camouflaged salamanders scurried as we swam to the edge of the bank and the glassy water exposed speckled trout as they wriggled past, lightly brushing my ankle. My nervous giggle and dancing feet hastened their departure. I bent down, ready to attempt a catch, only to lose my footing and tumble, arms flailing in desperate discomposure. Hugh stood, laughing at my misfortune.

"Here," he said, reaching his hand to mine. My embarrassment swam away, trailing the fish as I took his hand and he pulled me to him, his hands slick with water, gliding his fingers through my hair and down to the curve in my back. Our lips parted lightly as he kissed me. He lifted me and laid me down tenderly, searching my face as a roadway to our souls. Our passion ignited and released our desires, holding tight to time, to this day and not turning back to the world we must face.

We ate ravenously from the trout that Hugh caught and swam underneath the waterfall, then floated holding hands, drifting, lost to the world until hints of shadows and a whispered breeze infiltrated the alcove.

"We have to go back," he groaned as he backpedaled to land. It was past sunset when we reached the cabin again. Hugh curled his arms around me, intertwined within the darkened walls, and we succumbed to sleep without the hunger for food, but only the affection of holding and comforting, not knowing when we would be in each other's arms again.

Hugh and I awakened at the snort of Chestnut, as though he knew the haste of the waning day. Without words, we gathered our belongings and saddled him as he stood patiently waiting for us.

"We'll come back someday," he said as he turned our stead forward. I didn't answer but laid my head on his back, my arms around his waist as he nudged Chestnut to go. When we reached the rise above the homestead,

Hugh stopped, comforting me. "Don't worry, everything's going to be alright."

We put Chestnut in the barn, brushed him and fed him. Then, Hugh came to me, his hands caressing my face, and holding me securely in his arms. I began to cry.

"Don't cry," he said tenderly. "I will head over to Uncle Harry's in Mt. Airy, since it's on the way down from Virginia, and visit for the day. I'll arrive back here near sunset. Pick up my men and return to the mill up north the following day."

I nuzzled my head to his chest as he held me close, and in a breath, he was gone.

It was late afternoon when I was sipping on a glass of lemonade that the silence of my wandering daydreams was broken, and I heard the spit of gravel slung from the tires of Mr. Youngren's car as he approached the house. Quickly after, the chatter of their children burst through the front door.

"We're hungry," they said in unison.

"Well, ask your mother if you can have one cookie before supper," Mr. Youngren said.

They broke a gallop and rushed her just as she broached the foyer, almost knocking her off her feet. She relented, and after the family had settled in, I set the table and laid out the meal. I had freshly baked bread, fried chicken, fresh garden vegetables, and a sweet cake, all waiting to be devoured.

It was as Hugh had said and planned. I was drying the dishes when, later in the day, he swaggered into the house. The children wrapped their arms around his legs in glee, trapping him in an encumbered gait. I snickered as I stood in the doorway. Mrs. Youngren scolded the children to loosen their grip.

"Hugh," she said, "I thought you weren't coming back until next week."

He relayed to her the need for more manpower and the ensuing employment of more men to satisfy the demand. "I'll be leaving in the morning," he explained as he glanced over her shoulder toward me.

Melancholy and wistfulness became unwanted companions, but I could only rely on the hope that we had stored in our souls. Someday soon, Hugh promised he would announce his intentions to his parents.

"Would you like some supper, Hugh? Lillian can heat a dish for you."

I turned away, my cheeks warmed with blush just by the nearness of him. "Yes, ma'am," I replied.

As the children were scuttled off to bed, I set the plate of food before him. For a moment we were alone again, and Hugh whispered, "Come to the barn at daybreak, my love."

I shook my head, afraid to speak. But insistently, he retorted, "I'll find a way."

Perched on the leaves of the willow, even the katydids' raspy love songs hummed in mournful unison as I lay awake, wondering if Hugh also lay tortured in the same addled thoughts, like my own. Sheer exhaustion finally released me into a fitful sleep. It was there where I found myself standing alone on the hillside, my eyes shuttered to the light, that I lifted my face to the warmth of the sun, and I sighed in contentment. But then, in an instant, a dark cloud came and caught me up in it, tossing me about. Hail began to plummet me, and I laid down like a newborn baby curled inside its mama's womb. The whimpering became louder, more hopeless, crying out, waking myself. The taste of salt moistened my lips and ran down my face as I sat up in bed. My breath came uneasy, and my heartbeat pounded wildly. I heard the hail against my window, and in my confusion, staggered to the window.

But it was Hugh standing there, pebbles in hand, beneath a still sky. At the sight of him, I ached for his hands to take my silent storm of tears and toss them away. But he was there, in his boyish demeanor, motioning to me.

"Come!" he demanded.

"I can't," I protested weakly. But he was persistent and helped me over the windowsill, holding my hand as we ran to the barn. He led me to the hayloft, slid the upper door to one side, and then pulled me down beside him so we could watch the night go by.

"Look," he motioned. And he took his hand, spreading it across the sky. The stars twinkled in their leisure, weaving their magic. "If we can't say goodbye in the morning, then tonight is ours."

I began to speak, but he quietened me with his lips to mine. A lingering kiss, full of contradiction with moist, calming dew and surging fire. We lay in each other's arms through the night until a cloud shadowed the moon. A warning that our time had passed. We walked back to the house in silence, his arm around me and my head on his shoulder.

"I will miss you, but when I return, I will go to Papa and Mama, and your mama as well, to ask permission for marriage." He stopped, facing me, holding me in his arms, and lightly kissed my forehead before he lifted me across the threshold of my window. Our hearts had spoken of love, often to each other, but tonight the last touch of his fingertips ran across my lips, catching my breath and taking it with him, as he turned to leave. I hurried to bed, pulling the covers tight around me until I heard the screech of the back door. He had entered the house. It was the sound of two voices that stopped my heart as I placed my ear near the door. The mumbled voices rose in anger. It was Hugh's mama.

* * *

My eyes remained downcast as I served breakfast to the family.

"Would you care for more coffee, dear?" Mrs. Youngren asked as Mr. Youngren placed the morning paper down on the table.

"No, dear. That was aplenty. Seemed a little weak, though, this morning. Lillian, is that the same coffee you usually buy?" he asked.

"Weak?" I replied, only catching a word now and then that lay familiar in my heart.

"The coffee, dear," he replied impatiently, which was most unlike him.

"Oh, I'm sorry, sir. No, it's the same. I must have measured the amount incorrectly. It won't happen again."

The lines on his face softened. But not Mrs. Youngren's, who was studying me like a misplaced stitch on a hem. The shuffle of the children leaving the table broke her fixation, and I thankfully retreated to the safety of the kitchen.

Hugh was gone, leaving me with unperceived knowledge from last night's confrontation. I delved into the household chores before retreating to the garden, hoeing the weeds that persistently invaded, then strengthening the raised beds of tubers. Baby-like cornsilk poked through ears of corn, and I shucked them, occasionally digging an earworm away from its feast. The diversion was welcomed during the daytime, but night left me without concentration, and books lay idle on the nightstand. I stood by the window, yearning for the pebbles to grace a broken silence once again.

Each day melded into another, forming them into weeks. Mrs. Youngren began to accept an unusual number of guests on the front porch. Older women of an age past childbearing, whom I knew were not in her social circles. I served them sweet tea or lemonade, and then Mrs. Youngren dismissed me, sending me to the hillside to pluck any remaining berries. I felt a shiver go up my spine when she said that but shook it off as an ailment trying to get ahold of me.

Then, as suddenly as they came, they came no more. She offered an extra day off, and I gladly accepted, returning to Mama's home.

* * *

Our little holler rarely heard the sound of an automobile. My sisters, Mama, and I were stitching a patchwork quilt when the ruckus began. The car I recognized immediately, though once shiny, was now covered with layers of red clay dust, and the driver, familiar as well, was white-knuckled and gripped to the steering wheel, swerving to avoid the potholes.

I stepped out onto the porch and down the steps to meet him, in a quandary of his presence. He sat in the car, not offering the welcoming of an open door. Hesitant to look at me, his eyes darted back and forth, and my mind raced like a rabid animal, searching for answers that might be revealed before he spoke.

I swallowed hard and drew a deep breath. "Good day, Mr. Youngren."

He mustered up a tight jaw. "Hello, Lillian. I…I hope I'm not intruding on you or your family." He never gave me a chance to speak. "Well, I'll get straight to the point. Mrs. Youngren and I will not be needing you any longer. And Hugh won't be coming back. He has moved to Virginia."

As frigid as a plunging dip into an April's icy river, coldness rushed like a winter storm throughout my body, unable to speak. A wave of darkness covered me, and I grasped the downturned window to steady my stance.

"I've brought the rest of your items." Mr. Youngren's gruff voice now dropped to a whisper. "I'm sorry, Lillian. There was nothing I could do. We wish you the very best."

And with those words, he removed himself from his vehicle and started toward the house. But I stopped him, not wanting him to see inside how little we had.

"Thank you, Mr. Youngren, but I'll take those."

He tipped his hat and turned to leave but stopped and turned back around, his face flushed. He said, "You were very good to our children, and they all loved you."

For a moment I thought he was going to say Hugh's name as well. But he didn't. Alone, I was left with the bag in hand, watching him turn, and the roil of dust trailed the car, fading like an apparition. They must have known.

Gathering black clouds and flashes of searing light were all around me as I stood there like a sacrifice to God. I welcomed my fate, deservingly. A confusion of rolling thunder carried me back to the meadow, the storm chasing us. But now it was upon me, and even the tears no longer wanted me as they fled down my cheeks. Razor-like rain slashed my heart and emptied it. A voice called to me, but I stood paralyzed, not knowing how long Hell had taken me.

"Lillian!" The panicked screams came closer, and then beside me. "Lillian, come."

May and Sarah, also drenched, directed me as a mother would shelter their child.

"Lillian, it's going to be alright. We'll manage. We always have."

They didn't understand the impact of that day. Not only the loss of my job, but Hugh as well. My quivering body shed profound grief, like layers of skin being stripped from my body, as they tucked me between piles of quilts until the chatter of teeth was silent. It was deep into the night when I awakened to the rhythmic sounds of Mama and my sisters' sleep. Shadows played tag with the moon and moved silently through the distorted window glass, through the checkered curtains, and onto the log walls. I toyed with the hand-hewed chair, mindlessly wobbling the uneven leg, now realizing it was as crippled as me. I pulled my crocheted shawl tighter and stepped into the moonlight, wondering if he, too, was sharing the same sky, where stars winked at us and carried our whispers of love to each other. I leaned back on the roughened railing, not willing to leave him until the dawn silenced their communication.

It had been three weeks since I received the ill-fated news. I slowly regained strength and acceptance of my and Hugh's failed romance, when I heard May wail, "Lillian!"

She was waving a postal item. "It's for you." Breathless, May climbed the embankment, handing me a postcard. My heart throbbed in anticipation.

I read aloud, "Dearest Lillian, my days are empty without you. I now know that you aren't working at the house due to Mama's dismissal. Please forgive me. I take responsibility. Rest assured that we will be together, my dear. Lovingly, Hugh."

I closed my eyes and lay my cheek against the written words that had touched his hands. I smelled the cardboard paper, as though I might smell and taste the essence of him. He gave me hope. I leaped to my feet, drawing out paper and pen.

My dearest Hugh…

Our letters united us again, and on the same day of the same week, I perched myself on the porch step, waiting and watching for the postman.

Words shared on paper placed us next to each other, read over and over until the imprint of my fingers lay embedded, as though pressing into him. But it was on that day, the day when the postman ran late, as though he knew he carried a morbidity of which he wanted no part, that he came.

"Hello, Miss Lillian," the postman said as he lowered his head and handed me the mail. He had read the message, and the cloak of truth lay unveiled on his furrowed brow. My heart plummeted and my wavering smile lacked the earnestness that I had wanted to offer, as I nodded and waved goodbye.

The letter read:

> *Dearest Lillian,*
> *I will be detained in Virginia for another two years. Papa has forbidden me to return until the project is completed. I miss you.*
> *Lovingly,*
> *Hugh*

A shutter of chill came over me as if it had hidden in Hugh's words, only released when read. I wiped my brow and could no longer contain the spasms of nausea that had followed me for days. I had known now since last month that I was carrying Hugh's child.

Hope had wantonly teased me, then turned its head to step aside so that abandonment could slither in. Despair seeped through my veins and dulled my mind with confusion. We would never be together again. Emptiness battered my heart, knowing I would never be accepted. It showed in Mr. Youngren's tortured face the day he came, his hand touching mine as I rested it on the car door.

"I'm sorry, Lillian," he said, apologetically. Surely, Hugh knew as well. I imagined that he would come to hate me, and I would rather bear life without him than look at me in disgust.

My fretting pace only increased my anguished thoughts as I slouched down in the chair with a resigned sigh and wrote the following:

Dear Hugh,
   Time and separation have cleared a pathway for others to enter our lives.
It is with great respect that I free you of any obligations to me in the future.
I will remain forever your friend.
Sincerely,
Lillian

My words were as cold as the frost that burned the embittered wildflowers, but he must believe. A month passed when Hugh responded to the resounding dismissal.

Dear Lillian,
   Is everything cast aside because of my lengthy absence? My heart cannot
believe that you are dismissing our love so wantonly.
I remain yours,
Hugh

Like the farmer's scythe decimating the wheat fields, my heart lay in shreds. His letter went unanswered.

* * *

White bricks of layered snow lay on the ground throughout the winter. Our child within me was all I had left of Hugh, and its kick brought remembrances of our playful wrestle within our now lovelorn cabin. Nestled on my side, I cradled my rotund belly in soothing contentment as I whispered lullaby melodies. I was no longer standing by grasped curtains, peering out the window. Now, hope through our child came again as a ghost not to be trusted. Throughout the frigid winter, we sat by the crackling fire, crocheting a cradle full of clothes, and challenged each other for the best name. Mama was, at the time, distraught with shame that I was carrying a child, but it was only when my burst of pent-up tears released themselves that her relinquished anger encircled me with her motherly love.

Now, the March rain had melted the hardened snow, and it was the first Sunday that the sun was warming newly budded trees. Mama was tightening the garter to her cotton stockings and arranging the only hat she owned, a small black cap with dried flowers on the right side and a touch of frayed netting on the other. The dark blue gloves, the ones she had crocheted during the winter, fit snugly over each finger. Her blue flowered dress, as well as May and Sarah's pink, straight dresses, had been fashioned from the now empty grain sack. Mama taught us to sew on her old treadle sewing machine, and when the flour was gone, a new dress was made for the one that needed it the most.

"Mama," they pleaded, "we're going to be late."

Mama and I had known since last fall that they had set their eyes on two boys, who would be waiting for one of them at the front door. It was a mile to our church, a minuscule walk for country people. I longed to go with them, but my cinched waist dress, long ago, could no longer contain my girth, and the whispers saddened Mama's heart.

"Sing a song for me," I said as I kissed them goodbye.

The white clapboard church swelled to capacity when more than fifty came, sat upon a knoll, and if I stood outside, on my tiptoes, I could see the steeple. I used to be the little girl who, occasionally, was offered to chime the bell. It roared as though God was speaking, beckoning His people. I pulled on that twined rope all the way to a squat, and it carried me, feet flaying in the air, until Mama grabbed me by the ankles, lest Jesus took me right on up to heaven. Before the preacher, white yellowed handkerchief in hand, swiping away beads of sweat, before the warning that the devil was waiting at the door to claim us, we sang the old gospel songs and clapped our hands until the stained glassed windows rattled in their wooden frames. Sometimes even the rafters joined in bellowing praise to God. If I leaned out a little farther and stood, tiptoed, I would be able to see some people I knew walking toward the church door. But the frayed, porch edge crumbled.

I thought it was a dream that I was falling, my fingers slipping from the front porch rail post. But I awoke sprawled like a fattened chicken on the ground. Dazed, I ran my fingers through my hair, searching for the knot and source of blood, that stained my ripped dress. But there was none. Then, the pain trapped my silent scream, arched my back, sliding the dull, hot knife back and forth. As I tried to stand, the oozing crimson flowed between my legs. Somehow, I found myself in ebbs of dreams swirling, with faces vivid and fading at the same time. I heard Hugh's voice calling me but could not see him.

The trailing harmonies of May and Sarah stopped.

"Lillian!" they screamed.

The dream returned, and one voice growled, contained within me. Somehow, I could feel their pain. The others echoed as voices in darkened caves, and I strained to distinguish the sounds. Through the fog, I searched for Hugh, but could only find apparitions. Abruptly, I sat up in bed as a corpse unwilling to be laid to rest. How long I lay in this purgatory, I did not know. But both familiar voices and consciousness returned, pleading with me, "Lillian, you're okay. You have to help us."

Through gritted teeth and clenched jaw, I released myself to God, pushing through the ripping pain until the wail within me laid me down into a bed of peace. There was silence, then her shrill cry. Her breath of life.

"Lillian, this is your daughter," Mama said.

I opened heavy eyes and peered into depths of love, searching each detail for Hugh's reflection. At that moment, I thought I could never love someone as much as I loved Hugh. But she was part of him, and now my heart ached from holding so much love. Hugh would have loved her, and pride would be emblazoned on his chest. As May took her, cradled in her arms, I whispered, "I'll call her Lydia."

Contentment tiptoed into my heart as I drifted into a dreamless sleep.

* * *

In June, May and Sarah married at the Antioch Baptist church, on the same day, to the boys who swooned at their giddiness. The church was filled with parishioners, each one bringing a customary stacked molasses layer cake fried up in their cast iron skillet, with Mama providing the apple butter to hold the wedding cake together. It was a day filled with streaming sunshine through the opened windows, and the smell of violets waifed through the meeting room into an aromatic bath that clung to our clothes. Mama had sewn, with fabric offered by Mrs. Baird, our neighbor two ridges over, new robin egg blue, gingham dresses, with a touch of lace around the bodice, and choked neckline.

I picked wildflowers and bluebells mixed with periwinkles, tying them to a spare strip of lace. With the juice of a wild strawberry, I stained their impatient lips. And I held my breath as Sarah's precarious walk down the aisle might be misinterpreted as dancing. After the ceremony, there were church brothers Clay and Harry, the groomsman, trading bib overalls for suspenders and plain blue bowties anchored to collars of flax seed shirts, who fiddled and picked till I thought I saw the preacher tapping his foot.

It was the happiest day I had felt since the birth of Lydia.

"It should be you, Lillian, the one who's getting married," a busybody whispered in my ear.

"Nonsense," I chastened. "I have Lydia. She's all I need."

She was my joy in my uncertain and tattered world, even though I still sat at night on the porch stoop after Mama was in bed, and Lydia had long ago fallen asleep, speaking to the stars and, in their twinkle, asking them to carry a message to Hugh.

"I still love you," I whispered. "You have a daughter who looks like you."

May and Sarah's departure left us with only the sparse income I had saved. I found work on Mr. Danner's milk and apple farm five miles away while Mama looked after Lydia. The narrow, winding footpath trail crossing the Watauga River, which joined two other streams, was the path I liked the most, nestling me between the mountain ranges. It was the valley of the cross, and it emboldened me with God, giving me no fear. But when the river flooded over the splintered footbridge two hours before sunrise, I walked the cake-hardened dirt road, sheathed with a pasty face of dust, and the wind snatched up swirls dancing unpredictably my way.

The contrast between the two pairs I likened to my life. The narrow path, filled with living creatures and beautiful distractions, often stops me at the hum of a bumble bee sipping nectar like afternoon tea. Or a fawn, suckling on its mother before the anxiety of a fallen branch makes her flee. And trees filled with reds, yellows, and purples in a kaleidoscope of colors, with a gentle breeze of voices announcing the end of a paltry summer. And the other path, a dusty vise of loneliness and despair that can't be shaken off my shoes, a blistering sun with no shelter, and cracked, monotone leaves lay dead or dying from unrelenting pounding rain. The path now led to harvest time and little time for frivolities of self-pity.

When the first frost came, Mr. Danner hitched up the team of horses to the wagon, and with me and Sally Mae, a stout woman with four kids and a husband back home, laying in a daze of moonshine, we waded through cornstalk rows, the crunch of frost still under our feet, picking and shucking the hardening corn, destined for the corncrib, and later, during the winter, food for the pigs and cows. Sally Mae fell off the ladder last year when we were picking apples from the orchard. She lay whimpering when I reached her, and we both knew that she wouldn't be able to work until the swelling in her hand had gone down.

"Please don't tell Mr. Danner," she pleaded. "I can still carry a bucket with my other hand."

No work meant no food on the table for her hungry kids, and a no-good drunken husband who wouldn't work but expected to eat. We worked well together and helped each other. If an apple had been laying on the ground for a few days and a burrowed hole showed a squirmy brown worm within, we stuck it in our pocket and fed the neighing horses by the greying split-rail fence at our day's end.

Now, the harvest was nearly finished, and the apples had been churned into apple butter, canned in mason jars, and sat on the cellar shelves, ready for sale at the general store. Two of the fattest pigs, now slaughtered, lay in a salty brine of water, curing, soon to be hung in the smokehouse until the store patron summoned the need. Our aprons, filled with pig's blood, reeked with stench until we doused them with lye soap on our chapped calloused hands.

The Danners' working farm had provided jobs for boys and men, along with a few women throughout the years, but age and health had determined that Mr. Danner would no longer afford the responsibilities another year since his heartache last month. The milk cows would be taken to market, and only two people would remain.

"What am I going to do? My children!" Sally Mae sobbed, quietly.

I drew her to me and held her, comforting her. "It's going to be okay."

A raspy numbness loosened its grasp from my fear-gripped throat. Casting aside my unforeseen future, her circumstances lay dire before me, and I went to Mr. Danner, a kind-hearted man with weary sheltered eyes, and pleaded to him for Sally Mae.

"I'll do the best I can for her, Lillian," he said. "But are you sure you want to do this?"

With nodded head and pensive smile, he laid in my hands a sackful of potatoes, two jelly jars of apple butter, and a slab of cured ham. I walked away on that last day, appreciative of his kindness but knowing the food may not last us throughout the winter. The fading harvest moon shadowed me along the last two twisted miles, until the distant flicker of Mama's oil-lit lantern hung high on a wobbly porch knob, gently swaying like a beacon, guiding me home.

Deep in winter, the howling wind grew like resentful bitter herbs left too long in the garden, and sprinkles of snow seeped between the crumbling chinked logs. Papa had, long ago, taught us the makings of a mud plaster which we splatted into the crumbling gaps. But now the mocking whistle taunted us, pushing aside my efforts, boasting of the intrusion, and the logs groaned and heaved from baked summers and melting icy winters. We huddled, the three of us, beneath scratchy wool blankets, sharing our bodies' warmth, when the fire faltered during the night. My milk for Lydia was long gone, and the summer's canned garden food was almost empty. The remaining potatoes lay sparse in the cellar, along with our stray cat, Clover, who, after a row with a coyote and now bearing one scarred and blinded eye, feasted on wandering rats.

At Christmas, May and Sarah, along with their husbands, came, now bursting with good news of their growing family. They brought wild turkey, shot by May's husband, Charles, and Sarah brought mincemeat pie, along with freshly made bread, and canned preserves. There was a new shawl for Mama, leather-hewn cowhide shoes for Lydia, and suede gloves with rabbit fur lining for me. And for them, potholders, hand stitched with embroidery wrapped in brown paper and secured with raveling twine. The spirit of Christmas permeated my heart as we laughed, and I savored the good fortune of my sisters. After the last goodbye, the last crumb eaten and the remaining food stored away, with Lydia and Mama tucked in bed, I stood by the dancing fire, and like finely dressed ladies and gents in grand halls, Hugh and I waltzed and curtsied till midnight, and I whispered, "I love you."

In the spring, past Lydia's first birthday, I planted early greens, spring onions, and sugar snap peas. Mr. Baird, an outwardly gruff but inwardly kind man, brought his plow and farm horse to till the ground, along with a belated Christmas gift. A laying hen, for our empty hen house. From my last pay at Mr. Danner's farm, I had squirreled away in a tin on top of the fireplace mantel the remaining coins for seed. My garden would be twice as big, for I would sell the extra at the general store, enough to buy staples and kerosene for the next year.

Mama had gotten consumption during the winter, and between fits of blood-tinged racking coughs and bed-soaked night sweats, I boiled the linens and separated her from Lydia and me, making a floor cot on the far side of the room. Her affliction lingered through the early spring, and I sat her in the warming sun, hoping it would rid her of her discomfort.

By fall, though, I had no hopes of her thriving through the coming winter. The starkness of reality loomed like the dark sheen of a crow's wings in flight.

"I have an extra room," May said, with hands in mine. "Lillian, you've taken care of Mama for a long time. She can't help you with Lydia anymore, and you can't help her and yourself. It's time for me to take her."

My silent tears fell, and the salty brine invaded my cracked and aching heart. I could no longer deny that Mama—or dare I even think, Lydia—could stay with me any longer.

* * *

Orange balls of pumpkins lay waiting in the farmer's fields, along with mounds of hay and corn shocks, tied with rye straw, announcing the ghostly separation into winter. The house, now empty of Mama's loving care and support, rifled me with uncertainty. But Lydia was like the morning glories, a touch of sun unfolding all the possibilities of the day. Her long, straight hair was like streaks of yellow rainbows caught between the piercing blues in her eyes. Some days when I could no longer hide behind a blanket of pretension, she laid her tiny hand on mine.

"Sorry, Mommy," she said with calming assurance. My soul lay cowed of the days ahead as I held her, unwilling to cave to untenable wells of hollowness. Now I knew why May, on that anguished day, looked at Lydia with tears trapped in her troubled eyes. She knew before me but was afraid to say that I could not face losing both so close together.

Summer's harvest had been bountiful to me, providing me with an abundance of pole beans, which Lydia's tender fingers helped me snap, and plump tomatoes, along with Tommy Toes that tasted like honey nectar. I had gathered crabapples to dry and October beans. Also, green, hairy-shelled walnuts from our old walnut tree. All are to be sold, except for our own needs, to carry us through until the next planting.

Occasionally, Charles stopped by with fresh kills of rabbits and squirrels, which I later canned. He always skinned them for me, taking the pelts for May to prepare for a jacket befitting their growing child.

"How's Mama and May?" I asked.

Tipping his cap, he wiped the beads of sweat off his brow with his shirt sleeve. "They're doing just fine. We got your mama to the doctor, and he gave her some kind of medicine that seems to be helping her."

My heart was encouraged. "Please give them my love, and thank you for the meat."

Visits were less often, now that their child was born, and I didn't begrudge their absence, because their responsibilities had doubled, and I would not allow myself a wallow in self-pity.

Mama always said, "Decisions are crossroads, with some having many pathways, but for others, the road may be mired in quicksand and no way out." I determinedly refused to believe that, even though at night doubts came like swarms of locusts rising from the ground.

Mrs. Baird had lovingly showered me with kindness and concern in Mama's absence.

"Let me take Lydia for the day," she offered many times as I was putting up the winter's food. I was grateful for her generosity.

There were no children for the Bairds, an uncommon occurrence in the mountains. Since Mama left, we visited more, her serving warm glasses of milk and sugar cookies she had baked. Lydia licked the sprinkles of sugar off the top before biting into the delicacy, and she played outside, often following Mr. Baird to the barn to "help" him with his chores.

It was on one of those unexpected days that we sat on the porch in rocking chairs, padded with rose embroidered cushions and the labyrinth of crosswinds like looms of honeysuckle threads penetrating our silent thoughts, that she set her glass aside, folded her hands in her lap, and with resigned acceptance said, "I had a miscarriage years ago, the first year of our marriage. And then another the following year."

Her face turned drawn, one tear escaping as memories crept in like gall in the throat, choking and trapping the pain once again. The lines in her face deepened and sagged into aimless pathways. Her silver hair, top knotted and anchored with hair pins, now appeared uncharacteristically unkempt, as of no importance. "After the third, the doctors told me that the risk was too great." Her voice cracked. "I have often wondered if Mr. Baird should have or wanted to leave me, but did not have the courage to do so."

The chair that rocked, its rhythm lost, sat silent. I held my breath, not knowing what or if I should say anything, but wanting to touch her, hold her, but I did neither. "Oh, there's no need to say a word," she said, composing herself as though I may not have heard, or she didn't say. But then, she continued, "I've just needed to tell someone—not just someone, but you. Lillian, you still have directions that the winds can carry you toward. Some may be good and some bad, but there are answers out there. Don't close your mind to them."

Mrs. Baird had never been so open and now, for some reason, maybe her slower walk or trembling hand had hastened her to speak. "Lillian, write to him. Tell him about Lydia, before it's too late," she whispered.

"But his mama and papa?" I asked.

She put a finger to my lips. "He needs to decide to accept Lydia and marry you. Not his kin."

We awakened before dawn, and it was the kind of day that lifted our spirits. A day like a new preacher coming to visit and dinner on the grounds and the laughter of children playing hide and seek. And a day where the autumn sun, filtering through pallets of reds and yellows like mounds of apples, laying in latticed baskets. Cattails loosened their grasp as they floated and teased in mystical patterns until Lydia, absorbed by curiosity, relinquished her frustration of their elusive capture.

After the last heave of baskets and crates brimming with vegetables for a destiny of stew, were loaded onto Mr. Baird's long open wagon, I lifted Lydia to the narrow space tucked between the crosses in my legs, and wrapped my arms around her. Settling beside her husband, Mrs. Baird smoothed her dress, which was adorned modestly with lace around the sleeves and neckline. Not too fancy. Not too plain. And her hat, anchored with a satin tie and formed into a bow, leaned to the right side, so slightly.

Mr. Baird turned with a broadening smile of affection before a click of the tongue and a gentle nudge of the reins, and Mrs. Baird leaned into a light kiss on her cheek, which produced a pink mark of embarrassment. She was all that mattered to him. It was the beginning of a day filled with possibilities and Lydia's new adventures.

Today, we would sell our goods and purchase staple items for the winter, maybe a little fabric for sewing if the market price was good. To her excited applause, I promised Lydia a penny candy. Two stops today—one at the Mast, a small, isolated country market, set low in the valley, storefront filled with competing space for hitch posts and wagons. Then, another hour away at the township, where Mrs. Baird would fondle patterned, cotton fabrics and admire the newest hats in the milliner's window, while I attempted to sell any remaining canned goods.

"Whoa," Mr. Baird commanded as he pulled up to the Mast. The white clapboard doors swung inward, and the potbellied stove's commanding presence sat squarely in the middle. A small fire brewed inside, warming and mixing the air with pronounced repugnance, from plank floors separated by wear and caked with dung, dried and scattered from farmers' boots, like insulation, keeping rats and field mice away. Shelves were half-filled, and by the fall's end, they would be bursting with other farmers' wares. The owner bought half of what I had brought, defending his decision to support other farmers when they came, even though he bought the entirety of Mr. Baird's produce.

My hope remained at the larger store, in the township. Mrs. Baird extended a comforting arm and said, "We'll get the rest sold. If the township store doesn't take the rest, then we'll sell it on the street."

It was just before noon when we pulled underneath the shady branches of the rambling oak tree. After Mr. Baird fed and watered the horses down by the stream, we spread out the gingham tablecloth and sipped on lemonade and ate jerky and cornbread and fried apple pies. Mr. Baird told a joke, which I thought was totally out of character for him, but we laughed until tears inked down the sides of our faces. He was quite pleased with himself at the attention, and I began to see him as the father I once loved.

The bustling township gave Lydia pause, in wonderment, as we watched automobiles mixed with horse-drawn wagons vie for right of way. It was a town on the edge of growth and development, with mixtures of caution and suspicion of change. A town I once frequented several years ago to replenish the cupboards for Mr. and Mrs. Youngren, and beyond the far side, ten miles out, a grand ole farmhouse where Hugh and I had met and loved. With Mrs. Baird's encouragement, I decided to swallow my pride and write to Hugh and tell him the truth, although his father made it clear that day I was not wanted back. But I wrote it anyway and had tucked it in my cloth purse to place in the township postal box.

Dazed in thought, a distant car honked, rearing the two horses and exasperating Mr. Baird. "Damn cars," he moaned. Although a religious man, even he couldn't control his impatience when the two eras collided.

"Ahem," Mrs. Baird said, throwing a glance at her flustered husband.

Unwilling to apologize, he continued, "I'm going to let you girls off here in front of the general store. I'll help you with the baskets. Then, I'm going to take the horses down to the end of town, away from this nonsense."

Mrs. Baird and I snickered. "Let's go sell the rest of your goods," she said.

The Boone general store sat as a patriarch in the center of town. Outside the double doors, barrels were positioned for sitting and watching. Windows displayed advertising signage of tobacco and ligaments, and window shelves boasted dolls and fancy patterned plates and knick-knacks. A stack of newspapers lay on the counter, offering insight, opinions, and classifieds. One section was cordoned off, filled with big bolts of fabric, both cotton and satin and felt, alongside any sewing necessities for a complement to any attire. An aisle ran down the middle, separating the two walls that soared with brimming shelves straight to the ceiling. We had no more than put both feet inside the store when a voice acknowledged our presence.

"Mrs. Baird. Miss Lillian."

We nodded to Mr. Robbins, a jovial man with a limp from a bear encounter on Timber Ridge. Some people teased that the bear got one taste and decided to spit him back out. It was a way of avoiding pity, but instead was a good ribbing, which was of Mr. Robbins' benefit, with him joining in on the laughter.

"I haven't seen you in a while. You've been missed. And who do you have here?" He looked at Lydia, who had flattened her nose to the confectioner's glass case, peering into jars of peppermint twists and horehound candies.

"This is my daughter," I said. Sheepishly, I rubbed away her smudged fingerprints.

"It's good to see you both. What can I do for you ladies today?" His eyes darted back and forth to each one of us.

"I have some items for sale," I finally spoke.

"Well, let me see what you've got, young lady," he said. He followed us outside to where Mr. Baird had placed my produce. He studied each jar, examining the contents carefully. "It looks good, and I'm sure I can sell all of it."

A sigh of relief escaped my lips. "Thank you, Mr. Robbins."

He took Lydia's hand and led her back inside, where he opened the candy case, offering her a penny candy of which she had already spied as her choice. I was thrilled that I had a little extra for lace and buttons.

"Now," Mrs. Baird offered, "I'll take Lydia outside to eat her candy, and you take some time for yourself to look around."

I accepted, gratefully. There was so much to touch and wish for and dream for. I wandered slowly, studying needlepoint squares for formal dining chair seats and crocheted dollies to adorn parlor room couches, and hand-painted rose patterns on china. There were delicate teacups with matching flowered saucers, and I picked one up, imagining me hosting my Mama, my sisters, and Mrs. Baird, with lace tablecloths on the front porch, the wind lifting the hem like a naughty man catching a glimpse of a lady's stocking. I would serve special tea biscuits stuffed with raspberries, picked from bramble bushes on the hillside, and drizzle honey from the comb snatched within the depths of the bee's nest. We would talk of childhood mischievousness and pause to resounding echoes of laughter.

Daydreaming dwindled into a deep sigh of resignation, and I placed the tea set back on the shelf. It was the reverberant sounds of men that touched me on my shoulder, and from beyond the separated aisle, accusations hurled, followed by snorts of laughter that captured me in a silent chuckle, as one man trophied the checker game. Their rowdiness was matched by the strong stench of tobacco and the sound of spittle, airborne, skirting the nearest spittoon. An unexpected contentment covered me with peace like a newborn's swaddled sleep. I picked up the button jar and poured some into my palm, intent on finding the perfect buttons for Lydia's next frock. They were mostly yellowed with browns and dulled blacks and an occasional faded pink, with small, ripped pieces of cloth still attached. Some were cracked, and I eyed them carefully as to size and shape, until…

My focused concentration deafened me to the jingled bell at the opening door. I found three buttons of plain color and matching cloth and set them aside as I began to replace the others in the jar. The voice speaking to Mr. Robbins was calming and familiar, and it somehow prickled the nape of my neck and clutched my stomach, reviving a longing I had pushed aside. Perceptions of flower-filled meadows and pristine waters faded in and out like mockingbirds, taunting. My mind refused to accept both hallucination and presence until he spoke again, and I was able to isolate his voice from the clamoring chatter.

"Where have you been keeping yourself, Hugh? We've missed seeing you in town. When did you get back?"

My heart lurched, and the jar slipped through my numbed fingers, flailing buttons on the shelf and floor.

"We got into town two weeks ago," Hugh replied.

Weakness consumed me, and my trembling hands shook as I struggled to fill the jar. I wasn't prepared to face him now. My letter, still tucked in my pocket, was supposed to reach him first. Words would not form clarity and discomposure lay with me on the floor, on hands and knees.

"Where can I find the buttons?" he asked Mr. Robbins. Panic tossed all reason and thought away as the creaky planks announced my impending presence. "May I help you, miss?" As he extended his hand, I looked up, fear now an unwanted intrusion.

"Lillian!" Hugh remarked, startled. He stepped back as though struck by a precipitous wind. His eyes were still the deepest blue in an endless sky.

He grasped my shoulders, helping me to stand. The warmth of his touch flooded my soul with love. But he released me gently, searching my troubled face, me wanting to pull him back to me, fulfilling memories from days and nights of sheltering in his arms. Nothing else mattered as I stood there, helpless to my crumbled and aching heart. His voice was soft and caring.

"How are you? I-I didn't expect to see you here," he stammered. "It's so good to see you." His eyes softened even more as his smile broadened.

"I-I didn't expect to see you either," I said. "It's good to see you, too. Y-You came back earlier than expected." Nerves gripped my stomach.

"Yes," Hugh said, and his eyes narrowed, wincing. He looked away and back at me again.

"How are the children?" I asked, trying to calm the confusion in my head.

"They're all doing well." His smile fell, and he became sullen. I wanted us to remember the days that we took them down to the creek, the polliwogs, and the slippery rock soakings. And amongst the chit-chat, all the while our hearts reunite to the place in the cabin and the days following, in the breathlessness of our unspoken words, remembering. This was the moment I had dreamed about, upon the first light of day and the first stars of night. I wondered what his parents had told him. I started to ask, but he leaned toward me again, with whispered breath, heart-wrenched and angry, emotional wounds now visible from mixed wisps of crimson among his blue eyes.

"Why did you push me away, Lillian?" he pleaded. "I loved you."

Guilt caused words to fail me. I would never tell him of his papa's visit.

I stepped toward him again, my still trembling hand touching the sleeve of his jacket, commanding my voice to speak. Through pools of darkened waters and cracks of brokenness, I lifted my eyes and looked at him. "Hugh, I have always loved you. There were things I couldn't tell you. Afraid to tell you. That may hurt you, that may hurt us…"

Hugh stepped closer, urgently. "What, Lillian?"

It was the sweetness of his quickened breath close to mine and the nearness of our bodies yearning to embrace, remembering how we loved each other and planned for our future, that I began to say, "Our love will live on forever, because…"

A shadow that swayed and took form, advancing with forthrightness, caught my breath, hurdling me backward like the long arm of an executioner's whip, as it slipped behind Hugh.

"Darling, did you find a button for my coat?" The woman tucked her gloved hand through Hugh's arm. A dark fog of entanglement hindered fantasy from reality, and I stepped back, my heart somehow loosened and pounding in my head. Every heartbeat pulsed, urgent and desperate, like a church bell warning of imminent danger.

Hugh stood tautened, and pallor replaced the blush of our closeness. "Margaret," he said, clearing his throat as though it would cover his discomfort. "I'd like you to meet Lillian."

Without hesitancy, like the last light of a falling star, I grasped a feeble smile, my disarray of composure now unsuspecting as I jutted my chin, extended my hand, and offered, "I'm the one who took care of Hugh's brothers and sisters."

I hoped she could not feel the cold clamor of my hand that had now stiffened my bloodless palm. But she didn't notice. She was happy. Radiant and overjoyed with life. "Oh, yes, I've heard the children speak of you, and how much fun they had."

I lowered my eyes. "That's very kind of them to say."

I knew now how the fable ended, facing both beginning and end like a maddening orchestra of untuned instruments, meshed into unrecognizable speech that rang in my ears as she tightened her arm around Hugh and in her excitement, announced their engagement. Our lives were no longer our own but of different destinies. Unable to push through my anguish, I wished them well, not trusting myself to look at Hugh again.

I heard my name called, past Hugh and Margaret, to the opened door where Mrs. Baird stood, holding Lydia's hand, and I ran to her with no excuse, swooping her into my arms. I did not turn to see Hugh step to the store window and outside to the sidewalk, watching me walk away with his child.

Why had I not noticed at the day's start how it would wickedly fool me? In my shaken stupor, Mrs. Baird had guided me back to the wagon. "I can take Lydia if you like."

But I shook my head, numbed with reality, holding tight to Lydia until the rhythmic clop of horses lulled her to sleep. Dew was already clinging to the stilled earth, and splayed leaves wept as the color leached beneath them, when Mr. Baird pulled the horses to a halt. A sudden chill announced the bittersweet end to fall and the impending start of winter. Now, a needling headache pounded to the steady throbbing in my heart, and with resigned weariness I carried Lydia to the house.

Mr. Baird brought wood in, started a fire, and lit a lantern. I slumped into the chair, unable to withstand another step from my failing legs. Someone removed my coat. Someone fed Lydia. "You have to eat, Lillian," a voice said as I pushed the plate of food away.

Someone put Lydia to bed, then stood beside me, brushing a kiss to my forehead while placing an arm around me, whispering, it seemed...or was it something I imagined?

"Lydia is in bed, asleep. We're going now and will check on both of you in the morning. Try to get some rest, Lillian."

Absently, I nodded to no particular thought.

Now I sat alone, staring past the flickering flames, where the mirror of self-pity flings cinders of despair to my burning flesh. My shoulders curled, arms entwined to knees, as a strangled cry erupted and quaked to pools of gasping sobs. I had failed Lydia. And Hugh. And myself. Moans of agony, like bitter herbs, rippled my battered heart until I heard the soft rustle and call from her. I rushed to her side, comforting her, wondering if she had heard the sadness within me.

"It's alright, Lydia. It was just a bad dream. Mommy's here." And I tucked her around the curve of my body, smoothing her hair from her face, wiping away tears mingled with mine until she once again fell asleep. Her happiness was all that mattered now, and I pulled her closer, drifting in and out of tortuous illusions, taunting me to delve into their precarious world, and I succumbed.

Beguiling quicksand became a pathway leading to an endless road. Along the way, Hugh and Margaret stood, perplexed to see me. On the other side, Mama and my sisters warned me to go back. In the distance, a figure stood, undistinguishable, and speaking without words. There were legions of voices directing me, and in the confusion, I started walking on the wicked sand until I reached near the end. I looked back and suddenly felt the quagmire entangle me in its deceptive snare. I struggled to loosen its possession, but it came alive, and the rankled voice was unrelenting, assured of my demise. In my desperation, I reached for Hugh, hand outstretched to pull me free, but he was no longer there.

I woke with a start, dazed and breathless with anxiety. And I gasped, as a wailing newborn sucking in its first swig of air. The muck-like sweat of my gown clung to my skin. I stripped it off and washed the night from me, replacing it with a fresh but worn-weary dress. I held the mirror to my face, searching for the person I thought I was. But sunken, deadpan eyes like bores out of stone stared back at me. An annoying sun seeped through the tattered curtains, but I turned my face, lifting it to the warmth, willing my tortured soul to accept the moment's satisfying smile that crept in and calmed my heart.

My sweet, cherubic Lydia was still sleeping, and I leaned over and kissed the innocence on her face. Another smile broadened, and I whispered, "I will give you the best life I can. Somehow. Some way."

Bucket in hand, I stepped outside and pumped water from the well. White crystals of frost covered the glade, and a light wind brushed my face like a dusting of voices lifting me from my throes of self-deprecation. Soon the valley would be a raging storm of snow caps and mounds, like defiant clouds that wantonly abandoned their lofty domain. And when the frigid winter came, I hoped it would bury my heartache beneath a crust of icy snow and give me a new heart to feel again, so I could build a life for Lydia and me. Brushing off the chill that shivered me, I threw kindling into the stove. The teapot whistled and I sat down, clutching a warm cup of comfort, stoked the fire, and glanced toward Lydia. She scrambled out of bed, sleepy-eyed, tugging at my dress.

"Hungry, Mommy."

I scooped her up, planting burbles on her rounded belly. Her screeching giggle lifted me from the depths of my sorrow, tossing, for a brief moment, our dire circumstances upon a shelf.

Weeks passed, and the first of December brought a spattering of snow. Mr. and Mrs. Baird came by to check on me twice a week, sometimes thrice, each time bringing a homemade pie or leftovers.

"I always make too much," she protested. "We don't want it to go to waste."

They were such a comfort to both of us. Mr. Baird loved Lydia, and when he came, he brought a book and sat her on his knee near the hearth and read to her while Mrs. Baird and I sat in the kitchen, talking. In a whisper, she inquired, "How are you feeling, Lillian? You seem to have come through the worst. There's color in your cheeks again."

Gratefully, a smile gathered and slipped from my heart to hers. "I'm doing well, and I know that I must plan for Lydia. I don't know what's to become of us, but I will find work in the spring, hopefully farm work, and hoist her on my back, or put her in a basket beside me. I tried to speak with assurance, not letting my gaze falter. But we knew our eyes curtained with the same reflection, hiding the uncertainty.

Mama, May, and Sarah wrote to me every other week. May wrote the following:

> *I hope you and Lydia are feeling well. We miss you very much and hope to see you at Christmas. We lost our prized heifer two weeks ago, but we don't have the money to replace her. We are all healthy.*

Then, Sarah wrote:

> *Lillian,*
> *Mama is improving somewhat, although the cough returns at night with*

great force, and she seems happy here but misses you and Lydia. She said to tell you that she loves you, as I do. We sold all the apples this past fall, but Henry fell out of the barn and broke his ankle. He's in a lot of pain.

I returned with correspondence but could not lay another burden at their feet. It was the words of Mama, since I was a child, and long ingrained in my spirit that resounded and spurred me forward: "God helps those who help themselves."

It was on a frigid Monday afternoon, a day where rays from the sun melted the frost on top of the pond's icy hold, exposing the sheen underneath, and your hand rose immediately to shelter your eyes, which squinted from the reflection. The wind had disappeared, leaving the winter birds to escape their nests for snippets of food, when Mrs. Baird drove the buggy down alone and sat at my kitchen table, twiddling her wrinkled handkerchief.

"Is something the matter?" I questioned.

"Oh, no, no," she replied, avoiding my stare. "I just…Well, Lillian…I'm not quite sure how to say this."

"Go on, Mrs. Baird, you're like a mother to me."

She cleared her throat and swallowed hard. "Well…Mrs. Stump, at church yesterday, passed a note to me and asked that I give it to you. But I'm not sure I should." She shook her head in worry. My throat knotted in anticipation of a ridicule.

"It's alright, Mrs. Baird. I'm stronger now, and I can manage."

She handed me the crumpled paper. It looked as though it may have been discarded, and in a moment's hesitation was unfurled before it became charred wisps of voiceless words. I took it and slowly began to unfold it, glancing at Mrs. Baird's nervous avoidance of my crinkled brow. But, without warning, and most unlike her, she reached across the table and took it from me, holding unwaveringly with compassionate eyes and touch to my now unsteady hands.

"Please, let me tell you," she said as she adjusted her posture. I nodded, suddenly weary. "Mrs. Stump has heard of a man, a widower, who needs a wife. He has relatives who live beyond our township. But he resides in

Tennessee." She stopped, searching my face, allowing me the chance to hurdle the thought in the fire. "Mrs. Stump said he would provide for you. He has a farm and owns land."

I stood, a gesture that silenced her, and turned, gazing out the window, knowing that I had few choices if I was to keep Lydia. Ominous vines splintered the floorboards attempting to creep around me again. My heart quickened, trying to remember the words she had said. I felt hands slip softly to my shoulders.

With agony, Mrs. Baird pleaded, "I'm sorry if I've upset you, Lillian. I know it's been so hard to let Hugh go. But there has to be a way to make a future for you and Lydia. This could be your chance."

There was no one else who had shared my blinding pain as she had. I turned back to her, knowing her words rang true, and wept quietly as she held her arms around me, holding my head to her heart strength, each teardrop releasing the emptiness of his touch, and the sorrowful burden holding the last part of him.

Dear Benjamin,

It has been brought to my attention by a member of my church that you are inquiring about the need for a wife. I must tell you upfront that I have a daughter, almost three. I have never been married. Before there is any more correspondence, I will need to know if this would become a matter of which you would not find acceptable.
Sincerely,
Lillian

The defiance in my tone would surely deter him from continuing with a reply. At least he would know that Lydia was very much a part of my life, and she would not be excluded. The thought of me even considering the marriage proposal, or I should say proposition, to a man of unknown character had left me in a state of utter discombobulation. The letter had laid purposely in a poorly composed book I had read, whose content was so disagreeable that the distastefulness left me with a stomach of discontent. I thought it appropriate the two would be placed together, momentarily, to satisfy the respite from my situation.

A week later, I retrieved the book and its companion, to a quiet, dark corner and leaned hard against the cold wall, surmising where the wind seeped, between weather-beaten logs, and hobnailed its message to my resolute frame of mind and muted destiny. I wondered if Mama and my sisters would approve, or if they would be relieved of worry. Or even if he, the stranger beyond, would even consider Lydia and me. Now, I waited for him to make his choice.

It was nearing the week of Christmas when I heard from Mr. Cordle. His letter timed with a coordinating fluster at the expectant arrival of my family. Lydia sensed the anticipation in my excitement as I hummed Christmas songs to the rhythm of my fingers, kneading the sticky dough. She mirrored my cheerful mood, mimicking words that became trapped between tongue and teeth into a disarray of a newly formed version as she twirled into a circle with frenzied arms, flailing like nimble limbs from young, sprouted trees. After the floured table was cleaned, sweet pieces of bread blossomed, baking in the wood-fired stove. The dough balls, fried crisp and dipped in honey, were stacked like the nest, which contributed to the cunning steal in the tree's hollow. Lydia licked each sticky finger before her departure to the dreams that made her smile in her sleep.

It was then that I opened the letter and read...

Dear Lillian,

Your daughter will not be a problem with our arrangement. I will tell you about myself. I am a widower and have three boys and three girls. Sometimes the boys work in the coal mines, as they are in their teens. The girls are younger, the least is four. They'll give you no trouble. I can provide a good home for you and your daughter. I'm a hard worker. If you're willing, I would like us to get married as soon as possible.
Ben Cordle

Ice sickles hung sharp and pointed from the eave on the front porch. Words of love that I had previously cherished were now replaced with cold indifference. But I did not expect, nor did he, a reply of familiarity. At least we were moving forward into a suitable arrangement for both of us. Although I announced my forthright decision to Mrs. Baird, the thoughts of marrying this interloper laid as intrusions of panic beside me in my overcrowded bed. Now, Christmas was only a few days away, and I bundled Lydia to face the winter's prick of thorns and guided her to the cedar that I had been eyeing throughout the year, just large enough, above my five-foot frame, to serve as a Christmas tree this year.

"Stand over here, Lydia, so the tree won't hit you when it falls."

But she protested in despair. "I can't move," she cried.

I picked up my snow girl and brushed the powdered white from a nearby rock. "Sit still and watch Mommy," I said, tweaking her red nose into an upturn, ignoring her pouty lip. I lifted the bruised axe and swung it, with accomplishment, wood chips in flight like wingless birds. Each maddening chop released my pent-up exasperation until the tree was freed, and in exhaustion, I fell sprawled, teetering between tears and laughter. Lydia came to me, desiring to fall into the mixture and we rolled like chipmunks scuttling on a spring day down the hill, into that momentary valley of peace, together.

Dragging that gift of Christmas home, Lydia straddled between the prickly branches, providing great annoyance to her, all the while I was laughing until the split in my side loosened its grip.

The sound of my laughter had slipped so far away that I had forgotten the taste on my tongue and the touch on my skin, like water squeezed from mountain rocks on humid August days, and the smell of freshness cupped to a parched face. Now, the Indian corn I had saved from the fall, began to pop, as the lidded kettle hung in the hearth. Lydia found delight in the sounds, as though they were conspirators in her game of erratic bouts of jumps and flinging herself to the floor.

I felt giddy with her silliness, telling her that the corn were angels shedding their earthly clothes, and when she saw them, they would be dressed in white. I saw no difference in the whimsy since Preacher had assured his children that St. Nick, with his bag of goodies, would drop down the chimney, after, of course, he reminded them that God had already given His gift of Jesus to them. Lydia was in awe.

"Mommy, I want to see." When the last kernel uttered its moan, I removed the lid and she squealed with delight, "Mommy, look at all the angels!"

It was the best day I had had in a long time, and we sat after supper stringing angel popcorn, wrapping the tree with their goodness and anchoring my crocheted star to the treetop. We sat, sipping sweetened cocoa, an early gift from the Bairds, singing Christmas songs Lydia had learned in Sunday school. They continued until we said our prayers and drifted to sleep.

By Christmas Day, the snow had melted, and though the ground refroze, the road was passable. They arrived at noon, all seven. Mama, Sarah, May, their husbands, and toddlers. Mr. Baird had assembled two long benches, planing and sanding them to the touch of glass, allowing us to huddle around in a seating place together, instead of scattered like chickens throughout the sparse cabin.

"Are you two trying to compete with baby making?" I teased both sisters.

They laughed, rubbing their growing bellies. "The one who has the biggest baby has to keep all of them, so the other can have a weekend away with their husband," May bragged.

The men howled in agreement, confident that each one had supplied the necessary means for the most robust child. The table spread, as years before, laid with bounties of mingled succulence.

"Lillian, you have done a wonderful job of keeping up the homestead," Mama said. "Everything is so tidy and clean. And, oh, you dried the flowers from the summer. And the herbs, hanging in the kitchen."

"Thank you, Mama. I have been keeping busy."

Sarah and May echoed the same, showering me with affection. It was after lunch, mid-afternoon, when the children were napping that we lingered at the table after the dishes were put away, and the men sat sleeping before the open fire, that I approached them with my decision to marry Mr. Cordle. May and Sarah sat so wide-eyed and hollow-mouthed that they were lucky it was winter and a hornet didn't set up residence in the space.

I retorted, sitting upright, shoulders squared like cornerstones for a house. Mama shattered the silence with finality, leaving no discord for my sisters. "Lillian, if that's your decision, then I will pray that God will keep you and Lydia safe, and you will be blessed with more children that will comfort you when life isn't always the way we would like it to be."

I wondered, in flashes of scenarios, when Mama had acquired the garden of wisdom, planted and grown in words, ripe for harvesting. "Thank you, Mama," I whispered.

May and Sarah's chest relaxed, shoulders slumped in regret, offering me arms wrapped in smothers of love. Tears fell between us, not knowing which avenue to follow until the snort of a sleeping man broke and sent us into gaffs of laughter. Another hurdle and another ounce of relief with their acceptance made each step a little lighter. Goodbyes were wrenched with gnawing uncertainty, knowing the distance between us would stretch beyond our touch.

We stood on the porch and waved as they drove away, the procession straining to pull each hill and dipping into a narrow way, when, as a wave of a magician's wand, they were gone. I pulled Lydia closer, cupping her head and nestling it to my aching chest.

"Mommy, your heart's talking to me," Lydia said as she felt the throb inside me.

"Sometimes our hearts do talk to us," I said, smiling, "and my heart is saying how much I love you." I kissed her forehead and turned to step inside, when a distant noise echoed like a strangled coyote trapped in desperation, howling its last pleas, broached the horizon on the same pathway which my family had left.

Ahooga! Ahooga! Mr. Baird sat gripping a steering mechanism the size of a tractor wheel, fashioned in a spanking brand-new truck, and Mrs. Baird, in sheer terror, held tight to both dashboard and side panel, in proportion with securing a loose saddled hat. His smile broadened across the breadth of his face to capture both teeth present and missing. As he ground to a stop, Mrs. Baird attempted to regain her composure.

Ignoring her clenched teeth smile, which scolded him, he motioned, "Come on, Lillian, I'll take y'all for a ride."

I hesitated, warily glancing at the disheveled woman beside him. "Hello, Mrs. Baird, is that alright with you?"

She nodded, still retrieving color to a paled face, and said, "Maybe he'll drive a little more responsibly with you and Lydia in the car." It was my first time seeing an annoyance of any kind from her. But then she softened to her real self and added, "Of course, please come," apologetically.

I grabbed my shawl and blanket to cover Lydia, excitedly squeezing in beside Mrs. Baird. Mr. Baird, with soothing intent, patted her knee before jockeying the stick into gear. "Now, when we go to market, we'll get there sooner. No more horses—just horsepower."

And he heehawed at his humor, elbowing the missus, with me contorting from repressed snicker. Then she, too, burst into a bellow, like a sparkler on the Fourth of July. It was a perfect Christmas Day. One I would keep in my pocket and sometimes hold in the palm of my hand, remembering, when other Christmases would keep me far away from those who truly loved me.

I had not yet replied to Mr. Cordle, preferring to postpone my answer and not disrupt any pleasurable thought that might crimp my joy during the holidays.

* * *

Now, the cedar tree, which served its purpose of the season, lay in a wood pile, cut and ready to age for next year's winter. The stack of old newspapers, resting on top of the flour bin, beckoned me.

"These will keep you busy for a while, catching up on the news, and they'll make excellent fire starters in case the cinders grow black," Sarah had said.

While Lydia, warding off the last moments of stardust, drifted into a peaceful sleep, I thumbed through the crumpled papers, careful to wipe the ink smudges from my fingertips, lest I forget and scratch my nose, planting a black spot for Lydia's whim. It wiled away the afternoon, as I lazily turned each page. A few pictures, promoting Thanksgiving feasts and impending Christmas parties now long past were scattered between announcements and advertisements.

Each one read, I sat aside and rolled tight, placing them beside the wood bin. One more, I promised myself, as I languished over the last article, before flipping the page. A photograph, near the middle, evaporated all other content. The formal announcement of Hugh and Margaret's marriage, a winter date of January 20, had been written with details of time and place; an afternoon within the sanctuary of Pleasant Grove Methodist. What was the date posted on the newspaper? December 2, one month ago. The paper rattled as my hands trembled. *It was too soon*, my moaning heart cried.

My fingers grew numb, and I stared blankly, for a time I was not aware. Reality had knocked once again, unexpectedly, and caught me by surprise. I shivered and refocused, glancing at my sleeping child, reminding my encumbered heart of its new direction.

With a deep sigh, I closed the page, folding it into a neat arrangement, placing it between two already fired logs, their charred wisps flitting up the chimney in their last mocking tirade, and with dry eyes I sat down, pencil in hand, and wrote...

> *Ben,*
>
> *I accept your offer of matrimony and prefer to marry in February. Please return details and arrangements as soon as possible, so I may notify the landowner of my departure and prepare for the wedding. Thank you.*
> *Lillian*

His reply came swiftly but troubled my soul beyond anything I could have imagined.

Lillian,

I have enclosed a train ticket on the Tweetsie for February 9, assuming you will have transport to the station. We will be married at the covered bridge when you arrive. I will meet you at the station and will provide witnesses to our joining. However, after much thought, I feel it best, at this time, that Lydia's arrival should be postponed until you and I are settled. Give us a few months with my children, who have been without their mother and long for attention. Your child will be with us, then, and my children will have adjusted to their new circumstances.

Ben

This could not be! He had said Lydia would be of no consequence. A white-hot, stabbing pain raced back and forth through my head, blinding me from accessing any concrete thoughts. I uttered a cry of no sound, paralyzed by anger and betrayal, my knees no longer willing to hold me. I paced throughout the night, rereading his contrived suggestion, tempted to thrust it into the fire, but instead collapsed in the chair, the frailty of my strength gone. The realization crept in, like an infestation of maggots that soured in my mouth, retching the pit in my stomach. No wood was left to carry us through the winter, and shelves lay bare from lack of food.

I had to let Lydia go, for a while.

I had five weeks to prepare. Mrs. Baird found a dark navy suit and matching wool coat, which, she said, had belonged to a parishioner's young daughter from another church of great distance, her being of my size and stature, who had eloped with a boy, leaving her mother distraught and taken to her bed. She also overheard, at a Wednesday night church meeting, that they were headed toward Arkansas.

Mrs. Baird continued that her mother had wailed, "Law me, what in God's green earth can Arkansas have that we don't?" Now, Mrs. Baird said no ill will about anyone, but she added, "I will only say this. She was getting as far away from her mother as she was able, not that I could blame her." She stopped and stood, smoothing her dress that needed no primping. Perhaps an attempt at deflecting her blunt criticism. "But, we must write a note of thanks for her generosity," she finished, lifting a quick smile which then faded straight away.

I wondered if she had, in this recollection, remembered an unpleasant happenstance from the woman. "Two more pins at the waist," she continued as she adjusted the suited skirt, now fitted to my frame. "There, it fits you to a T, but you must eat more, Lillian. Are you not hungry? Or is it that you don't have enough food for you and Lydia?" Her chin dropped in sync with her upward glance.

"I have enough food," I simply stated, but not quite as truthful as I should have revealed. She always sent me home with a little meat, and mason jars filled with canned vegetables and fruit. I didn't mean to be ungrateful, but it only reminded me that I hadn't been able to provide for my child. "It's just that the rumblings in my stomach seem to scare off my appetite." My weak attempt at humor had not altered her concern. "But I will try to eat more."

She fiddled with the hem, making sure not to lift it beyond acceptable norms. "You look beautiful, Lillian," she said, standing back to admire her handiwork. "Does Lydia have anything to wear?"

I remembered the clothes tucked away in Mama's journeyed trunk, scars of notched wood and rusty metal that creaked like rickety wheels on a wagon when I opened it. Papa had made that for Mama when he worked for another blacksmith back in Virginia and gave it to her when they married. Mama said it was the most beautiful piece she had owned. She had lined the inside with a patchwork of fabrics from her favorite colors. Deep crimson and purples. They filled the mountains after the harvest, when the earth pulled up a rocking chair and rested, gathering its inhabitants together for foot-stomping dances and tall tales, before its bitter and unrelenting relative visited from the North—winter!

Now, it was half full of tattered quilts, outgrown dresses, and a few knick-knacks from her childhood. She asked me to keep it. "Someday, Lillian, you might want to fill the trunk with treasures of your own," she had told me. I grew weak, yet unable to acknowledge my decision.

"There's a dress, tucked away," I said. "It was May's Easter dress that Mama had made when Papa was alive."

"What color is the dress?" Mrs. Baird quizzed.

"It…It's blue, like a robin's egg," I stammered. "But—"

"I've got just the thing," Mrs. Baird interrupted. "White lace against the blue. Does she have a coat, not threadbare or torn?" Before I could answer, her frenzied excitement swelled, "I have some wool. Navy. Like your coat. I would love to make it for her."

I staggered backward into a chair. "Lydia isn't going with me now," I blurted.

Mrs. Baird had turned her back to me, head thrust into a small closet, shelves bursting with fabric in an ambrosia of colors, with trims matching sunsets melding with swirls of sky blues. Now she stood frozen and upright, her head perked like a deer, frightened, intent on an unknown sound, that might capture and kill.

"I'm sorry, dear, I don't think I heard you correctly."

I swallowed to a whisper. "He…Ben asked that I wait to bring Lydia. His reasons, I have qualified." Surely, she knew my heart. I turned and stepped to the window, a distraction that offered light from the room that lay in shadows and hid the tears that ran like prisoners, unshackled, from my cell. "It's only for several months," I had convinced myself.

She sat, with no semblance of speech. I felt bathed in dirty water at her disappointment. But my confession continued, "I have found an orphanage, and they responded to my need and will welcome her."

The words echoed and pounded in my head like a hollowed drum, confusing me with a voice now distant and unrecognizable, as the floor started to sway. An uncontrollable shudder swept through my body, and I tried to focus on an object of stability in the room, but the dizzying rotation pulled me downward, and the light backed out of the room before I yielded to the darkness that consumed me.

"Lillian, Lillian," the voice repeated. My body lay in disagreement with a will of consciousness, but the cool moist touch of water on my brow brought life to my being, as I willed my eyes to open.

Mrs. Baird sat, my head cradled in her lap, her tears now abandoned. "You scared me to death."

I struggled to sit up, leaning against the chair, my hands cupped to my face. "I'm sorry, Mrs. Baird."

"Hush, child. I have no condemnation of you. God did not put me here to judge. You are doing your best for you and your child. I could take—"

Now, I would interrupt. "Mrs. Baird, I cannot allow you to take Lydia. You have your husband, who's been sickly. And I cannot ask my sisters. I am responsible for my circumstances. My burden and guilt would be twice-fold on my shoulders if I allowed that. Mr. Cordle is not banishing Lydia. He is simply asking for a little time so we can all come together as a family, eventually."

I hoped that my voice had persuaded her, as I had not accepted the words myself. She helped me to my feet. Her hand rested lightly on my shoulder before she left me and said, "I'll get us some tea."

I was changing out of my wedding attire when she brought rose water to freshen my peaked face, and then took my arm, guiding me to the sitting room. Warmed tastes of cinnamon tea and touches of comfort were served, as I succumbed to the overstuffed chair. Its arms were draped with white linens and stitched with miniature pearls of delicacies and my fingers gently hovered over the knotted threads, reminding me that in spring, I would have Lydia back with me again. My ears perked at her advice, offering assurance that time would pass quickly for our reunion. Lydia would adjust to her circumstances.

"Children are resilient," Mrs. Baird persuaded with confidence. "So, go outside if loneliness, always an unwanted and uninvited stranger, chooses you for its next victim, and look up. Let yourself feel the people who love you, that will their hearts through many miles to yours."

It had been symbolic of nights, when the cool night breeze teased a lazy rustle through my hair, when I blew love rhymes through the darkness and the wind carried them, mapped by a trail of stars, to tap the shoulder of the one who would acknowledge the whispered post. Her words tripped over the goosebumps that lay in ridges up my arms, as I allowed myself a brief remembrance of Hugh.

The front door screeched before Lydia burst through, followed by Mr. Baird. His chest puffed and a chortle lay in his eyes as he sidled behind her.

"Mommy, look what I found." The hen house had been raided by the two, and a spotted brown egg lay wrapped around her fingers. "He said I could keep it." And Lydia turned to confirm his approval. He nodded wistfully. Her joy bathed me with the love that Mrs. Baird had just spoken of. And I smiled.

* * *

The first week in February, snow pillared throughout the mountain slopes, lapping like huskies to the cabin's outer walls, burying the decaying steps. The blinding snow tasted like bitters on the tongue as I swept a paltry clearing. Cold raged war with waning heat, and the wind whistled around corners as referee to their bout, as I stomped the snow from my shoes, pulling the door shut. Powdered heaps usually lay during the winter in hay-like mounds for an unsurmountable time. By the first morning of the second week, however, a warm spell blew in with soft rain, dimpling the snow, and the roads ran awash with mud. But on Tuesday, the sun shone and hardened the spew, which rain had left behind.

It was on that night that Lydia and I stumbled into bed, having packed the last crumb of memory into hand-carried bags, along with the splintered travel trunk, the one Mama had passed on to me. I settled us to bed and held her, book in hand, and read to her until her bobbled head lay limp on my chest, and with the rise and fall of her slumbered rest, I cut a square from her blanket, not more than she would notice perhaps, and tucked it inside my purse to retrieve on command and breathe in the essence of her until I returned.

The night wrestled with the morning, pulling me into their struggle, with tortured consciousness until the dawn intervened and the day stretched before us, uncharted, like aimless roads veering from unhinged cliffs. I pulled myself out of bed to the remaining tasks at hand, shoveling the silenced firelight and clearing the hearth for the new family who would shelter here, marshaling their tragedy, which coerced their plight. Maybe the men, brothers of good health, would provide the strength to eke out a living, and the head would not cast his widow and children to the dust with him, left to feign on their own.

Saved from the jam I had made, I scattered the last of the chokeberries on the back stoop, finches and thrushes vying for the most plump and tasty. My nesting child still slept, but I tossed her hair into prodding play, and she grumbled sleepily until I produced a cookie, sugared, the last one I had squirreled away.

"For breakfast?" she questioned, now sitting cross-legged, reaching.

"Just this once," I teased. And when she had finished, I covered her hands, still softened with the skin of her birth, and lifted them to my anguished lips. I led her mind to a new place, a journey where she, for a while, would meet new people who would also love her and provide food to warm her belly and light to guide her footsteps at night. But my throat tightened to a whisper, and I told Lydia that I would be gone for a while.

"You're not staying with me, Mommy?" Her words now formed with understanding, and the blue that held her eyes in place grew fearful.

"It will be only for a little while," I choked back my dread. "I'm going to make us a new home. A better home, where you'll have other children to play with. Mr. and Mrs. Baird will come to see you. We'll be together soon."

It was all I could give her. A hope and promise she didn't understand. I stooped to her, now standing before me, dressed in warm cloth stockings, a knotted thread, near the ankle, leaving evidence of the hole I had sewn together. I struggled with the buttons, my hands trembling to fasten her coat, shortened in the sleeves from her growth. She stood perfectly still, hands to her side, while I straightened the sash on her bonnet. Her cornsilk hair flew like seeds we blew and wished upon in dandelion fields. Time slipped backward in remembrance. I tried to catch her eyes, but she cast her sight toward the door.

"There, now you look beautiful, Lydia. I'm so proud of you." I gently touched her chin, turning it toward me. But her face remained stoic and cold, like the frost on windowpanes. A horn blew, shattering the moment, and with relief I grabbed our belongings, setting them on the porch, and waving to the people who had become family to us.

"Good morning, Miss Lillian," Mr. Baird said. "Miss Lydia. My, it's a fine winter's day. God has blessed us with good travel." He remained vigilant in his good nature and gathered the bags from the porch, while I carried Lydia and greeted Mrs. Baird as she took her from my arms. Their heartening disposition had been my mainstay, and now my trusted champion scooted closer to me, taking my hand. Her warmth soothed my frayed nerves.

We traveled leisurely through the bleak countryside, unwilling to hasten our departure from each other. Chimes of ice sickles now reformed on weakened branches, each slow melt catching the glint of the sun. I removed my glove and cast my hand on the side window, wanting to pull the cold in, then place it to my face, reviving my numbed senses. Lydia was cradled in Mrs. Baird's lap, the hum of the engine quickly lulling her to sleep, and the three of us rode in silence, not of a disturbance to Lydia, but to sort our thoughts, which spoke in contradiction to each other.

It was mid-morning when we rounded the last bend in the road, Mr. Baird throwing the gear low to climb the last hill.

"We're almost there," he announced.

I felt suffocated and gripped my throat in an attempt to calm the panic that roiled in my mind. Mrs. Baird aroused Lydia, her protest still rooted in a stupor. But I, in my panic, strained to see the house coming into view. Only a pencil drawing of the home had I seen, at the top of the stationery, which Mrs. Tufts had replied on, to the correspondence of my initial inquiry. A house with two stories, broad columns supporting the structure, with a wrapped porch. The drawing was faint, but I was able to make out the image. She, the keeper of the children, relayed in pen the care they gave to the children.

"A home filled with love for your child, who will be treated as my own," she had written. The words had given me fleeting comfort, but I returned the papers, filled with instruction of perhaps too much detail, regarding Lydia's routines.

"She'll need to be read to each night, with her blanket wrapped around her. And she likes a little snuggle in the morning, and…" I attempted to erase the words, but they smeared into messiness, befitting my unquieted life. How silly of me to think they would have time to give all the children special attention when so much attention was needed. I could only pray someone would tuck her into bed.

Mr. Baird jerked to a stop, refocusing my presence, and we sat, gaping at the residence where I would leave her, the starkness now formed into shape, and certainty seeped, like fumes from odorless poison, paralyzing us. It was Lydia who breathed for the rest of us, pointing to the child of about the same age as her, though more rounded, with reddened cheeks and a shy smile, waving to us as though requested. Her hand held another, an older woman, her raven hair pulled back into a chignon, silver wisps unfurled, and a gentle wind caressing them around her cheeks. She cast a bright smile, holding her hand above her head in an announcement in case we failed to see her. A weary sigh released from my soul as I took Lydia from Mrs. Baird.

"Would you like for us to come with you, Lillian?" Mrs. Baird asked. Her arm now supported my wilted frame. I nodded, unable to speak.

Mr. Baird hurriedly exited the truck, now having permission to follow along, and assisted the missus and I while toting the small bag of Lydia's clothes. My child tucked her head to the drum of my heart and wrapped her arms around me, unwilling to look at the other child, as we approached the bottom steps.

"Welcome, welcome," the woman beamed, still holding the other child's hand. "I am Mrs. Tufts. We are so glad you made it. And the roads were passable after this unpredictable weather?"

We ascended the steps, my legs wobbling like cattails in murky water. "Yes," I responded dully. "The roads are hardening, preparing for the next snow."

I searched her sincerity, now facing the woman who held Lydia's safety in her hands. Mr. and Mrs. Baird advanced behind me, hesitant to approach too quickly for concern of intrusion.

"This must be Lydia," Mrs. Tufts said, lowering her head for a profile of Lydia's face. "And you are Lillian." She stood erect once again. I'm not sure I answered. Lydia tightened her grasp, burying her identity. I let her be, not forcing an admission.

"Well, it may take a little time to adjust," the woman said. "But Lydia, I wanted to introduce you to a new friend who wants to play with you, when you feel comfortable. She would like to be your friend. Her name is Ruth."

Lydia stirred, turning her head for a glance at the girl who stood smiling at her. Ruth seemed too familiar with the routine, but pleasant and herself at ease. Mr. and Mrs. Baird now stood behind me, and introductions were made before entering the house.

A whiff of homemade bread and vibrations of shooed feet huddled in a mass, scuffling for position just around the corner, sounded like foals trapped in a stable. The lobby was small, uncluttered of knick-knacks and other breakables. The floor lay bare, unstained, rubbed away from wear in the walking lanes. A wiping mat, well used, for cleansing shoes from the winter's sludge, presented itself just inside the door alongside boots and shoes of various sizes lined in a row. A small faded burgundy couch of no particular pattern rested against a wallpaper of pink roses, displaying a disproportion of blooms.

Mrs. Tufts offered us seats, the Bairds refusing, insisting I sat with Lydia. Without resistance, I obliged. We sat, still leaning to the muffled chatter, our ears perked. Even Lydia raised her head, warily at first, then curiously she probed her surroundings, listening. The addled clamor, through thinly veiled walls, uncloaked their anticipation it seemed, in interpretation. Of course, the other children knew. Probably from behind curtains in the upper story, when we arrived, peering into the curiosity of the unknown child. Their memory, peering in self-reflection. Now a distinct and familiar voice rose above the rest.

"Hush," a reprimand was sternly given. Followed by an admonishment with a clap of the hands, "Get back to your chores." Whispered giggles and breakneck confusion rummaged for escape, like scurrying mice deprived of reward. The conglomeration brought smiles to our faces. Even Lydia's. With the disbursement, I hoped their hearts would remember their first day here and offer her kindness and patience.

Mrs. Tufts, breathless and quick in step, as though settling a matter of urgency, returned. "I'm sorry it took so long."

We shrugged with no concern. Visibly flustered, she sat down beside me, an unopened file positioned on her lap, while hands, aged and knotted in joints, smoothed the unruly vestiges of hair. "There are three papers I need you to sign. The rest is for you. Our telephone number and address are included."

I read each word carefully, making sure I would not be signing away Lydia permanently. "When you write to Lydia," she continued, "either I or one of the older children will read your letters to her."

Mrs. Baird reached for Lydia, while I finalized Mrs. Tufts's instructions. My attention wavered as Mrs. Baird slowly walked away with Lydia, Mr. Baird following obligingly. I squirmed, not wanting her to leave my sight, but Mrs. Tufts patted my knee, smiling.

"She'll be alright, Lillian," Mrs. Tufts said. "You're coming back for her. Many do not."

I relaxed my posture and nodded in agreement, accepting her truth.

I was lost in time, her showing me picture albums of families reunited, when Lydia rounded the corner, her holding the girl's hand.

"I have a new friend, Mommy," she said.

It was Ruth, united in a blanket of compassion, with my Lydia. Mrs. Baird stood behind her, fingers entwined in a relaxed pose, head tilted, and she smiled clearly in a motherly fashion, saying, "She's going to adjust."

Lydia ran to me, pulling me. "Come on, Mommy, I have something to show you."

Relenting, we followed her footsteps. I turned and stood in the doorway, aghast at the number of beds, neatly made, lined in rows like gardens prepared for planting. The bedding bellowed a scent of lye soap but assuredly cleansed of any ill-begotten germ. The room's center boasted a potbellied stove, the heat slipping under bed covers, tickling toes like wooly caterpillars nuzzling their brood. Curtains held the disparity between light and darkness, the color bleached and uneven. This was the girl's room, I was told. The boys slept upstairs. Mrs. Tufts' burly husband, a minister by trade, guarded the night's ruffians. We were led, room to room, no question left unanswered, no corner left unturned until I was assured of Lydia's daily comforts.

The noon lunch hour soon approached, and we were invited to stay but declined due to the remaining journey which lay before us. The lobby was now empty, each person slipping silently away, leaving Lydia and me together. I sat with her again, pulling her to my lap, while I reached inside the bag that would be left with her.

It was the end of autumn when the last corn had been husked, the kernels canned and placed in the dark cellar. But the husks, I hung to dry, and when Lydia had laid asleep, the flickering light dancing across her face, I took it down, forming and fashioning a doll with a blank face, and jointed with twine, giving life to hands and head. A red felt, of a small amount, I cut into two hearts and stitched them, one atop the other, where hearts are meant to be. Now, we sat in the vestibule, away from the others, and I laid it gingerly in her hands, which brightened her sweet face.

"This, Lydia, is our hearts together, and when I come back, they will never be separated again," I said. I smothered her to my chest, closed my eyes, and unbeknownst to her, silently wept to the soul that held my tears.

A young girl appeared and took her hand, guiding her to where the other children played, having done this before, to ease the new child's discomfort of separation. A familiar arm wrapped around me and directed me. A motor started and the landscape blurred to nothingness.

I stared out the window and whispered to the wind, "Carry a message to my Lydia that each day away will be one day closer, back to her."

* * *

My unconsciousness had fallen into purgatory, only to be released abruptly from the shrill whistle's command. I jerked to attention, trying to gain a sense of perception from my surroundings, realizing my head had been crumpled on her shoulder. I straightened my suit and pulled a fluff to my hair, apologizing, "I'm so sorry, Mrs. Baird. I slept little last night."

With a wave of her hand, she shushed me. "I'm not surprised, my dear. I would be asleep in the lap of God if I had gone through what you are facing."

We had left the orphanage, with a space ghosted between us. Mrs. Baird's arm cradled my heavy shoulders until my wounded heart could take no more.

Now, the train, a black mass of forged steel, sat glaringly before me, the object which would be furthering my journey away from Lydia. The vapored steam swirled languorously beneath the main engine. Its slow steady breaths in wait for passengers to board, while the railmen, faces blackened with coal dust, shoveled chunks into the bin. Soon, the steam would raise its pounding heartbeat, with nostrils flared like snorting workhorses, and each warmed breath of the engine, exhaling into a cloud of mist, would prod itself from the station.

It was only a few years before that the company had chiseled its way from the mountain community of Cranberry, rich with iron mines, past the fledgling community of Foscoe to Boone, and as my mama had said, "a hop, skip, and a jump" from our Valle Crucis community. A small platform had been assembled, simply made, from discarded lumber, which the mills had provided. It stood nearby for luggage and supplies until the travelers could retrieve them.

I was grateful that the drive into Boone was no longer needed in case an inopportune moment of greeting might arise with Hugh or his wife, as I had already heard they were married three days before. I cast the thought aside promptly, with a swift kick up my backside for allowing a feather of that thought to tantalize my mind…and gathered my bags.

Families bustled near the boarding ramp, none of whom I recognized.

One gathered, hooded in black, their distraught separation in grief. Perhaps a death. And a lone man stood, black dress hat snugly secured atop wisps of grey, protruding from beneath the rim. His impatience was most noted by the twiddling of his pocket watch, and pacing back and forth as though that would be noticed by the conductor, hastening his call. A father, his height shadowing two young boys, aged about six. Their hair, flattened to a spit shine, spoke with uncomfortable emotion to the mother. They tugged at her coat, urging her to board quickly, them not to be denied another moment's adventure. Departure from their father was of no concern. Yet she lingered, and he took a step toward her, lifting her chin, an approach of affection not usually seen in public, and kissed her lightly before she turned and said goodbye.

My heart seized with pain, crying out for Hugh. Everything I had known and loved, I was leaving behind. I wasn't ready for another goodbye. I was tired of goodbyes and tried to squelch the anger that rippled inside me, but panic consumed me like a rolling fog covering deep water, with no determination of step or direction. Then, somewhere in the crowd, a child cried, drawing me back into focus and calming my soul to the purpose of my commitment.

Mr. Baird, reluctant to intrude on my thoughts, took a step closer. With a lowered head, his hands circled the rim of his sweat-stained hat. Then, he reached out, took my hand, and placed in it a burlap pouch.

"A little food for your journey, Miss Lillian," he mumbled, as he turned and walked away. A swipe of his tired eyes displaced the tear. Mrs. Baird embraced me, holding me tightly for a time that I wanted to linger, her caressing arms soothing my anxiety. As she released me, her cupped hands held my face.

"I love you, Lillian," she said. "You're the daughter I never had, and I will miss you."

They had become my friends, Mr. Baird a grandfather figure to Lydia and Mrs. Baird a confidante to me. We had spent the last few months saying all the words we wanted to say, all that we wanted to share. Our hopes and dreams. Now there was nothing left to say, so I turned, shoulders squared, and boarded the train. No glance behind me, for fear of running back toward them, my courage in defeat.

I searched for a resting place, distanced from the others. The families were now seated, still waving toward relations who lingered, and the impatient man, head buried in a newspaper, reading, gave no notice to me. A seat, discarded by choice, the last one near the door leading to the ore car, was the one I chose. The rock, mined from the mountain, was the reason why the railroad had furthered its route. Its metallic scent was offensive but left me in solitude.

I tucked my bag under my feet and released the sigh that I had held since morning. The seat, wrapped in sparse padding and a worn state of leather, annoyingly prickled my bones, as a ghostly shiver traveled from my toes and covered my body, nudging goosebumps from my arms. I took out a shawl and wrapped it tightly around me, the cold from the nearby door already an intrusion to any comfort. Then, I pulled the last letters I received from Mama and my sisters, from the frayed, cloth purse beside me. A splotch of flowers had been embroidered on the side long ago, and I brushed my fingers over them, lightly, wanting to touch the fingers of the person who stitched the threads. In hopes of catching her lingering scent, I lifted the purse to my face, but only a smell of must remained. A gift from her mother, she had said, as she dug deep, pulling her treasure from the trunk.

"It's yours now, Lillian," she had offered. I grasped every word, and they filled me with encouragement. A smear of ink lay between the pages, perhaps a tear misdirected during the correspondence, of their concern. On our last visit, I assured them of my comfort from their support, and that we must each find our way and continue to pray for God's help in our time of despair. They had not abandoned me and neither had God. I tucked the letters away, peering wistfully out the window, wanting the train to start its journey.

The iron horse sat waiting, steam hissing from underneath the wheels like a black stallion rearing in announcement, as the engineer sounded the call. The train lurched forward, in a slow chug down the tracks, the stack from the engine in a puff of billowing smoke. I pulled to the seat's edge, searching for them, wondering if they were still there, but the space lay empty, and the loneliness crept in and sat beside me like an ill-gotten companion. Children stood on their knees, for a glimpse of the wheels, as they turned, while their mothers steadied their stance. And the mourning family, missing the man, dabbed at their eyes still. My heart grieved for them in remembrance of my father. But the grey-haired grandmother, who sat five seats up, her knitting bag snugly beside her, had already pulled out her needles, in deep concentration, intent on finishing the booties, which would adorn, presumably, her grandchild. A satisfied smile nestled between her face, each creviced line worn from age capturing a story in her life. I longed to sit beside her and capture a glimmer of happiness, in her stories. No! Actually, I wanted to hear her pain, of which none now shown, so she could teach me how to cope when I felt downtrodden, as I had today.

With a jolt, the railcar swerved around the narrow-gauged track, catching the passengers unaware. She looked up, holding me in a stare, but I snatched my eyes downcast to my empty lap before she could respond. An appropriate time had passed before I got the courage to look up again, this time pulling my face closer to the window, feeling the rasp of wind slide against the pane, as the engine pulled away from the mountainside. The conductor sounded the whistle again, the shrillness echoing against the last portion of the mountain wall as we shifted toward the inner depths of our journey.

The railway company had named the engine the Number 12, but folks around the mountain named her "Tweetsie," a contradiction in sound and power. Having never left my homeland, I wanted to capture every moment of the mountain's beauty, but hunger pangs now growled in annoyance. Grasping my stomach, I reached inside the bag for the pouch of food, my first of the day, which Mr. Baird had given me. A jam biscuit with a piece of cured ham and some dried fruit. But underneath lay a note and paper money. I unfolded the letter.

"Squirrel this away in a hiding place away from prying eyes," he had said, "and use it to come back for Lydia."

It was enough money for me to return to her. My heart swelled from his generosity, and I ate heartily, knowing that he had opened a door that gave me hope. And I smiled. Licking the stickiness from my fingers, not a crumb was wasted. But an uneasy feeling began to grow, and I looked across the aisle, only to see the snoring man, hat tilted to cover his face, asleep.

Then, my eyes swept gingerly up the aisle until I saw the grandmother, knitting now set aside, her smile like a gently warmed afternoon, nodding in approval of my ravished cleansing. A shy smile grazed uncomfortably across my face before we breached an unsuppressed chuckle, sharing my question-able etiquette. I loved her at the moment for not judging me, even for the small occurrence. Perhaps that was her secret. She cast no judgment of peo-ple or circumstances. In her way, the lesson was well taught, and I would always remember it. We nodded and returned to our preoccupations, but I knew that I no longer sat alone.

The book I had brought still lay within my neatly folded garments. Too many thoughts danced in and out of my head to concentrate on another story. My head reeled, wondering what Lydia was doing. A nap, certainly, or fitfulness and whining from her confusion. And Ben, who would be waiting for me at the end. I tried to imagine the man and the children I would raise. His children. However, I could not imagine their acceptance of me, and would certainly not attempt any action or thought of replacing their mother. A slip of apprehension snuck upon me, as a clutch of air escaped my held breath. "*One day at a time,*" I whispered to the person who lived inside, and I turned, reaching for the beauty of the land that landscaped my window.

The ever-changing photograph pulled me, my fingers rimmed to the win-dow's base, shoe tips lifting me a pauper's penny length, from my seat. We had left the rain-tossed snow behind as we climbed the mountain range. Snow-capped pines now hung with white gowns of shimmering ice, in tease from clouds and sun, competing in appearance. Even with closed windows and the prattle of tracks, I could hear the snap of ice sickles plunging to the frozen ground below. The slow chug inched higher, and in the valley below, a spatter of snow began to whip between branches, claiming its place among the prickled limbs released from their capture. A rushing river, fueled with snowmelt, swept under a fractured opening, providing an opportunity to quench the forest's thirst. The silhouette of a deer with broad proportions and rack-mounted with great weight lapped unafraid, while a famished hawk soared and glided rhythmically, orchestrated in a silenced lullaby searching for food.

The slow crawl continued up and around the rugged mountain tracks, and I slipped out of my seat, stepping outside to the rear platform. The crisp fresh air filled my lungs with tranquility, and I felt the presence of God. The untamed nature clung to me, like the misty fog that lay languid on the forest floor. But in a snap, the rustling wind churned and swept upward, loping the fog along, squelching the sparse sun. The train suddenly reached a plateau, but the wind followed, now with an angry spit of tumbling snow, and I held tight to the railing. The rawness was invigorating, and I leaned out and closed my eyes to let the snow fall on my face. It cleansed me of my sorrows, and I drank in the moment until…my hand began to slip from the rail, losing my balance, when she appeared and caught me with the crook in her cane.

"It's beautiful out here, but also dangerous," the grandmother said. "Let me help you back inside."

I took her hand, weary and exhausted, and fell back into my seat. She then left me and returned to her seat, chatting with a child across from her.

The rhythmic tussle of the railcar summoned my sleep, as the approaching tunnel furthered my departure when we slipped through the gateway.

It was the saber tooth rattling that snapped its fingers against my ear which awakened me, stiffened, holding tight to the seat in front of me. The rails clattered, and I gasped when I turned to throw my gaze below. The gorge threatened, like an angry troll, shadowed underneath with no permission given to cross its path. The vastness and beauty stole my breath, no mountainside to protect us, the train vulnerable as an open wound. I leaned forward, my forehead pressed against the window, praying the trestle, snow now piled between the angled supports, could carry us across. But the engineer blew his whistle, and it echoed down the ravine, bouncing off the craggy rocks as he coached the caboose over the last hurdle, a blast of unfurled wind pummeling behind us.

A woman shrieked and cried out, but the conductor kept the train steady, leading us into the narrows, along the softly rippling waters of the Doe River, until we reached a breakthrough sun, which brightened our spirits in welcome. By the time the train master eased around the final curve, I had already straightened out a wrinkle caught in my skirt, pinched my cheeks to color, rewrapped my chignon at the nape of my neck, and secured my hat.

Passengers were beginning to gather their personals, but I sat stoic, calming my nerves, refusing to turn my head to search for him. The train glided to a stop, my unknown companions in disarray from excitement as they hurriedly reached the door. But I still sat in a stupor, until…she was suddenly standing beside me, the grey-haired grandmother who had previously beckoned my heart from afar. I raised my face to meet hers, and she took me by the hand, assisting me to stand.

"Whatever has taken you this far can be endured, my dear." Her words flowed like gentle waters. "The path may not be of your liking, but your will is your strength. Search for the nuggets of hope and goodness when they become buried. Sometimes, you may have to dig deep, but they will be there, waiting for you. Now, let's go together."

She didn't tell me her name, but I had known her somewhere before, some time before, and I would never see her again. When we reached the descending steps, she motioned for me to proceed before her, and I stepped off the train to my waiting groom. A glance back and she was gone. *How quickly she had disappeared*, I thought. But the older man, graying near the temples and hat in hand, had already stepped forward.

"I'm Ben."

I stood before him, unable to speak. He was a robust man who stood tall in confidence, but short in stature. A jacket of ill fit, strained from the buttoned fastening, because of his expanded girth. His beard, full, with mounds of curls, jostling for position, lay between a quizzical upturn on his lips, waiting for me to speak.

"I'm Lillian," I finally uttered, my voice filled with uncertainty and my body shuddering from a prick of nerves.

His dark brown eyes pierced me, but then he stepped forward, taking my bag. "Welcome to Elizabethton, Lillian. How was your trip?" He didn't wait for me to answer before continuing, "There's a diner down the street, and I wanted to take you for some food."

I nodded in acceptance, my stomach hollow and rumbling as I followed along a step behind him, unable to keep his pace.

Through our letters, we had discovered that, although we had not met, there were cousins of second and third relations who knew of me and Ben. The news was relayed around the mountain by folks willing to share neces-sary information, which would ease us into our agreement.

"He's a fine man," one had said.

"A hard worker who had taken good care of his wife and children," another relayed. "Why, he'd make a good husband."

No one had said anything that would cause me regret. I willed my thoughts to the present.

The eatery sat among the other stores, sandwiched to each other and lin-ing the street. Gingham curtains had been threaded through a curtain rod hanging at the window. A sign above it boasted its name, Amanda's Café, and beneath the name, it said, "Homemade food like yer mama's."

Inside, a few tables were scattered about the small room, with the same gingham material covering the tops. Between dinner and supper time, no one else was there. A sprightly young girl came from the kitchen, draped with a freshly pressed apron and a short black hair bob of curls bouncing around dark eyes that danced. Perhaps the owner's daughter.

"Howdy, folks. Y'all need a menu?"

And before I could speak for myself, Ben ordered for me right away. Quick enough, the food came.

He ate without hesitation and without offering prayer, not even seem-ingly noticing that I bowed my head, or even cared. I started to pick up my silverware to eat, but a revolt grew inside, which bolted me from the table. Fortunately, I reached the outhouse, around back before I retched the foulness. By the time I returned, he had finished his meal and was waiting outside for me.

"Feeling better? She wrapped up a couple of the ham biscuits you left on the plate."

I drew in enough breath to respond. "Thank you, Ben. Yes, I'm feeling a little better. It was probably the train ride that made me a little woozy." But I knew that wasn't true. It was something else.

"The Justice of Peace will meet us at the covered bridge. That's where we'll hitch up." His voice trailed as he started walking toward the river.

It was too late to turn back. I pulled my eyes tightly together and opened them again. The distance between us grew greater, and I had to run to catch up.

"Come on, woman," he said. "You're 'bout to git married." His voice, full of dust and grit, and forehead lined like garden rows planted in the spring, reminded me that he was two decades older than me. His hair, balding in the back, further attested to that fact.

It was a February winter's afternoon that held the bitterly cold wind at bay. As the covered bridge came into view, it stretched appropriately across the parcel of land with its purpose of connecting two sides of the town, as Ben and I would be connected in life. The sounds within echoed to the slow clop of horse and carriage, passing through. And when they emerged, the driver then prodded the horse to quicken his trot, hastening their destination toward their warm shelter.

Underneath the timber-truss passageway, a roaring river sped past before late summer could dry its feet. The rapid water showed indifference in its rush, as the Bible lay open, and the pounding in my heart drowned out its discourse. At last, we stood facing each other, and the Justice's rallying cry from the scriptures led us down the road of matrimony until the penetration of his eyes told me I had missed my cue.

"I do," I said, shaking off the numbness, when the man with the Bible shut it with a clap. My now husband had permission to kiss me. I closed my eyes as he leaned over and placed a peck on my cheek. Nothing more given. Nothing more wanted.

A tear bled from my heart before I opened my eyes. Before I washed away the vision of Hugh. Slowly, stepping back, a blush warmed on my face.

It was the sudden polite applause that turned my head to see a few women from the town, who had noticed a celebration and had stood at a distance to witness the union, gather around me with comforting embraces and well-wishes. They pulled me into their joy and laughter. A few offered matronly advice, and a few more admonished those who gave it. In a matter of minutes, I had thanked the ladies for their encouragement and managed a weak smile and wave of the hand, as the back-slapping, hand-shaking men finished offering congratulations to Ben. The driver he had hired then pulled away en route to our home.

Home. How odd that sounded having known only one home where Mama and Papa had raised me and my sisters. Where Lydia was born. Now a different house...but not home.

I strained to see around the last curve and over the last hill as the horse poked along the frozen dirt road. Now, the cold lay deep in my bones, and I pulled the blanket closer around me. Not much longer, I thought, when the horse snorted a breath of nostrilled steam in the same conclusion. Ben and the driver had talked along the way, but I didn't mind, for I searched from side to side in discovery of my new surroundings.

The treelined forest walled most of the view, occasionally exposing patches of cleared land, and the makings of small farms, where families had carved out their piece of refuge for their family. Finally, we reached the perch where I could cast my eyes. His homestead sat among open fields. Forty acres, he had said. The late afternoon sun, with blending shades of crimson and violets, mixed like stained berries on cake frosting, stretched across the land, highlighting the clapboard farmhouse and outbuildings.

As we descended the hill, a curl of smoke escaped from the chimney top, and four bodies in motion clamored to reach the front door, pushing each other aside. The boys—two of them, he had shared in his last letter—were gone for weeks at a time, working in the coal mines. But his youngest boy, Baxter, age 15, and the three younger girls worked on the farm.

The acknowledgement of his family reminded me of his deceased wife's memory, him most likely still loving her, of which I couldn't deny him his affection. And her children, who held her close, still. I could only hope they would eventually accept me. The possibilities were daunting. By the time the horse and buggy pulled to a halt, one girl, a tallness to her which didn't match the youth in her face, scampered out the back door, a tin bucket swinging by her side. She was headed toward the barn, which sat on a knoll behind the house.

Ben lifted me down from the carriage, paid the driver, and gathered our suitcases. I cast my gaze to the wide spaces where signs of nubby cornstalks were plowed under in the fall, waiting to become part of the earth and start new beginnings. The field, enclosed with split rails, zig-zagged like a shallow creek trying to elude its dried-up banks. A smokehouse sat close, outside the back door. Although unseen, the smell and rut from pigs made their presence known, somewhere on the property. A frozen pond lay quiet, its road map of cracks patterned on the surface, where the sun had bore down and weakened its structure.

A fresh scent allured me, turning me on my heel to see the forest, standing thick with large oaks and pines. But I felt drawn to the dwelling and slowly walked ahead. It held a second story, astride a portion of the lower section. There was a covered porch for sitting and when I approached the bottom step, a stench grabbed my nose, and I held tight to the post, pulling up a layer of coat to cover my face. Splotches of chicken poop lay rutted in the grooves, and the animal from which it came suddenly flew from the open window of which I stood. A shriek came flying out of my mouth as I fell backward against the wall. I wanted to run. As far away as I could. But I had no place to go.

"The kids do the best they can, and I ain't no house cleaner," Ben told me. "My day is spent in the fields."

I nodded, holding back the tears as he passed behind me, taking my belongings with him. I followed him inside. The small living space bore a stained brown couch, ripped and torn, with a deep sag in the middle. Two rocking chairs sat on each side of the fireplace. One his. One hers. A grief came over me, having seen her empty chair, and resentment from all shrouded my dread if I sat in it. There must be someone near who could make me one of my own.

The fireplace light grew dim from lack of wood to feed its fever. Though nearly empty, I grabbed what was left in the wood bin to restore the heat. Whispers and giggles seeped through the ceiling. I could imagine if I was their age, I would have my ear to the floor as well.

Ben came out of the back room, motioning. "That there is our bedroom. Now, you make yourself at home. Feel free to look around all you want. The girls will cook us some dinner, so don't you be concerned about that. I need to go to the barn to make sure the pigs are fed. I'll be back after a while."

I shook my head in acknowledgment, still stuck like molasses to my soles to the room that gathered his family together at night, before being tucked into bed. Before a kiss on each forehead sealed their dreams until the morning, knowing they were loved.

Continuing to gather my thoughts and study the room, I took a lamp to the far corners. There, a wrapping of silk display with woven, intricate cobwebs, spiders hid near their lair, waiting for their next trapped prey. I hated spiders and would never allow an entry to my home.

A dousing of lye soap water, rag-soaked and wrapped around the broom, was swept throughout the cabin from top to bottom every day. A shiver crawled up my leg, and I hopped a jump, thinking the creature had been misguided in my direction. But my imagination, instead, was the culprit. I pushed the thought aside and ventured to the dining area. A smudged, glassed cupboard sat in the corner with a layered film of dust clouding the cracked plates, cups, and saucers. And in the middle of the narrow room was a plain wood table, chipped and notched with markings, by dull blades, used by mischievous boys. Worn benches were placed on each side and two high-back chairs at each end. The rungs on the back of the chairs had teeth marks, where I could imagine a mama had held her teething child with one hand and eaten with the other. But scattered on the floor were the remnants of dried food and crumbs from milk-soaked bread, now soured. The ranked mix turned my stomach and not having anything else to hold onto, I steadied myself, reaching for the table for fear of swooning to the floor. The adjoining kitchen fared no better, with a dusting of flour sealed beneath my feet.

Voices tumbled through my mind, in confusion, taunting me: "Flee back out that road. Catch the train again, and never look back." The message deafened me, but then spun me around, mocking me repeatedly, saying, "You have no place to go."

I found a nail to hang my coat and purse, changed my dress, shooed the other chicken out of the house which hid beneath one of the beds, and found a scrub brush and lye soap underneath a wisp of cloth that was fashioned around the kitchen sink to hide its contents. Within an hour, I could see the grain of wood in both the kitchen and eating room floors and had cleared the corners of each room from its web of inhabitants. I was admiring my handiwork when I looked up to see the girl who had scampered off to the barn, standing before me.

She was sullen, crossed-armed, and holding a bucket of fresh milk. Tight black curls escaped her wool headdress. Her eyes, brown and cold, like her father's, stared unblinking. I wondered if the other children had the same intense color and gaze that made a body appear transparent. I brushed the wisps from my face and smiled.

"I'm Lillian. It's so nice to meet you. I—"

But she swept past me to the kitchen, her cold contempt following. I rubbed my arms to warm them, but it was a cold that couldn't be rubbed away. Grumbles of anger and bursts of clatter from iron skillets clashing with the iron stove hastened my steps away. She wanted no part of me, or my interference into her house. My heart cried out to her, realizing the responsibility that had been thrust upon her, and the emotional separation from her mother.

Lydia must feel the same emptiness, wondering if I'm ever coming back for her or lost to her forever. A tear edged down my cheek and I wiped it away, staring back to the dwindling embers, wondering how a breath of happiness could once again spread like lavender in the fields throughout this dwelling. It was with relief that I ventured to the porch to finish the cleaning task. I found a stack of wood out back, brought in as much as I could carry, and stoked the fire to a healthy blaze. All windows, now closed and locked, contained the heat and filtered the warmth throughout the house. I placed my palms toward the flames, then touched them to my cheeks and closed my eyes, remembering my Lydia. Remembering Hugh.

The scampering feet above my head sounded like a family of mice being chased by a ravenous cat. It was both the creak in the steps and unbridled curiosity that gave them away when they peeked from behind the curtain, which covered the doorway, separating the sleeping room from the night-gathering room. The whispered snickers passed behind me slowly, like baby turtles in mud, and then suddenly they darted as though they had picked up their shell and grew longer legs for running. They too had mops of raven curls tossed about their heads, miniature replicas of their sister, still harboring herself in the kitchen.

The youngest was only slightly older than my Lydia, and the other was a few years older. I guessed the oldest, preparing the meal, to be of an age when girls turn from children to the beginnings of young ladies. I started to speak, but they skedaddled to the kitchen where their squeals were suddenly hushed, reprimanded, and issued orders for their chores. I leaned backward to try to see them again as they took the plates from the cupboard, their eyes now downcast, not daring to look up at me. I wanted to help but feared the one in control would step out of her domain, glaring at me. Their innocence warmed my soul, and I knew I wanted to love them. I would not discount the one whose manner was off-standing.

While they fiddled with supper, I stepped out onto the porch, the last inkling of light in conflict with the darkness of the sky, and the post of stars beginning to shine. It would take time to fit into Ben's family. I whispered to Ben's wife, "I'll do the best that I can for your children."

Two faint shadows walked from the barn toward me through the fading light. I squinted to see it was Ben and a strapping boy beside him. They approached quickly, Ben's voice preceding him, in anger. However, by the time they stood before me, Ben greeted me with no apologies, introducing his son, Baxter, hat in hand. His features danced off the oil lamp light from inside, but I could see the kindness in his resolve. He appeared to be slightly older than the girl in the kitchen.

"I'm pleased to meet you, ma'am." He barely looked up at me, not with disregard but a shyness about him.

I smiled broadly. "I'm pleased to meet you too, Baxter. Looking forward to getting to know you."

He snatched a quick look, bringing his deep-set eyes to meet mine.

"Now, you go on in there and wash up, and don't forget to do what I told you," Ben commanded.

"Yes, sir."

And he left us. Ben's authoritative voice unsettled me. I retreated to my familiarity with Papa and couldn't recall the same. The sound of his voice soothed my hurts and tears. I could still feel his gentle touch, protecting me. But Ben was a different man. He had endured the loss of his wife, loneliness, and struggles with raising his children alone.

"Sometimes, you gotta be tough on boys, so they don't get out of hand," he explained.

I had no right to judge him, not knowing the circumstances that happened. "I'm sure," I said, and I remained quiet until he stepped closer and pulled me to him, kissing me urgently, his burly arms entrapping me and sliding down to my thighs, inching my dress up, pressing me against the wall.

I couldn't breathe and tried to push him away. "Please, Ben, not here. The children, please."

He released me just before the door swung open and the youngest child announced that supper was on the table. I straightened my disheveled hair and clothes and stepped inside, hoping the children wouldn't notice my shaken demeanor. Ben sat at the end he had long ago claimed as his, and the children followed in order. One open seat remained at the opposite end, the place that was rightfully *hers*. Ben motioned for me to sit, and I complied, acknowledging each one with a nod and humble smile.

"Kids," he bellowed, "I'd like you to meet my new wife, Lillian. She's going to be taking care of you, and I expect y'all to mind her and do what she says. Now, y'all tell her your names, you hear?"

The little one began, "I'm Rachel!" Her big, round eyes and quick smile bounced with light as she spoke, until a nudge under the table snuffed it out.

"I'm Hazel," another said, looking across the table for direction from the oldest girl.

"You've met Baxter," Ben said. Baxter nodded and smiled softly. "And this is Callie. She doesn't talk much, and she's stubborn sometimes, but I can't help but think she's as pretty as her mama."

Callie stiffened and didn't raise her head. Her jaw set and the muscles in her face twitched. I knew the pent-up anger that churned inside was lit by more than losing her mother. My heart yearned to understand.

"Okay, let's eat," Ben announced.

I looked at him, but he was already filling his plate with food. Cured ham and Irish potatoes. No prayers were offered. It was so foreign to me to sit at a meal and not ask for blessings. So, I bowed my head and spoke silently to God, who had cared for me and Lydia, for the children who sat before me. That I would be a good wife and a blessing of thankfulness for our food. I raised my head to see everyone had stopped eating, staring at me.

"Just a quick talk with God," I chuckled. "It always makes the day brighter."

And I dove into my plate of food, my stomach craving second helpings, but the bowls now sat empty. Gently prompting the youngest into a conversation, hoping that would be the most pleasant, she followed the lead of the others, in silence. I couldn't help but compare the differences in our families. When we gathered there was lively chatter with rolls of side-splitting laughter. But Ben and his children's routine was focused on the task before them. I wondered if this was how it had always been before his wife passed away, or if she was the ray that showed throughout the house.

At the end of supper, the girls gathered the wares from the table. Ben had already settled in front of the fireplace, pipe lit, drawing on the pleasured taste of tobacco. Baxter lay sprawled on the floor, a book opened, preparing for the next day's school. I followed Callie and Rachel to the kitchen.

"Please tell me how I can help," I pleaded.

Rachel, already planted on the high stool, spoke quickly in hopes of relinquishing her chore, "You can help me dry."

Callie's glare snatched away Rachel's smile, but I responded before I could be dismissed, "I'd love to help you, Rachel."

Hazel had already gathered the scraps and toted them to the hungry grunt of pigs. Now reaching the doorstep with great announcement, and clearing the mud off her shoes, she said, "It's getting colder, and it feels like it's going to snow. I wish we didn't have to go to school tomorrow."

Callie continued to clean the dishes, only acknowledging Hazel's request. "Stop complaining. Or Papa will pull you out of school like he did the others."

Silence settled in, and I struggled to remove it from the room. Ben had told me that the older boys were away, working in the coal mines, and I now wondered if that was of their choosing. But I cast that aside and finally was able to grasp Rachel into talk befitting a small child. She soon welcomed the conversation, and then I told her that I had a little girl almost the same age as her.

"Where is she?" she asked excitedly.

I told her that she was staying with some people for the time being. Callie whirled around, accusingly, teeth clenched, "You left her!"

Her fiery eyes confronted me, arms to her side, hands held in fists. Her voice was clear in the depth of her accusations.

"She's staying in a safe, loving place until I can settle in here and help all of you," I replied, softly.

Callie turned back to the dishes, and I mustered up the courage to speak: "I'm sorry, girls, that your mother isn't here with you. I know she would want to be if she could. I can't imagine the pain y'all have been through, but I want you to know that I'm here to help you, but not to try to take your mother's place."

No acknowledgment of my words was offered, but at least they knew my intentions. "Come, Rachel, I'll help you to bed," I said, taking her willing hand in mine.

All three girls slept in the attic, with Baxter sleeping on a small cot in the only other bedroom downstairs, besides the one Ben and I would sleep in. The attic stairs stretched to the ceiling, where the door lay flush, and a gentle push opened the ceiling to the bitter cold room. I raised the oil lamp to capture the faint image of the rough-hewn beams and walls, which allowed the wind to penetrate any comfort. A whiff of damp wood and stale air mixed with the dust of dead moths reminded me of my task tomorrow. At a narrow, peaked eave, one window beckoned the moonlight into the room, allowing shadows to turn small children's minds to thoughts of discomfort and twisted imagination. In the center of the room sat an iron bed, large enough for three children to sleep on their sides. It was covered with quilts, the top one filled with colors of wildflowers and overlapping rings. I knew that design. It was a wedding quilt. The stitching was precise, unlike my own. I sat down on the bed and ran my hand over the quilting.

"My mama made that," Rachel said. "Callie brought it up here after Mama went to heaven."

I understood why they would want her quilt on their bed. Something, anything, to hold onto when the person isn't with you anymore. How I missed my Lydia. Rachel brought me back.

"You can't leave me up here alone," she said, her eyes grasping mine. She curled in my lap, like a caterpillar before the cocoon.

"I'm not going to leave you," I assured her. "I brought a book to read to you."

Her eyes widened and she settled in closer to me as I read her a story. Soon I heard footsteps and saw Callie and Hazel carrying the same object I had used at night for Lydia and me.

"Mama always heated a brick and wrapped it in wool to put at our feet," Hazel explained.

"I do that for my daughter as well," I said, quietly reminiscing.

Hazel lifted a quick smile, but Callie had already pulled herself to bed, back turned and unyielding. Rachel found her place between her sisters, and I slipped down the stairs, pulling the ceiling door behind me and whispering, "Goodnight."

I knew he was waiting for me, but I lingered, drawing from the water pump on the porch, a pot of water which I then heated on the wood stove. Washing the long day away, I bathed at the sink, clenching my eyes to the night. Then, I resolved myself to tarry no longer. He sat perched against the headboard, the firelight strong and revealing of a man eager for his wife. I slipped into the bed beside him, my heart and head thrashing about in unison. No time for tears. No time...

The sleeping man now rolled to his side, snoring lightly. I had hoped my weariness would carry me to sleep, but I lay, thoughts mingled in mindlessness. And belated tears now awakened the gamey smell of constrained feathers, long ago stuffed to frame the pillow on which my head now rested. Gathering my shawl around my shoulders, a wool blanket that had been set aside on the chest, along with the woolen socks Mama had crocheted years ago, I slipped out of the room. The door creaked as I opened it, but he did not stir. I tiptoed to the far end of the house and opened the kitchen door without sound, but the screened door screeched like an old hoot owl. It must have been me that gave an audible *shh* as though it were human.

The graying clouds played hide and seek with the full moon, teasing the earth with waltzes of shadows, celebrating the coming snowfall. The darkened mountain range peaks also fell in rhythm with the sequence of the game. I curled up in a corner along the porch, where the gaining wind could not find me, breathing in the chilled air to numb my senses. I had known love once and the touch of a gentle hand. I tried not to remember. To compare the cold, calculated response of a loveless union. But tonight, I needed the remembrance.

Toilsome eyelids denied their sleep, pulled me into the darkness, and I succumbed to their demands willingly. The shadows walked toward me, in the lavender meadow, where Hugh and I had lain, where the wildflowers intoxicated the senses, and toes were tickled by velvet petals. The sun shimmered and reflected their laughter. He held Lydia, their arms entwined, and they waved to me. I run to them, and we are one, complete and happy, lying against his chest, his arm cradling both of us and feeling the love of his beating heart. I wanted to stay there forever, but the wind began to buff the flowers and snow fell from the sun. We ran, catching flakes on the tip of our tongues. It tasted like sweet cream mixed with wild strawberries. We collapsed happily on the ground, making our mark with snow angels until the flowers started to wither and the sun began to fade, taking both Lydia and Hugh with it.

"No," I cried, as I dropped to my knees. "Please come back."

But they were gone.

I awoke with a start, lying in the dead grass of winter. The snow I had brought with me. The bitter wind had found me, and the reclusive moon and mountains were now shrouded with white crystals. Although snow still lightly danced around me, the clouds parted briefly, and the stars shone with grace. A gift for my heartache. Whispering to him once again, I beckoned, "I will carry you in my heart forever. Our Lydia will be with me soon, and I will treasure her and look into her eyes and see you."

I wasn't sure how long I had been asleep outside, but the numbness and tingling in my feet warned me of the consequences as I rushed inside. After gathering another spit of wood for the fireplace, I tied a piece of cord to a lodged nail, stretched it across the mantle, and hung my waterlogged socks up to dry. Settling in the rocker, I thrust my feet toward the embers of warmth, the flickering light trying to pull me back to the meadow until I heard his voice. He stood in the doorway, his ballooning nightshirt emphasizing his stoutness.

"Come back to bed, Lillian," his voice said blankly, like a book with no words. Obediently, I rose and followed him, his sleep sounds quickly returning. The tips of my hair, gathered from the waist of my back and laid across my bosom, were strangely fragranced like a sachet pillow of subtle lavender, lulling me to sleep, cleansing me of my weariness. The rooster still slept when I crept out of bed once again. This time to surprise the family with sweet pancakes, browned around the edges with crackling butter, in the old cast iron skillet. A drizzle of maple syrup on top, a jar given to me by Mrs. Baird, would perk the children's sleepy eyes. Determination seized me to take my place in this broken family and try to mend them back together with kindness, patience, and love. I knew it wouldn't be easy, especially with Callie. But I would not give up on her.

Then the rooster crowed, and I heard grumbles and first-day steps walking across the attic floor, as the creaky planks played like an untuned fiddle. Soon they would come, and I would be prepared. In my nervous excitement, I touched the hot stove and yelped like a wounded dog that had been scratched by an unruly feline. Baxter rounded the corner and rushed to me, his kind heart skirting his shy demeanor.

"Mrs. Lillian!" he exclaimed. Tears had yet to spill as he fled outside and returned with a tin cup of icy snow. "Come," he directed me, and went to the sink and scooped a handful of numbing cold on my hand. He was different than his papa. A soft heart, filled with compassion.

"Thank ya, Baxter," I said. "I'll be alright. How stupid of me to touch a hot stove. I wasn't thinking."

He dipped again and replenished the frozen slush. "We all have thoughtless accidents. Why, one time I was guiding ole Jack, our mule, him pulling a plow, and I didn't see the twig that was rooted in the ground. Well, I'll tell you right now, I tripped over it and landed right on my face. I didn't have any idea dirt could taste so bad."

We burst into a chuckle, and I suddenly realized his shyness had flown the coup, if only briefly. "Now, you git goin', you hear," I said. "Your papa is going to be calling for ya."

Baxter scooted out the door and headed to the barn. Callie came next, expecting to serve up the family in her usual way. She stood in the doorway, stone-faced. A chiseler's tool would be unable to carve out any emotion.

"I thought it might be nice if you didn't have to get up so early to prepare breakfast," I smiled.

She turned, silent, and walked away. The others soon followed into the eating area, Ben coming last. Baxter, now back from the barn, sat waiting at the table. I bowed my head again, with thanks, but the others didn't wait.

"These are the best pancakes I've ever eaten," Rachel gulped. Baxter, now quiet, nodded in agreement. So did Ben and Hazel, but Callie never said a word. Though, when the plates were cleared, she took her finger, pulled the last drop of syrup off the rim, and licked her lips with satisfaction. A moment that pleased me.

Although the fields and pathways were now laid in a blanket of snow, the children prepared for school. I was glad Rachel was a year away, so we could become better acquainted. With their packed lunches and a wave of goodbye, they didn't look back. Not even Baxter. It would come, I reminded myself. Ben had already left after examining ole Jack.

"He looks a bit sick," Ben said, "I'm going up in the holler and see if I can buy some moonshine for him. That'll perk him up."

Now the house was quiet, given a few pops and crackles from both the wood kitchen stove and fireplace in the room that gathered his family at night. Rachel and I settled into the kitchen, measuring flour and sugar and milk, taking a moment to dust her nose. After kneading and rolling the dough, I formed the pie shell in the tin pan and took Rachel's finger, pushing and marking a crimped path along the rim. The way I did with Lydia. *Ah, my Lydia.* How I missed her.

She and Rachel are so different in appearance. Lydia, with straw blonde hair and blue eyes, caused the bluebirds envy. The other with tightly woven, raven curls and cow-brown eyes that reflected my own in a mirror image, pulling me to her, wanting to love her even more.

"Will you be my mommy?" Rachel asked.

The question befuddled me. But I dropped to my knees, leveling our eyes to each other.

"Of course, I'll be your mommy." I wrapped my arms around her and held her, and she held me. I knew then I would do anything for Rachel and Baxter. I would never leave them. They would always have me to love.

It was mid-afternoon when I put Rachel down for a nap. Ben had still not returned. I pulled on a toboggan, my winter coat, and gloves, and stepped out into the bright sunlit day. It was the first chance I'd had to explore the farm. Snapping off an ice sickle, one of many across the tin edge porch roof, I crunched on it, letting the pure water quench my thirst. The sun warmed the snow, now glistening like stardust, as though fallen from Heaven. I took a moment to breathe in the frigid air. The kind of air that burns your lungs yet brings them to life again. Daylight brings clarity and hope. Nighttime crawls into your bed, your thoughts, and twists them, leaving you with hopelessness. That's what Mama used to tell me, and most often she was proven true. As I walked along the snow-covered fields, I felt alive again. I could be happy here. And I would close my eyes at night, imagining the daylight to always be there.

Lazily I strolled across the dormant land when a sudden movement startled me. A stressed-out rabbit darted and zig-zagged across the frozen field and disappeared beneath a dugout burrow, just before a lop-eared bloodhound sniffed at the creature's front door. He paced back and forth but eventually retreated with no reward. I never saw that rabbit again. Hopefully, a new home was made deep into the woods. Songbirds rested on top of crosshatched fences, scouting for bare patches of earth, where a stray seed may have been missed by field mice. A hawk sprang from the depths of the woods and circled and dove, grasping its prey, and in retreat satisfying his hunger. His steel sharp eyes had been watching the grey squirrel leave its habitat to scuttle across the open field. A missed opportunity for one, an opportunity for another. So was life and what those lessons entailed. Regrets, but hope.

With a stream of smoky breath, I reached the ridge. That once invigorating air was now like rose thorns, stabbing my chest. I wrapped my scarf tighter around my face and slowly circled my sight to the expanse of the farm. Straight ahead sat the farmhouse, miniature in size, compared to the rolling hills. Behind it, a smokehouse stood with grey stilts of aged wood hammered together, and a tin roof. Pigs, rooting in their pen, would be slaughtered and cured during the fall harvest and hung from the rafters for our winter's food. Wood was stacked to season and bring comfort from the cold.

Beyond lay the outhouse, similar in size and design to the others that I imagined were dotted around the neighboring farms. The pond, now frozen but willing a person to step cautiously onto its icy form, is silenced now, near the tree line of the forest. The barn, worn like a pauper's clothes, its ragged hem splintered and rotting, sat on a closer ridge not far from the house. The bellow of the milk cow caught my ear, and I walked toward the shelter, out of the numbing wind. The barn cat, belly hanging low, stuffed with babies or her pick of the mice, lazily inched toward me as though her duty to rub herself around the ankle of my boot was inconvenient. I reached down to smooth her thick fur, but she, aloof and dismissively, strutted away.

The weeks became repetitious, snow and ice freezing in layers before the last could melt. Previously chopped wood for heat was dwindling, so Ben and Baxter loaded up the axe and took the horse and wagon into the woods for replenishment. I wrote to Lydia each week, hoping my letters would be read to her. Each letter with a promise: "I will come soon."

But Ben kept putting me off, saying it wasn't the right time yet. I worried when he would let me go. His children had become fond of me. Even Callie, although still brusque, would now answer me when spoken to, and they all bowed their heads at the table when I blessed the food. By the end of April, the planting season was near, so the fields were turned, and rows were hoed. Spring onions and baby lettuce were planted before the rest. Ole Jack, harnessed up and trudging along, his baying an announcement of rebellion, and a kick from his hind legs would cause Baxter to do a sidestep. I never let him see me laugh, but the little dance was entertaining.

Women know when their bodies are changing, and it was the same feeling I had with Lydia. It was the smell of warm milk, straight from the cow's teat as I encouraged the flow to the bucket, when I turned my head to retch that confirmed my suspicion. Ben's child would be born before next winter's end.

The days before had been tense with emotions cascading like rolling hills, loosed from their stable ground. Ben was happy when I told him of his coming child, but the children were less than prepared for a sibling not made from their mother. I tried to offer an encouraging smile at the dinner table in an attempt to convince them that love can be shared with all.

My morning sickness continued for several more weeks, and Callie had to return to the kitchen in the mornings. By noon, though, I was able to work the broadening plantings in the field. At night, I crocheted a baby bunting by the fire while the children studied. Ben sat, nodding off from a day's long work. When my sickness subsided, I approached Ben after the children were settled in bed, behind our closed door with persistence of fetching my child and not denying her my absence any longer.

His jaw tightened, and his eyes grew darker. He said, "It's not time, Lillian. You're having our child."

But this time, his child within me gave me courage, and I told him that I was going.

"You have no money for the train," he blared.

"I do have money," I said, standing firm. "It was a gift from my neighbors."

His voice relaxed. "Where is it? It's needed here."

I feared he might force me to submit the money, now hidden in a rusty snuff tin behind a loose plank in the attic wall, but he relented. Maybe it was his unborn child that softened his anger.

The train chugged slowly out of the station, and my heart quickened in anticipation of seeing my Lydia. I had written to Mr. and Mrs. Baird, Mama, and my sisters that I was coming.

"I will be spending a night before I must return."

I wanted to see them all, to touch them and let them hold me, but not before I had covered my child's face with smothering kisses and told her I would never leave her again.

Lydia

Now, I admit I don't remember much. But just enough. The house was bigger than I had ever seen, with large rooms where beds lay in rows like the garden Mama made. Only she grew vegetables, not children. There were lights at night of which there was no need for kerosene. And a strange box on the wall rang quite often, causing a scurry for someone in charge to shush away the tagalongs, as they talked to the box's handle. But what I noticed the most was the incessant noise that mingled into a chatterbox of laughter and sobbing, anger and frustration, and the stillness of night, when children, great and small, tucked themselves into bed and lay with the whimpering loneliness that wove into their quietened minds.

Mama was gone! At first, I was taken in by the kind girl, older than me, and clearly I was happy to have all the attention. They doted on me. They picked me up and carried me. They twirled me into a dizzying laughter. Others joined and were in awe of my striking blue eyes.

"She's captured the sky," they said, although they tickled me and played silly games, and I rallied with pleasure until a strange mood came over me and I twisted out of one girl's arms and headed toward the door.

"I want Mama."

They ran after me, but the woman I saw Mama talking to earlier stood in the doorway and caught me. She lifted me to her and brushed my hair behind my ears. "Lydia," she sighed, "Your mama had to leave and wants you to stay here with us. She will come back for you. She loves you."

But all I heard was, *she was gone*. I didn't have her to kiss me goodnight.

To wake me in the morning or crawl into my bed and snuggle with me. I reached toward the empty doorway, willing her to come back, then threw my head against the unknown woman's breast in an outburst of tears.

I soon learned there was a routine of order in place. Most children quickly conformed to the rules, without being told. Only occasionally was there a revolt, usually from one of the boys who dwelt in an upper room and felt infringed upon, with a disproportionate level of work. I was only required to dress myself and make an effort on bed making. There were a few children my age that I felt comforted to play with, but with the dimming light, we all lay with our thoughts, longing for our family.

Being a child, I had no comprehension of time and was not aware of how long it had been since I had seen her. But one day, she appeared in that empty doorway, and I saw nothing of her clothing or manner. Only her face, filled with longing, arms outstretched, her moist eyes smiled as her lips quivered. I ran toward her, and she scooped me up into her arms. Me crying with her. I thought all tears were the same, of the same feeling, but I was wrong. My heart burst with happiness and reached up to cover me with tears of joy.

The annoying whistle of the train trumpeted through the mountains. I covered my ears and buried my face to her. Since she came back for me, I had not left her side, even the night when Mrs. Baird prepared an extra bed beside Mama. I refused to sleep in it and curled between her arms, so she could wrap them around me. Now the train carried us to where Mama had said she had been living. To the waiting driver who would take us to Mama's new home. My home, now, as well. But time and my youth lulled me to sleep before our journey's end.

I woke confused about my surroundings. For it was late afternoon, when the sun touched the back side of the mountain, bringing long willowy shadows, which increased my anxiety. Mama paid the driver, and he in turn carried our bags to the dimly lit porch. She looked weary, and a heavy sadness came over her. Was it the long trip? Or was it me? But she knelt and took my face in her hands.

"Lydia, please know I love you, and nothing will ever separate us again.

I will always be here with you. There are other children here whom I must take care of, but no one will *ever* take your place. Do you understand?"

I nodded, not understanding the complexity of which I would be thrust into.

As she cracked open the front door, I hid behind her, tucked in a fold of her long, scratchy, wool coat. I peeked to the side and saw a sullen-looking man, pipe in hand, a smoke circle trailing above him, who sat in a rocker, seemingly content as three girls of various ages played a game on the floor. A game of which I was not familiar. They all stared at me, and I retreated to safety behind Mama. But she tugged at me and brought me out so they could look me up and down, and though I was at a tender age, I felt the judgment to be severe, including the gruff man's scowl. Afraid. Except for the girl a little older than me.

"I'm Rachel." She stood so quickly and came toward me that the older girls were unable to grasp the tail of her dress to stop her. Mama prodded me to speak.

"Hi," was all I could utter. But I liked her smile and somehow felt we would eventually become friends. Mama found a little to eat in the kitchen. The others had taken their meal earlier.

The girls had already kissed their Papa goodnight and retreated to their attic bed by the time we had finished. Their brothers, Mama had said, were working away from home and would be here in a few days. There was so much to remember and to accept, but as long as Mama was with me, I knew I could shelter in her arms. She took me to the attic and showed me the bed where I would sleep, and the other girls would share. At the foot of the bed, she said, for the three at the top had chosen their places long ago. A poor attempt was made to soften the announcement.

"There is so much room at the foot. Far more than the top."

And to no comfort, Rachel popped up and said, "I'll come down there with you."

But I would not have it. I didn't want to be in their bed at all! And they didn't want me. Well, maybe Rachel. I began to cry and cling to Mama, and she took me downstairs and rocked me by the fireplace. Soon, the warmth of her body and the firelight shadows danced across my face until I could weep no more, and the dream makers came and took me to their secret place.

Did I hear a sound? A whisper? Or the scamper of a mouse across the floor? I only knew that I was awake in an unfamiliar place, an unfamiliar bed, and three girls whom I had just met were sprawled with legs entwined across each other into a sound sleep. In the darkness, I scurried down the steps, looking for her, fearful that she had left me. Baxter lay sleeping and I passed him, silently, until I found a closed door and turned the knob, opening it. There was still fire, in the cradle of the bedroom fireplace, and I could see Mama asleep in the bed beside the man she called her husband. I tugged on her arm, which had fallen outside the covers. She was barely aroused as I crept in beside her. She instinctively pulled me to her, wrapping her arms around me. This was the bed I wanted to sleep in.

After many nights of my habitual retreat to her bed, I was eventually scolded and told that I must stay in the same bed as the others. I cried and whimpered and pouted but, having no other recourse after she found me lying outside her bedroom door, asleep, I accepted my fate.

Soon Rachel started crawling down to my place of exile, laying beside me. We became fast friends. But Callie and Hazel would catch me alone outside and spank my hinny, just for their amusement, it seemed. One day, when we were older, they confessed their anger had been formed and molded because I had a mother, whereas they were thrown into the disparity of their own mother's untimely absence.

Rachel, however, became not only my friend but also my defender who stood in front of me, fists raised, and dared anyone to touch me. Including the man I had been told to call Papa. But Papa's swift hand was laid on everyone, including Mama. I hated him, with not even an ounce of guilt, although Mama taught me that hate was wrong.

Mama's belly had grown as large as one of the pumpkins harvested from the fall, and there was no longer room to sit on her disappearing lap. It was in the depths of winter when Rachel and I, along with Callie and Hazel, became alarmed, as Mama's cries became wails of unfurled gasps and searing screams. I overheard that a woman who often came for ailing women was being sent for, without success. For the ground lay covered with more snow than I had ever seen. And for the first time, I saw fear in Callie's paled face.

Papa asked for hot water and fresh cloths. Callie leaped up from our circle on the fireside floor, fetching what he needed. It was in the wee hours of the early morning when we were awakened to the replacement of Mama's painful howls by the blustering cries of a baby. We scuttled down the steps and ran to her. Mama was sitting up in bed, her dark black hair falling past her shoulders, and a bundle of wrapped blankets was held comfortably to her chest. She laid a finger to her lips, then motioned for us to come closer. We strained to see the shriveled-up head that lay quietly, sucking on Mama's little finger.

"Awww," we sighed. So, *that's what a newborn looks like*, I thought. We clamored for the best view, and even Callie seemed pleased.

Mama appeared happier, cuddling her newborn and nursing her. And when she let me hold her, I felt a part of her, too. Now, us four girls worked together in cooperation, stepping into chores where Mama was unable to. As I recall, this time may have been the moment that bonded us together in ways I would have never foreseen.

Jacqueline, or Jackie, as we nicknamed her, had just taken her first step before Mama bore another child. This time, a boy, Ernest, with generous dark eyes like the broad center of a black-eyed Susan.

When the older boys came home, we ate at different times—the men first, while the girls waited table for them. Papa's children of six and Mama's three, now. The chores were plentiful and never-ending. Lines began to form on Mama's face. The kind of lines where each one led to a road traveled, or a heartache, which wound around curves and hid in the mind. Normally, a child would not notice, but since Mama came back for me, I searched for any sign that she might leave me again. I held her hard, calloused hand, chapped from the cold and too many wet dishes, feeling beyond the physical, and into her heart, where the weariness and sadness lay together. But she still pulled me to her, no matter what time of day, and held me and kissed my red cheeks, which gave me comfort. And I wondered why she loved me so much.

Many seasons had passed and I, growing taller and in years, had adapted as well as the other children to this hard life. Now I walked with my sisters to school. Callie had reached seventh grade. She was tall and stout from jockeying hale bays to the upper barn floor. Hazel, a few years behind, mirrored her stature, and Rachel, just a year ahead of me, remained behind in growth unlike her sisters, mimicking my short image.

Baxter had been pulled from school to work on the farm, as his older brothers before him. Papa didn't believe in schooling. Callie had been told this was her last year. She lay in bed and sometimes cried until sleep finally came. We tried to soothe her, but she pushed us away. Her anger with us was brief in comparison to Papa, though. In his presence, she was timid and contrite. But when we told stories, after the light was snuffed out, bitterness leaped from her tongue, toward him. I had not noticed her repugnance until then.

I loved school! The excitement sat in my seat with me, but I was often called upon to harness my squirming, which made my cheeks warm in embarrassment. Although the one-room schoolhouse with a potbellied wood stove sitting squarely in the middle reeked of smelly boys and burnt wood, nothing of which I was unfamiliar in our own home, it was a time when happiness filled my childhood. I was the first to finish my morning chores, dress, and carry my books to the front door stoop, waiting for the others to walk with me. My sisters stared at me in annoyance when I skipped and hummed along the way. But they didn't dissuade me, 'cause I was ready to learn.

It didn't take me long to learn how to read, and I would sit beside Mama at night, and we would read together. Of course, recess was an easy course. Why, I learnt "Ring Around the Roses" and "London Bridge" real quick. And the schoolmarm trusted me to put my potato on top of the stove to heat. She was very strict but needed to be, 'cause one time Billy Russell, a boy whose overalls were as short as a grasshopper's legs stuck in the mud, put a worm down Sue Ella's dress, a girl who never had to work in the cornfield.

It set off a chain reaction, which was whispered around the school for years to come. For she leaped to her feet faster than a bee can suck out honey and yanked her dress off, right there in front of everyone. Of course, she had her petticoat on, so we saw nothin'. But Billy paid with the seat of his pants. I could swear that I saw smoke coming from the back pockets of his britches.

If one of us got a spanking at school, we were sure to get another at home that night. Knowing Billy, I'm sure he got a piece of tree bark and slid it where his daddy's paddle would soon land. Callie had stopped whopping up on me years ago and began treating me with kindness. Like I was her sister. Why, when the schoolteacher wasn't looking, she even motioned for me to come to the schoolhouse's open window and lifted me out to the playground, even though it wasn't my turn, and played with me. Then she peeked over the windowsill to see if the coast was clear and plopped me back inside. And I loved her for that.

Ecclesiastes 3

To everything, there is a season. A time to weep and a time to laugh, a time to be born, and a time to die. A time to love and a time to hate. A time to kill and a time to heal.

Lillian

It was after the leaves had fallen and lay trapped amidst the mud-soaked rain, and the trees stood bare-boned in the woods, signaling the beginning of winter. The pig had been slaughtered and prepared again, like any other time of year. The cornstalks were sheared and used for fodder after the eared corn was harvested from them.

That's when death came to me and my family, like black soot that lined the chimney and made its mark on the wall. The encroacher came disguised and had chosen the one to take back with him. We didn't know. Lingering coughs and snotty noses were common and transferred like ropes knotted together. I had summoned the doctor, and he came, giving advice of which I already knew.

"A potion of this will help the cough," he flatly stated. His concoction of rock candy, glycerin, and whiskey was widely known and used throughout the community. The medicine gave no relief from the pneumonia which ravaged her body, and now I held her, rocking her outside on the porch where I often sat in the evening spring, breathing in the silky fragrance of wildflowers in the meadow. Now, though, I sat holding her, wrapped in blankets, willing her to breathe in the fresh air.

I pulled my face from hers and glanced at the meadow, listless and barren, not even scraps of food left behind from the summer for the deer, and felt the last heave of her chest fall. I looked down at her again, still and at peace. She was gone. I had no wish or prayer to bring her back to this misery, but I mourned for my loss. Anger roiled from only having her love for a few years and yet, I, in my agony, was grateful to have her and know her for just a little while. And there were others who loved her who felt the twinge of guilt that they survived. We all shed tears. Even the older boys, but not Ben. I had never seen him cry. He no longer tried to hide his apathy. And yet, as I buried my Jacqueline, another child of his within me would be born in late summer. A time to weep and a time to mourn.

Weeks collided and blurred my perception of time. I was without words to the children, and Ben kept his distance for a while. Maybe he did have some compassion, hearing the quiet sobs as I lay in his bed. At night, I picked up a book to read, but the words were meaningless, so I rocked in front of the fire to the dance of the rippling flames until a fitful sleep came. There was no time to mourn. There was work to be done. Cooking, cleaning, and washing. Looking backward wasn't an option, but my heart remained heavy, unable to shake off my hopelessness.

Ben presented himself dismissively and without any pain or loss. Callie withdrew from the others once again, and the boys hitched a ride back to the mines. They hastened their escape from the unwanted house intruder that lingered, sitting silent and invisible in every corner. Baxter, however, mourned, and Callie mourned too. Her set jaw was now weak, and sometimes quivering. I felt remorse that I, in my melancholy, had not noticed her withdrawal, not only from me but also the others.

It was during the early spring when the earth began to warm and tender sprigs of grass pushed through the ground after a gentle rain. And the lily pads surfaced on the pond, providing a pedestal for bullfrogs to broaden their chests, luring the females to a romantic hideaway, that dragonflies began to emerge from the warming pond and dance to the delight of the long reaching embrace of a weak sun. My garden, plowed and planted with the first produce of the year, sprouted early greens and lettuce, giving me hope for the new life in me. Daffodils, bordering the edges of the porch, began to bud from their spindly stems just in time for Easter season, and the children began to bring laughter to the table at the evening meal.

A time to laugh and a time to heal. It was during this time when, on a quiet afternoon, Ben and Baxter had hitched up ole Jack to the wagon for a day trip to town to purchase more planting seeds and fertilizer. Callie had wandered away to her reclusive hiding place, of which no one knew, and the other children sat at school, learning their readin' and writin' while my youngest, Ernie, lay asleep, a belly full of bread and jam, that I chose to take a solitary lunch beneath a tall, budding oak tree far into the woods. The sound of chattering squirrels rustling the towering branches, and birds calling to each other to pursue a mate that would further the creation of their family dynasty, awakened my senses.

Mists of soothing pine scent filled the air, and a jade green carpet of earthy moss clung in patches around rocks. Trees of great age could no longer contain their roots, and they spread and dove in and out of the ground like earthworms after a heavy rain, surfacing for air. The stagnant smell of a decaying log lay nearby with a multitude of insects clamoring for a tasty morsel. I learned early on in my life to be careful where I sat, because one time and one time only, I sat on a sturdy log. Just long enough for the chiggers to burrow underneath my skin. Mama made a plaster of snuff and rubbed it all over my middle. That's where they liked to hide. Neither I nor the chiggers liked the taste and smell of that snuff.

I found a flat rock, laying out my spread. My appetite had only recently returned, and the breath of life flowed easily within me. As I bit into the last piece of bread, a honeybee dove and swerved near my face, and I swatted it away, hoping he'd mosey along to the honeysuckle which had rooted next to the new growth of saplings. With no success, I laid a crumb of apple pie on the dining rock to entice the little pollinator as I walked away.

The depth of the woods gave rise to snapping twigs and upturned leaves that had long laid beneath the snow and rain of winter, decaying and preparing the earth with fresh growth. My ears perked, and I stopped to listen. From a distance, I heard a tree fall, strength sapped after decades of life, and made its exit well known to all who were there to hear. I wasn't afraid, and I walked on, bucket in hand, toward the cave, where, last summer during the drought, the older children labored to haul water from the natural spring that ran through it. I approached a clearing where a patch of blackberries huddled in the warming sun, ripened for the picking of anyone who discovered them. Their branches were plentiful and their bodies plump. Irresistible, I plopped a few in my mouth, but the bucket soon filled, and jam would be made and spread on warm bread. I hesitated to leave the light, the powder blue sky and the mellow sun, but my baby boy would wake from his nap, the children would be home from school, and Ben would come home wanting and demanding.

Not one to tarry, I hurried to the mouth of the cave and its formidable opening, even though the boys had cleared the entrance of bushes and underlings which continued to hasten its closure. They carved out two lowering steps and as I stepped down, I covered my head with one hand, balancing the bucket of berries, careful not to spill any. A few steps in, a cloak of darkness veiled me and strapped my feet to the hardened clay floor. Unable to find the oil lantern, which I usually brought, I fumbled for the candle and match in my pocket. With a spark of the match, the candle now lit, I looked up to the soaring ceiling, where the chimney-like opening filtered light onto the appendage that grew from the ground.

We called it "the ghost," and eerily it greeted us each time we came. I lifted the candle higher and slowly turned, watching the shadows sway and hide along the jagged walls. A slight shiver ran through my body from the cool moisture that dwelled throughout, and I was glad I had borrowed a pair of coveralls and flannel shirt from Baxter's clothing chest. With closed eyes, I listened to the rhythm of the cave. An occasional drip of water splattered on the earthen ground, and a nervous mouse scurried to its hiding place. But a shuddering fear suddenly ran through my veins, and I froze in place, realizing I wasn't alone.

My throat tightened as though a hangman's noose was cast around my neck. For within the shadowed room where I stood, whimpers echoed through dark passages and traveled along corridors like a rush of wind, though in a windless cave. The reverberating wails of a trapped animal released my ensnared feet, bolting me toward the exit of my escape. Clawing my way up the measly steps, my chest heaved, and my heart pained from the throbbing, leaving me dizzy and weak. A catch in my side formed. The kind of catch you get when you run long and hard, stopping you right where you're standing, not able to move another inch. Grasping my side, I gulped the fresh clean air, drinking life into me again, as I lifted my face to the sun. I tried to sort out my distraught thoughts.

What if it was a small animal, a wayward dog, perhaps? I must go back in to see, at least, and retrieve the tortured creature. But if the animal was large, such as a bear roaming for spring berries down from the mountain, which was of rare occurrence, I would retreat hastily to the safeguard of men who carried guns. Snatching a fallen branch, insignificant in size, for reassurance, I ventured to the opening once again, only to realize I had dropped the candle with my panicked departure. The bucket also. I reached for another match and lowered myself to the darkness once again. Sweeping the fleeting light across the barren floor, I spotted the silenced candle and spilled bucket of berries. Quickly, I lit it as the flame began to burn my fingers and stopped to listen. The absence of sound, like lifeless stones, stagnant and cold, played with my already confused mind, causing panic to rise within me. Had the animal died? Or had two animals fought and one retreated in defeat? I had no choice but to continue. The squat walk room, as the children had named it, was the only way to the dark expanse where the water was gathered. It was a low ceiling, where any defense was impossible and certainly advantageous to an animal.

I had never felt so vulnerable. Droplets of water stippled the crown of my head, penetrating my anxiety and determined to annoy me, to flee. But I ventured on, reaching the end of the squatty room where the faint sound of flowing water could be heard. An envision of the dawdling waterfall released a peaceful melancholy like an entrancing fire in the winter.

The room's darkness became the light before dawn, still clinging to shadows, though the glow penetrated and settled onto dim and nameless objects. I remained in confusion that no natural light source was ever present this deep in the cavernous earth. The light overshadowed the use of my candle, and I blew it out while placing my retrieved bucket of berries down and raising my ill-suited weapon. Drawing in a shaky breath, I stepped around the bend. The arena was vast and spacious and proud, with a ceiling of mud like icicles clinging to its roots, and curves like winding roads which hid a new wonder.

The whimpering began again followed by a long harrowing yowl, and the weakness returned to my legs, as though it had crawled on the ceiling, following me like a spider, its legs interwoven around me in a death grip. I trembled to the point that my teeth mimicked the rattle of bones in a grave, and for a brief moment, I considered running back into the safety of the sunlight. But instead, I sidled further around the corner toward the waterfall and the source of distress. The pounding of my heart now throbbed in my temples, my breath caught, from no length of which I could determine. But a gasp could not be contained as I stood as a pillar of stone like the ghost in the first room.

Callie stood beneath the waterfall. Naked. Water flowed over her face in an attempt to wash away her misery. Her rounded belly was full with child. She had not seen me, and I stepped back, rambling thoughts ending in thoughtlessness as I tripped over the bucket, the pail of blackberries released and unrestrained down uncharted paths and around the curve from which I hid, their insignificance now of no importance.

"Who's there?" her voice quaked fearfully.

I stepped around in full view, her now dressed in the loose frock which she always wore, belly once again unseen.

"It's me, Callie. I-I came to get a drink of water," I stammered, unable to swallow.

"You're spying on me!" she shrieked, flailing her arms despondently.

Hesitant, I walked toward her, her tears and clenched fists in conflict. She tried to walk past me, but I stepped in front of her again. "Callie, I'll help you through this. I can raise the child as my own. No one will know. Or your papa will make the boy marry you."

She looked at me, a wild and wide-eyed fear carved into her face, and unflinchingly, my eyes locked onto hers. So many questions suddenly tumbled over themselves and left my mind in mass confusion.

She lunged at me, screaming, "Marry me! Marry me! Papa can't make a boy marry me! It's Papa's baby! And why didn't you stop him?"

Her words spit like venom from a snake that had slinked its way between us, and then she fell to her knees, crumpled like a dried flower, delicate and untouchable. A knife-like feeling gutted me and drained the blood from my body, veiling sight and sound from me, and carrying me away to where thinking is lost and feeling is neutered. I wandered back and forth, unable for her words to penetrate my understanding.

Ben! Ben? Yes, he was ill-tempered and abusive with words, and the belt was often lashed upon both the child and myself. But not this! Why would Callie lie? She wouldn't. Why didn't I know? My mind felt trapped as though in the thorn branches of a briar patch. There were so many questions, and rage began to grow like weeds at the realization of his betrayal, of both Callie and myself. Had Ben turned to his daughter to console himself after our child died? My mourning had been profound. A darkness I had not known followed me for many months. I wanted to ask how long the darkness would stay but could not bring myself to say.

Numbness shrouded me, but I pushed it away, stooping down, cautiously approaching Callie. She was still sobbing and took both arms to support her weak legs. I stood with her. She now allowed me to embrace her, while a muffled wail vibrated against my chest. But she retorted again in crippling pain. The wracking pain of a child contorting the body of a woman, in laboring agony.

"We have to get you back, and quickly," I whispered when the pain subsided.

Callie obliged my support, my arm nestled around her, and we left the cave, anger now a passerby. But fear and uncertainty walked beside us.

"It began after Mama died before you came," she whispered.

And we walked on through the woods, silently, to the clearing where the farmhouse sat, where we became women who would blame ourselves and each other…and the man who linked arms with the devil. A time to hate…

The fresh scent of lavender-tinged lye soap made during the harvest perfumed the air as I fanned and tucked the clean sheets and laid extra padding on the mattress. There was no time for selfish thoughts. Only Callie's care mattered now. The small bedroom containing the attic steps and a curtained doorway was the only place of comfort and a semblance of privacy. This was the boys' room, although they were away working with no intent of returning until the mine foreman permitted them to leave. And Baxter could sleep in the breezeway now that spring warmed the day and only a whisper of wind cooled the night air.

I slipped in to check on Ernie, still sleeping, though in a restlessness to wake. Lydia, Rachel, and Hazel's voices, now as a tussle of magpies walking from school, gathered themselves through the kitchen door in need of a morsel to tide them over till supper. Callie stood from the rocker, and I settled her into bed and placed an extra pillow under her back.

"I'll make you some catnip tea. It will ease the pain. The girls will cook tonight, and I'll stay with you. All we need to think about is you and the baby. Callie, look at me."

She was turned to the raw slatted wall, her shoulders heaving as the tears rolled down her flushed cheeks.

"I'm not going to leave you," I said.

Her face remained unmoved, but her hand reached out, and I clasped both of mine to hers. How alone I felt when I had Lydia, even though my sisters and Mama were there. That I understood! But not this! I pushed the thoughts back to where thoughts are stored and brought out throughout a person's life, unwanted yet persistent to take you back to a time to be relieved. Quietly, I slipped out of the room.

The girls were all a flutter with girlish stories of boys they liked and the schoolmarm's new dress. "Shh," I scolded, "Callie isn't feeling well, and I have made her a bed in the boys' room. You're not to go in there and bother her, you hear? And y'all got to git supper tonight. I'm going to be in with Callie."

They all began talking at once: "What's wrong with her? Can I go see her?

Does she have a tummy ache?"

No, and no, I had said, which made them all the more curious.

"If I find any one of you at her door, you're all going to get your fannies whacked," I threatened. "Now, Hazel, I would like for you to boil me some water, and Rachel and Lydia get some clean scrap cloths out of the chest."

They scattered, their assignments underway. But Callie's writhing scream startled them into numbed silence.

"Go and do your chores," I demanded and rushed to Callie's side. I grabbed a cloth, wet with cool water, and placed it on her forehead. "Breathe, Callie. Slowly. Until the pain goes away."

Fear lay on her face. "It hurts so bad," she whispered.

"It won't be for long," I fibbed, not knowing how long her labor would last, or if she, like her mother, would even survive. She must be wondering, too.

"I have the tea," Hazel spoke softly beyond the curtained door.

"Thank you, sweet girl." I stepped out from the curtain and bent down, taking the tray, and brushed a kiss on her forehead, knowing she was as worried as me.

Rachel and Lydia ran and stood behind her, their arms loaded with the cloths which I had asked for.

"She's going to be alright," I said. They looked at each other, not knowing or comprehending the predicament. "Now, scoot, and do what I told you."

I turned back into the room, carrying the tea, but Callie had fallen into an unsettled sleep. I sat the tea on the dresser and knee-buckled into my rocking chair. A taste of vileness churned in my stomach and crawled up my throat. I grabbed the night pot under the bed, no longer able to contain the foul taste in my mouth. Ben had betrayed his daughter. Now her life was run amuck. And what am I to do? Stay with him? Where would I go? Share his bed again? The thoughts tumbled like rocks in a tin can, the noise deafening. And what about the others? I must ask the girls, and I would demand truthful answers. I retched again and dry heaves stalked me. I sipped on the now cold tea to settle my stomach. The child within me moved, making known its disapproval.

It was late afternoon, before the beginning of the setting sun and the end of a day rife with a servitude of upheaval, that I heard Ben and Baxter at the water pump, refreshing themselves after their travel. Callie still slept, except for the spasms of pain that woke her and thrust her into the nightmare. I took leave of her when I heard them, my smoldering rage unchecked. They leaned on the porch railing, as casually as a house cat lying on a windowsill in the morning sun.

"Ben, I need to talk to you. Alone." I could hear the drum in my chest slide upwards to my temples. He barely glanced my way.

"Woman, you can wait till we finish here," he replied. "It's been a long day. And there's nothing you can say to me that Baxter can't hear."

I didn't want Baxter to hear what I had to say to him, but Ben gave me no choice. A curdled scream tasted sour on my tongue as I stood bold-faced in front of him and said, "Callie is having a baby! Your baby!"

Hate and rage gathered like a demon slipped inside of me, instead of him. Never had I confronted him on anything. He stood there like he never heard me and looked away toward the empty field. Then, turning to me, a darkness in his eyes bored through me, and I swore I saw the devil himself in there when he lowered his jaw and a smirk curled his face up like the dead skin of a snake. The curve of his fist lay fast and hard on my face, knocking me to the ground, and day became night, enveloping me.

When I awoke, Baxter was knelt beside me, dabbing at my discomfort, but I winced, pushing his arm away. I tried to sit up. "Where's Ben? And Callie?"

I tried to stand, but Baxter rested his hands on my shoulders and said, "Don't get up. He's at the barn hitching up ole Jack again. Said he was going to the store to use their phone. I don't know who he's going to call."

And as soon as the words fell out of his mouth, around the corner of the house, Ben came. He slid off the mule's back and tied him up to the post. Ben approached, nostrils flared and fists opening and closing rhythmically. I dug my heels in and tried to move backward, but he was upon me, lifting me with one hand to my feet. I trembled, not knowing if he was going to hit me again. But with a sweep, he backhanded me, and blood pooled in my mouth.

The snarl on his lips spewed spittle as he blared, "It's Baxter's baby, not mine!"

Baxter stumbled like a puff of wind had taken him right off his feet. He looked aghast at the accusation, as though an arrow had struck him through his heart, and he pulled his hair, walking wantonly back and forth. "No, Papa! You know that's not true!" Tears ran down his cheeks like a swollen stream after the winter, but Ben ignored him.

"Woman, don't you ever say that again," Ben said. He dropped me and I crumbled, curling myself into a twined ball, holding tight my unborn child. He raised his foot to kick me, but I rolled to the other side, taking the brunt of his boot in my back. The pain settled in my ribs, and a voice unknown to me moaned and grew and released a bellow of agony, rushing from my mouth.

I heard Baxter, in a fit of fury, say, "Get off her!"

I looked up, and he was pulling Ben from me. "You know that baby's not mine. It's yours! And you're not going to blame me for it."

Ben raised his hand to strike him, but Baxter ducked and picked up a stick, busting Ben's knees, making him fall. Then, the boy, only a lad of fifteen who I loved as my own, took off running down the road. The wail of Callie's misery brought me back to my senses, and I left Ben in the dirt. Under the dusty soil where pocket gophers and meadow mice lived and dead roots eroded was where he belonged.

In the middle of the night, Callie's baby boy was born. Neither Ben nor Baxter had returned. I didn't care where Ben was, for he had left a prison of walls surrounding us, but I cared for Baxter and felt the pain of a father turning on his son for something he didn't do. Callie lay at peace after I placed her son in her arms. I sat beside her and showed her how to nurse him. Holding her eyes to his, she uttered his name.

"I'll call him Vern."

In these moments, he was her child and her child alone with no thought of the father. Swaddled and fed, I put him in a bread trough and placed him on the low dresser. Callie drifted off again, but I lay awake, the weight of this new reality crushing me like stones on my grave. No way of escape. No relief from Ben's sting. How would I leave, with the children? And me carrying another child. I could see no recourse but to stay and protect, as I could, the other children. And Callie. I had questioned the others before the goodnight kisses, before the prayers, and they said Papa had whopped up on them but otherwise was of no concern. I worried if I should believe them. But no girl in my house would ever be alone with him again.

Then, I remembered his shotgun resting on the back wall inside the closet.

* * *

A pot of coffee was perking, an extra split of wood added to the stove, and eggs were dancing in a pool of lard in the cast iron skillet, when I saw a car pull off the dirt road to the front of the house. Its wheels settled into a spattering of weeds and muck. The new grass was tender and hadn't taken hold. Voices trailed and I strained to put them together, one out talking the others. Ben must have slept in the barn last night, for I could distinguish his as the loudest. The others talked almost in whispers. Still hanging on to the dish rag, I cast a glance out the window. Ben's sister, Dora, and her husband, Ebb Tripp, were standing outside the car huddled together as Ben flung his arms up in the air in exasperation. Shaking his head, she laid a consoling hand on his arm. I squeezed my eyes tight to block out what I surmised the conversation to be.

They lived half a day toward Mountain City. Throughout the year, their automobile would roll in, Ebb persistently honking about a half mile away, to let us and the neighbors know that they were coming. When I married Ben, Dora promoted right away how Ben had loved her sister. Replacing the children's mother was like putting a foal to a cow's tit. They were not having it! And I understood. Goodness knows I worked hard to fit in with these kids and let them know that I could never replace their mama. They learned that I cared, though. I was there to wipe their noses and hold their head over the bucket when they ate those green apples I told them not to touch. But they learned to love me as well, and each time I had a child, even the boys when they were home, would fetch me coffee in the morning. But the other kin folk...well, they were harder to love.

The men hardly noticed me, and the women, well, I was held up in disapproval no matter how spit-shined my house was. And don't think I didn't notice when their noses went flying in the air, sniffing around to catch a stench of stink or lingering sweat. The kind that men carry with them if they even miss one iota of flesh when they bathe, or the kind of sweat that lingers in hair. We didn't have much, but we were scrubbed clean, and I or one of the kids dragged the tin tub in from the smokehouse, or we washed in a basin.

What a time for them to come! The breath came right out of me, and I suddenly realized Ben had called them. They'd come for Callie and her baby boy. A roiling cloud of smoke burst out of the kitchen and passed me like a runaway train. I ran to the smoldering skillet and burnt eggs, pitching them out the back door, and fanning the smoke out with them. Panic covered me with a flinch of fear that shook my body, as though I was caught in a thrashing machine.

I had no sense in me at the time to know that she wouldn't want to go or stay. No one had asked her what she wanted. Ben had decided for her. For her to be taken this way so soon was just, well, wrong. My head spun, and the light began to fade when I realized my breathing was caught up to near passing out. I stuck my head between my legs, the way Mama had taught me to do if I felt the wobble come to my knees, and took slow deep breaths until the shaded light came back to my eyes. I went into Callie, touching her tenderly on her shoulder.

"Callie, I need you to wake up." She groaned, clutching her belly, pushing my hand away. I touched her again and said, "We have company. Your Aunt Dora and Uncle Ebb are here."

Her eyes, large and brown, flew open like a startled deer.

Dora walked slowly up the narrow path and greeted me, already gawking over her rimless glasses. A crooked smile lay on her lips like a dead stick, void of movement. Her handbag, stitched with needlepoint in a bouquet of roses, rested in the crook of her pudgy arm and a brown, boiled, wool hat sat low, covering her ears and pruning her full cheeks. Nervously, I returned a half smile.

"Why, Lillian," she greeted me without a hello, her face crinkling in the space where eyebrows tend to forge together. "Whatever in the world happened to your lip and eye?"

I had forgotten about the bruises and pulled a lock of hair over my eye to hide as much as I could. And instinctively, I covered my busted lip with my fingers. "Oh, I fell off the porch step yesterday. I'm so clumsy."

"Tsk, tsk, tsk," Dora said, shaking her head. "You should be more careful, my dear. Ben needs a strong woman to help him."

I lowered my eyes, knowing it was futile to say anything contrary to that tale, for no one would believe me, and the punishment would fall on me twice fold. Dora reached the top step, putting us eye to eye. She continued, "Well, I hear we have a new baby in the house. You know you have to watch these teenagers every minute. It's part of our responsibility as mothers. Of course, I know that Baxter and Callie aren't yours, but you should still, as a Christian woman, have noticed those two carrying on."

I bit my lip, forgetting that it was already bruised.

Sweeping past me, I followed Dora, fearing she would burst in on Callie. She would never see it differently, and I was not the one to change her mind. Of importance was Callie and her child. I had no say so in their lives. Or my own. I never had control of Ben. Nobody did. He wasn't even the least afraid that I'd leave. He knew I had nowhere to go. *Keep 'em barefoot and pregnant*, he always bragged and chortled with the men folk like I wasn't standing there.

I directed Dora to the kitchen, pouring her a cup of coffee, delaying the presence of Callie as long as I could. "How was your trip?" I asked, making small talk as though their visit had long been planned.

Dora stretched her neck around the door, searching for any movement in the far room. "Why, it was," she said, her face taunt, "unnerving."

There was no need to respond, and I busied myself with flour and milk, adding a little salt and sugar to the dough. Just when she started to stand, I kneaded and pounded and picked up that dough and slammed it down on the working table. Startled, Dora sat back hard in her seat.

"Callie is nursing right now," I said. "I'll fetch her when she's finished. She doesn't need no disturbance right now."

I didn't even bother to dust the flour off my hands when I went to pick up the coffee pot and pour her some more. I could see in her eyes she was taken aback, lifting the cup and studying me over the lip, but I didn't care to notice until the wail of the newborn locked our eyes together in dark pools of reality.

"She'll want to get dressed, and I need time to pack her things."

Dora tipped her head, signaling that she had heard me. It was just understood that she was leaving.

"And Callie hasn't eaten yet," I added. I quickly gathered some biscuits from yesterday and slapped some honey between the halves. She didn't like my jam.

"Doesn't taste like Mama's," Callie reminded me. But I had learned to accept her and knew it was just a way of keeping her mama alive in her mind.

I stood over her for just a moment, this child who was nowhere near a woman or knowing what a woman would know about birth, life, and living. My heart longed to turn away and let her linger, but tarrying would only prolong the inevitable. She was curled on her side, her newborn tucked near her.

I lightly brushed her shoulder and said, "Callie, I have some breakfast for you." She stirred and pulled him closer. "Callie, please. We have visitors."

Rolling to the edge of the bed, she sat up, glancing at her son who was now sleeping soundly. "I'm not hungry."

The flatness in her voice reminded me of my own after I lost my baby. But I persisted, "You have to eat. Eat for your child. You need the strength, and he needs the milk." She took the plate and nibbled on the biscuit, so I continued, "Your Aunt Dora is in the kitchen and wants to talk to you. I'll get your robe."

"No! I want to get dressed."

I left her for a moment of privacy before she pulled back the curtain, the only other loose sackcloth dress she owned now draped on her frail body. Her hair was coifed and pinned; her jaw hardened again. But it was the vacant darkness in her eyes that caused a lonely tear to escape and roll down my cheek when I saw her. I wanted to pull her to me, but I knew that I not dare. She turned without a word and walked toward the kitchen, shutting the door behind her.

Stirrings from the attic and the tromping of feet down the steps, where Callie's bed had been set underneath, aroused my senses back to necessity.

"A baby!" the girls exclaimed, as they turned and saw Callie's son. "Mama, you had a baby last night?"

I could no longer hide the truth. "No, child."

"The baby boy belongs to Callie?" Rachel asked, who stood close by, listening. "Why did she have a baby?"

This caused Hazel to come up from behind and poke at them, "Hush! You don't need to know."

Lydia and Rachel shrugged their shoulders, and I followed Hazel's reprimand.

"Never you mind," I said, scolding them.

Callie had started sleeping at the foot of their bed, and they never questioned why she was so generous, giving up the warmth of the others' body heat to keep them warmer.

"Now, move along. You've got chores and school. Your Aunt Dora and Callie are in the kitchen. Knock before you go in and get some breakfast. It's waiting for you in the cupboard."

They scooted back up the steps and dressed, giving me time to change Vern's diaper and retrieve some clothes that I had stored away after each of my children's births. I dressed him in a light blue crocheted knit I had made with a soft white lamb centered on the gown. He looked handsome and I forgot, for a moment, whose child it was. But this baby had no say in his birth.

I touched his cheek, remembering the innocence in the softness, and whispered to him, "Your journey will be long. May God see you through it." My brief absence from the others melded into obscurity, having no recourse or opinion, not that I could think of anything that made sense for the rest of the family's survival.

If Dora and Callie were in a disquieting discussion, it was abruptly ended when Lydia and Rachel, now dressed and bursting with excitement and inquisitiveness, interrupted.

"Someone else is coming," they squealed.

A second car rumbled down the road, the morning dew still gripping patches of dust. It was unusual to see another automobile on our road, and I gathered the bedroom window curtain back to see where it would stop. As the tires slowed and inched up behind Ebb's car, it bereaved me to see yet another couple step out, Ben greeting them as though he knew them. My mind tried to grip on what was happening, and yet I had no notion. Another motor car sat at my house, and the spoken chatter reeked of the unknown. I rushed to the kitchen.

No matter what the troubles, they would want their stomachs filled. Callie had stepped out onto the porch while Dora traipsed down to Ben and the others. The girls came, before the walk to school, and told me goodbye. I wrapped my arms around them, holding them before they saw the smile fade and another tear fall, knowing Callie wouldn't be here to greet them when they came home.

"Now, y'all go on, you hear. And be sure to hug Callie."

It wasn't my place to hasten the loneliness of her absence. I stood by the window and watched them all gather around her into one giant force of nature. Love. And she kissed each one on the forehead and watched them scoot down the road, a skip in their step, carefree and unsuspecting. Callie, sensing my witness, turned and held my eyes before her shoulders slumped, and came into the house.

The screened door creaked as she stepped in, and I took a hesitant step toward her. Her eyes, filled with brokenness, said what we knew was already there. "Vern and I are leaving with Aunt Dora. At least I'll have my child. Would you let me know when they're ready to go?"

I nodded and she turned, the weight of her tragedy consuming her, and returned to her son. My heart shattered like a hammer laid to wood, which was in no comparison to Callie's own, but both hearts ached and mourned our losses, knowing we would never be the same women again. A clutch of sadness would hold us forever.

I called them the posse, as they approached my open door. Plates, already in the small china cabinet when I arrived, had been a wedding present for Ben and his wife. The faded roses adorning the rim and the chip here and there were now set on the table, along with bowls of breakfast foods. Dora, taking the lead, strutted into the dining room, the men following closely behind her as though she rightly owned the homestead. She introduced me to her sister, a woman more stately than herself.

"Lillian, this is my sister, Clarice." And before I could bring up a brief smile of introduction, she went on, "This is her husband, Tom. Tom Peterson."

Authoritative, a trait Ben would never allow in any other circumstance, Dora added, "They've been driving all night from Winston-Salem."

Although I hadn't been there, I knew where it was. It was about three hours east of Mama's home, where I grew up. But my mind still lay in confusion, not understanding why they were here. Had it not been decided which sister would take Callie and her child?

"Would you like to wash up before breakfast?" I asked. My manners stood intact.

"Yes, just to wash our hands and face," Clarice replied, gratefully. Her voice, full of grace and kindness, lay as distant from her sisters as the northern and southern winds.

I laid out the linens and pumped water into a bowl, then we all sat down at the table. Dora prayed.

"Where's Callie?" Clarice questioned with concern. I glanced at Ben, and a muscle in his cheek twitched, but he didn't look up, stuffing his mouth with bread.

I blurted, "She's already eaten. Wanted to lie down for a few minutes."

No one spoke, and only the clank of a fork on the plate was heard, until Tom bragged, "It was mighty good, Lillian. I feel like a stuffed pig, but I'm sure if I tried, I could hold a third helping." He pushed his plate away, and his chair scraped against the floor. "However, I'm going to resist."

Tom was a robust man, whose belly hung over his belt, his eyes unable to meet his feet. With a twinkle in his eye, he finished the meal with a good-hearted story, and, pleased with himself, his chuckle seemed to start from his toes and fill him up like a well full of water into a full chortle, ending in a belly laugh that shook his whole body. Wit and humor had become foreign to me after I left my family, and my eyes flitted around the table to see if the women were laughing.

Clarice scolded her husband, "Now, Tom, you cut that out. I declare he must have the attention of everyone."

No one laughed, and I dared not crack a smile until they had left the table, and I gathered up the dishes, hiding my snicker in my apron. I needed that reprieve, just for a moment.

A breath of fresh air to my soul. The decision makers settled into the gathering room, where a small flame still flickered in the fireplace to take the chill off the spring air. The men had long ago left the house, leaving the women to do the convincing. I busied myself sweeping up crumbs that had fallen underneath the table, only an earshot away. Sidling up to the wall, I pressed closer, against it, to hear. But their voices became whispers, and whispers became hushed tones.

I had no inkling of time passing when Callie stepped through the doorway. I peered around the corner. The room became silenced, and they sat upright, stiff as a poker, as she came into the room. Her eyes, puffy and rimmed with red streaks, betrayed her staunch posture. The dark shadows beneath them lay like midnight, compared to the pallor on her face.

"I won't do it! You can't do this! I won't go!" Her voice was raw with conviction. She had caught enough of the conversation from her listening wall to understand their intent for her. I stood, hoping my breath was unheard, in my tucked-away hiding place. Leaning on every word, a churning in my mind tried to make sense of an absence of understanding. Callie had seemed resolved to leave with Dora, but now a change of heart appeared in her reluctance.

"Callie," Dora chimed in, "we all want what's best for you and your child."

And Clarice supported her, saying, "Yes, Callie, this is the best option for both of you. How would you make a living with him? You will both be well taken care of."

My lips parted, and I grasped my mouth, silencing the scream that unfurled from the hollows within me. A numb tingling spread and weakened my legs, and my hands clung to the wall, holding me up as my stomach stirred into a sick, empty pit. I knew now how Callie's life would unfold. Callie would not be leaving with her child. One aunt would take Callie, and the other aunt would take the baby to raise as her own. "Auntie" would serve as Callie's title; not Mother.

Her face fell, and a bitter coldness swept over her. Her determination crumbled, and a glimpse of fear was caught in her eyes as she turned on her heel and withdrew. Dora and Clarice followed, unwavering.

Ernie stirred in his crib; either the uncertainty that hung in the air or the rumblings in his stomach awakened him. I went to him and allowed him to suckle, but my milk was dried. I had prepared for this, but not on a morning when my body was ravished by confusion of one child's needs of my body, along with another, yet born. I took him to the kitchen, now bare of intruders, and put some cow's milk in the pot, slowly warming his nourishment. Weaning him would be quick, although not painless to him. He choked down a bit, coughing and sputtering like a stalled motor car. He hung onto my dress tail while I cleaned the dishes, my mind in a daydream, filled with conflict. A whimpering cry brought me back to him, his discomfort of a full diaper, annoying and piled full of smell.

"Phew, stinky boy, you need a change."

And he then settled back to a nap, his thumb suckling in his mouth on instinct, for comfort. The age of innocence, how short it seemed to be.

I waited for them on the porch in the swing where, in the warmer weather, I had swung with the children, both the young and the older ones. I often sat a pitcher of sweet tea on the table. There had been laughter amongst them and a time to play, after the work was done, usually at the setting sun. Rachel found a lost baseball at the school, which no one eventually claimed, and the schoolmaster permitted them to bring it home. The boys fashioned a large stick, whittling it to smoothness and form, creating a bat of sorts. Callie and Hazel joined in at my insistence, while Rachel and Lydia retrieved wayward balls and served as the cheering team. Occasionally, I joined in. Ben never participated.

"It's a waste of time," he implored and would remove himself from our presence.

Now I sit, with both voiceless words and opinions, pushing my shoe-wrapped toes on the porch floor, the swing swaying back and forth, ceiling creaking where the heavy twine is anchored. Slices of blackberry pie and a hunk of ham powered between biscuits wait in a basket for them. I had busied myself in the kitchen, the only place I could try to shut out my rambling thoughts, a refuge where smells of pleasant things happen, and my hands steady themselves in pastry, forming and shaping a creation that will satisfy only a physical hunger, not a fulfillment for the soul. The thing that shelters and appeases me from this hopeless oppression.

I looked up, and with a puff of dust behind them, two cars were zigzagging from one side of the dirt road to the other, dodging rutted-out holes as best as they could. I could hear them laughing, the Smith boys. Their papa owned the feed store in town. Sometimes they would take their papa's cars and create trouble. I could see the pleasure that it gave them, but my jaw tightened, and I heard the grind of my teeth like fingernails scraping against a chalkboard. My breath quickened, and I thought of the axe in the woodshed and how it could quickly splinter the tires and scrap the metal that shined like tin pans in the cornfield, catching glints of sun, scaring the crows away. How dare they feel any happiness! Happiness didn't live here! My fingers dug into the palms of my hands, blanching my knuckles.

But I knew our course would remain unchanged, and I retreated inside, only to be met by the two women who had come to grasp, retrieve, and leave me in this emotional wilderness. My raging thoughts provoked me, and I cried to my desperate soul, "Resentment, let me go! Abolish my selfish feelings."

And I looked past the women, their hands full, one with the child, the other with a tote of Callie's, to see her standing behind them, no longer the headstrong girl I had come to love. Head hung low, she refused to look at me. The two brushed past me, leaving us alone.

Taking a step toward her, she backed away from me. My voice cracked, "Callie, I'm sorry. I didn't know they were coming. I didn't know they were taking him away from you."

She said nothing but raised her head slowly. The darkness in her brown eyes was terrifyingly dim. A cloud of weariness showed her cheeks drawn. Then, an unexpected sigh of relief escaped her breath, and her voice spoke with a toneless whisper: "He can't hurt me anymore." And she walked past me, leaving a shiver to run across my arms and the hairs on them, standing on ends.

My heart numbed and the words replayed again and again, not realizing I still stood where she last spoke.

The spew and spit of the car, motors turning, grabbed my attention and panic railed within me. They were leaving. I rushed to the kitchen, grabbed the food baskets, bolted out the door, and called to them.

"Wait!" I pleaded. I remembered I had forgotten the most important thing. "Please, wait."

I sat the basket down on the porch and ran back inside to the secret hiding place where, stolen away, was the smidgen of material things that mattered to me. A remembrance for Callie—my crocheted gloves, which Mama had made for me when I left my childhood years and reached my becoming. On Sunday morning, each finger had caressed the hymnal, and between God and Mama, I never felt so happy and loved. I was so proud of them, but now freely gave them to Callie, folded and wrapped in my lace handkerchief, tied together with a blue satin ribbon.

I laid it in her hands, from where she sat in the back by the open window, resting my own on top of hers for just a moment before this auto car, of no feeling on its own, was directed to transport people and things both to and from destinations, carrying with it also luggage of emotions, packed tightly and long-suffering.

Ben now stood beside me, throwing his hand up in a wave. His crooked smile lay across his face as though that slither he held inside his soul had been released and curled to its resting place on his lying lips. I strained to see if Callie would look back, for any reason, but I only saw the nape of her neck, her shoulders, and her head downcast. Paralyzed with the swiftness in which our lives had been changed, I waited until the last roil of dust had settled before I let my eyes pull away.

They had barely left the driveway when Constable John Cleaver inched past them and rested his official automobile in the shadows of their space. He was a stout man, aging out of his job in a few years, I had heard. His once salt and pepper handlebar mustache was now white and fluffy like the puff in a rabbit's tail. It sat proudly on his upper lip. It was the only hair left on his head. He was never seen in public without the hat, which bore his shiny badge, and reminded the folks he still bore responsibility for the arrest of illegal doings, especially of certain moonshiners who ran from him. He did, in time, brag about the occasional chase, and it seemed to give him a thrill. A rare time to visit, if John came, unless it was on business. My arms tightened around me as he pulled himself out of the car. Ben didn't move, hands thrust into his overall pockets. Not even a twitch.

"Howdy, Ben. Mrs. Lillian. It's a mighty fine morning, isn't it?"

Ben nodded. I did too, unable to speak.

"Well, I won't take up much of your time, but I thought I'd let you know about your son, Baxter. Seems like you had a tangle yesterday that got out of control."

Ben's feet shifted in the dirt like he was digging in for the rest of what he had to say. I had forgotten about Baxter in all the melee that had occurred. "Well," Ben's voice was calm and collected as though he were sitting and spitting tobacco, and of no concern, "he's always been trouble. Why, he has messed up his sister."

My head spiraled and my jaw dropped, then clenched like a mad dog. I felt the fury in my eyes as I turned to look at him. But he didn't waver from his straight-on stare at John.

"Look, I don't know what's going between you two, but I'm here to tell you that I got word yesterday that Baxter got a gun in town and was on his way here to kill you," John said. "I put him in jail last night." His face lowered as though it pained him to say the rest. "I told him I'd let him go," then he looked full-face at Ben, "if he promised me he'd leave and never come back."

I shook so hard that Ben's shirt sleeve was the only thing to hold me to my feet. But when I realized I had touched him, I pulled away, staggering, and turned, not wanting to hear, not wanting to see or feel.

A flood of finality and loss like a raging river of death poured over me, pulling me under, and all I could breathe was the murky water. My hands clasped my burning cheeks, and I ran and ran, wantonly, trying to raise my head to the surface for air. But the whispers in my head pulled me deeper, and I was frightened and could not seem to run away from them. They ripped my clothing, stripping my arms of their flesh. I stumbled and fell, but then awkwardly scrambled to stand again, and kept running.

I was unaware of the time when I woke, curled in a bed of moss on the forest floor. Dazed and confused, I sat up, both sight and body darting from side to side, heart pounding as I tried to clear my mind as to what had happened and where I was. Trickles of blood had weaved their way down my arms and legs, a thorn here and there. I pulled them out, wincing, and with the stance of a four-legged creature, lifted myself and staggered like a Saturday night drunk. Then, a cool spring breeze lifted my face to beads of sunlight, passing through the budding branches, willing my eyes to close and lay down again, but as I brushed the hair from my face, I saw the cave opening drawing me to it.

Where Callie went for refuge. Where I found her in her misery and this unwanted journey chained us together. In the expanse of the darkness, with no candle to be lit and no lamp to guide me, I felt my way around the walls, in the room where the "ghost" stood and the light from the ceiling opened, shadowing it. Still, and menacing. Why had I not noticed it before? But I was no longer afraid! And I walked toward it, fists clenched. Then, I lunged at it, pounding it, and a feral scream came from me, the depth of which I had not known, and the scream in me didn't stop, like a runaway train. Screeching and unfaltering until my battered hands clawed their way down to its feet. I lay there, tearful sobs drowning me again like a baby wren fallen from the nest, its feathers matted and laden with water, unable to fly. A weighted blanket of grief lay on me until a whimpering cry, like the last moans of an animal desperate to flee from its agony, gathered my knees to my chest, and I rocked them as though comforting a baby. When no tears were left and spent from torment, I peered at my hands, caked with mud.

Like God had created at the beginning of time, taking His hands to blow a breath of life into man, so had he breathed into me in that moment. With renewed strength, I returned to the light of day. A gentle rain had begun to fall, leaving the earth with new growth and life. I drank in the sweet aroma of hope. The leaves glistened and the plop of each raindrop sounded in musical harmony like a bass fiddle, plucked. And with uplifted arms, I embraced the bath, cleansing me of clay and blood. Cleansing me of hopelessness.

A clap of thunder rang in my ears, and I began running back. Back to where I had to be. Back to my children. And Ernie, my baby, who now was bound to be distraught and hungry. And the others who would come home from school wanting and expecting their lives to be the same as when they left. Ben spent away my dignity, my strength, and my resolve, but he would never be able to take the love of my children away from me. As I reached the clearing, the house that held sorrow, life, and death, would not be relieved of its fate. For its future stood, uncertain. But a new voice came from me, comforting me in a way I had not felt for many sunrises and sunsets, and the voice sang...

Soft as the voice of an angel, breathing a lesson unheard,
Hope with a gentle persuasion whispers His comforting word.
Wait till the darkness is over, wait till the tempest is done.
Hope for the sunshine tomorrow, after the shower is gone.
Whispering hope, oh, how welcome thy voice,
Making my heart in its sorrow rejoice.

Callie

My home and everything I knew it to be, good or bad, was gone. Everyone who had spoken to me in my young life who had smiled at me, or even had a cross word with me, was gone. I had not looked back when we left, afraid that my heart would become human again. I should have felt fear, but I had already faced that. And hopelessness. But hope had come after me, even though I didn't realize it at the time. My chest heaved in silent sobs, not knowing why they still tortured me with feelings I could not comprehend. Tears should have been falling, but they were dry as a cold winter's wind. I turned away, mindlessly unfocused on the road before us, and set my jaw like I had done many times when I didn't want people to know how I felt, and my tortured spirit knocked on my door.

When Mama left me, she might as well have carried me to Papa's bed. I first blamed her for my circumstances, then Lillian. Eventually, I blamed the person who actually deserved the blame, and ruined me...Papa.

We had rolled past the Appalachians into the Piedmont valley, only stopping for petrol. And lunch was spent sitting on the runner, beside a lone oak tree on the side of the road, to partake of the bounty in Lillian's basket. I had never seen the lay of a land so flat, even though it wasn't exactly that. The fields stretched farther than I had ever seen and made me wistful of the mountains. But this land showed me a kaleidoscope of ever-changing colors, and a treasure chest of possibilities, which brushed the treetops and pushed the clean, fresh air in a whiff up our noses.

Aunt Clarice and Uncle Tom had hardly spoken a handful of words to me before we stopped. I hardly knew them, only seeing them one time when Mama died. We were all strangers to each other, tied up like hostages, barely willing to accept our sudden departure from our used-to-be lives. I nibbled at the fried chicken, not thinking I was hungry, but the taste on my tongue felt pleasant, and I wanted more. And I asked for a second piece, of which they were obliging. Auntie tucked a wayward strand of hair behind my ear, and a gentle smile followed across her lips, unsettling me a bit with her kindness.

"We're going to be a family, Callie. You have your whole life in front of you, and we want to give you a good home."

I couldn't speak or even nod, but I held my dark eyes to hers for just a moment before I took another bite of bread. They never had any children, of what reason or why I never knew. But I let my heart, in its stupor, feel just a little, before the door locked again.

I had seen things already today that I had never seen before and had no inkling of roads that were made of anything but dirt, but here I was riding along without an ounce of jostling, with roads that had been smoothed and paved. Occasionally, a motor car had careened down our road, and I wondered what it would feel like to ride in one and lift my face to the wind. Now I knew, and the wind was strong on my face, not the way I had expected. But I closed my eyes, thinking about my baby and wanting him back, and my sisters and brothers…and Baxter. He, of all my brothers—the quiet one, the compassionate one, who caused no harm to me yet accused and dejected—would tug at my heart of guilt. Another tear rolled down my swollen face as the pastures spread farther, and the cornfields blurred into nothingness.

Weariness had found me along the way, nodding my head like a marionette, and sleep soon sought me. I don't know if it was the whispered voices in the front seat or the engine's hum that woke me, but a warm blanket caressed my shoulders, and I pulled it around me tighter. The flitting awareness of where I was briefly lingered, then I succumbed to sleep again.

The sun had swapped places with the moon by the time we arrived, their shift of time. One finished, and one had just begun.

Before I opened my eyes, flashes of light danced all around me. I sat up and blinked, trying to anchor myself to my setting, shielding my eyes from the glare. Poles stood upright, with a ball of light on top, as though God had taken a piece from the sun, knowing people needed an extra dollop of light from the darkness. They lined the streets and thrust light toward tall buildings and storefronts. A misty spring rain was falling, coating the pavement with shimmers of light, reflecting like ice on our pond during the winter. It was magical, as though the sky had become the earth and millions of stars had fallen on the streets. I sat up in my seat, wiping the moisture from the window to try and see more. But for an occasional passing auto and the patter of rain, silence resided in the absence of people. At a turn, one building seemed to reach heaven and stood taller than any forest tree I had ever seen. Upright windows were stacked on top of each other and anchored with stone, holding them together. And there were lights in some of them, yellow and dim, like lightning bugs that had stilled their beam. I wondered how many people lived there, and who bore the children. The words flew out of my mouth before I could stop them.

"Who lives in that house?" I asked. Both Auntie and Uncle burst into a chuckle, which came near to raising a wave of anger in me.

"Well, Callie, that's an office building. People don't live there, although sometimes they may feel like it because they spend so much time away from their family. They work there."

I was in awe and left my misery behind me for the time being.

There were other buildings as well, not quite as tall, but similar in stature. My excitement quickly waned as the light faded, passing each abandoned street. The darkness grew brash as Uncle guided his auto down tree-lined side streets, away from the harsh emptiness of the city. I sat up on the edge of my seat, concerned that I would miss an important shadow or dwelling. Houses began to grow like weeds and stretch like laundry on a line, with hardly any grass between them. Even though Uncle proceeded at a snail's pace, I was unable to pinpoint their details within the shadows. Wondering, still, how the people had room to coop their chickens and pen up their pigs, I braved another question.

This time, though, Auntie covered her smile and answered me, simply, "We don't have farm animals in town."

This led me to think of other questions, but I dare not ask.

The street began to narrow, and Uncle slowed the vehicle, tapping the brakes as he turned into a driveway. The flash of auto lights glared at the windows, reflecting an illuminating of their home. There was colored glass in the upper half of the front door, as though melted crayons had dried in the sun, with odd shapes and sizes which fit together perfectly. The porch, with many steps, unlike our one stoop, was bricked and cuddled with hanging pots of flowers, already in bloom. There might have been a swing on the porch, like back home. I couldn't rightly tell in a split second, for Uncle didn't stop until the car settled in front of a separate building behind the house that was made just to store it.

"Well, Callie," Uncle began, his voice in a gesture of cheerfulness, though he sounded weak and tired. "This is our home, and now it's your home too. We're happy you're here."

Auntie chimed in, "Yes, we'll get you settled in, show you your room, and I'll fix us a bite to eat."

Gathering my belongings, I followed them up the back steps, a porch light paving our way. Uncle Tom, now with a little catch in his step from the long drive, persuaded the door as he turned the key, then flipped a button on the wall, causing a flood of light in the room, which made my hand cover my eyes. In a moment, they opened, and I gazed around the room. The kitchen sink had water coming from the spigot. He was drinking a glass of water that had simply flowed by a turn of the handle. A white stove sat in the corner, with no sign of a need for wood or fire. And another box sat in the opposite corner, where he was taking food from. I walked closer to it, and the coolness chilled me.

"Come, my dear," Auntie said, not stopping for a second. "Let's go upstairs."

The hallway was long and narrow, exposing a walled garden of papered roses. Her quickstep pulled me behind her. Then, in a turn to face me, her arm outstretched, and she motioned, "This is the parlor, and come, here we have the dining area."

Dark wood furniture edged with intricate carvings, trimmed the upholstered couch and chairs, and lamps with white glass, flowers etched upon them, sat on wood tables that matched the carvings on all the wood furniture. Hanging curtains of heavy tapestry, bordered by sheer lace curtains, lined the windows, gently brushing the polished floor. In the dining area, a table rested, waiting for guests to arrive at any time appointed, and chairs tucked under, ladened with needlepoint, waited to seat them. Above the table was a chandelier that showed like ice crystals. I wanted to touch them, imagining the sound as their music played like a soft breeze. But it was the hutch with glass doors that drew me closer. Inside, teetering on instability, stood rows of plates upright, all matching with a gold rim around them, followed by a streak of blue alongside as well, and the center was stamped and sealed with tiny periwinkles.

I didn't realize it was my sigh that I heard, admiring their beauty, until Auntie laid her hands on my shoulders and whispered in my ear, "Tom's mother gave them to us when we married. I'm very fortunate to have my husband, Callie. Life could have been much different for me. And you, too, will have a good husband someday."

I looked into her eyes, searching for the truth in her voice. Hoping. "Now, come on," she continued. "You have more to see."

And with that, she took my hand and directed me up the steps to the upper rooms. The first was a shared bathroom for all of us. A tub with claw feet bolted to the floor, and best of all, a toilet, she had called it, for the "necessities." My bedroom, as she opened the last door, held a white wrought iron bed adorned with a fresh quilt, hand sewn with bits and scraps like Mama used to make. One table, small and square sat beside the bed, and a lamp, plain and simple, supported a soft green shade, the color of grass just sprouting, and tassels hung at her hem like a veiled woman's hat on Easter morn, pulsing a glow around the room. This was more than I had ever seen or experienced or tried to understand. My lips began to tingle, and beads of sweat covered the back of my neck as I stumbled, my legs no longer willing to hold me, and Auntie caught me before I fell, shuffling me to my bed.

"You dear child. So much has happened in such a short time, and here it is after a long, tiring day, that you're exhausted." Auntie left me briefly, only to return with wet cloth and a basin of water, washing my face and arms. She continued, "Now, you finish up and I will bring you something to eat."

I insisted I had no hunger, but shortly a bowl of warm soup and bread was placed on the side table near my bed. After she kissed my forehead and said goodnight, the tempting aroma heightened my desire, and I took in every bite, swiping the last morsel of bread around the bottom of the bowl. Then, sleep came quickly after I turned out the light, but not before I muffled the sobs in my pillow.

The morning slipped into my room, quiet and warm, cradling me, and I stirred to a drowsy wakefulness with my arms wrapped tightly around the same pillow of security from the night before. But now a wayward feather nudged a tickle on my nose, and my body stretched without permission then retreated as I pulled the cover back over my shoulders before I even opened my eyes. Never had I slept in a bed of such design and solace, and I wished to stay. It was the creak of a screen door and the following footsteps below that reminded me of my obligations to the household, and I dressed, washed my face, and primped my hair the best I could. Having no knowledge of the morning hours, my hurried steps greeted an empty kitchen, breakfast dishes washed and dried, and only a sniff of bacon lingered. A clock hung on the wall beside an opened door, and the pantry was stocked with canned food. Not canned the way we made back home from the garden, but cans of tin with paper labels, stating their nature. It was nine o'clock, and my embarrassment had already flushed my face when Auntie came from the outside.

"I'm so sorry, Aunt Clarice, that I overslept."

Before I could utter another word, she shushed me, "Dear child, you needed your rest. Now, no more apologies. We have a few things to do today if you feel up to it." And before I could answer, she said, "Sit down and I will get your breakfast. You can watch me. You've never seen an electric stove, have you?"

I shook my head.

"Or refrigerator?"

I shook my head again.

"Well," she continued, "there's a lot to learn, and we might as well get started today."

And with that, she pulled out eggs from the cold chest—the fridge, as she called it. Bacon as well. And milk! There were no farm animals in town, like she said. I began to feel more confident and asked, "Where do you get the milk?"

She turned from the stove, a spatula in hand. "The milkman," she said, covering the smile that was hiding behind her words. She hesitated, choosing her words carefully, and continued, "A man drives through our streets delivering milk in jars and sets them on our porch three times a week. We place an order from him, and he takes our empty jars back to the factory to be sterilized and refilled. The factory buys milk from the farmers."

She scooted the plate to me and reached for a cup of coffee, sitting with me. I had so much to learn, but now I only wanted to delve into the food she had prepared. Tomorrow I would make my breakfast, and theirs as well.

She doted on me for a week, not allowing me to take on chores. She'd say, "Your body needs to rest. There'll be time for work."

It was, however, on a morning after breakfast that she announced an outing for the two of us: "I'm taking you downtown today. You will need some fresh clothes. Clothes for church and social gatherings."

The thought gathered fear and wrapped it around me, smothering my breath. She must have noticed and said, "You're going to be alright, Callie. I will be with you. It's time you make some friends and start living again. I know it will take some time, but there has to be a beginning. A fresh start."

Her words held truth, but I still shuttered at the thought of those new beginnings.

* * *

There were many waiting for the bus. Mothers and their children, sharing motherhood with each other. Babies in strollers, like mockingbirds crying out to each other, reminding me of my own again. Also, women with grey hair pinned and wrapped into a high chignon, clutching a wooden cane. A husband here and there, escorted them with a helpful hand up the steps, all the while him needing the same assistance. It was upon the roar of the engine and a jolt forward that a rush of excited nervousness pursued me and captured my view out the window. A strip of sun warmed my face, and soon the bustle of the city opened with a wave of people on the streets, hurriedly seeking their destination.

Hanging lights of red and green instructed pedestrians and vehicles when to move in an orderly fashion. Storefront windows boasted specialty merchandise, and awnings shaded the wares from the sun. Men wore dark suits, some with vests, and a chain leisurely swayed from their pocket, them checking the time of day. Polished shoes with wing tips completed their attire. Women also strutted in skirts with jackets and sensible heels, their hair short, curled, and shaped, some with curlicues. Mixed in with the crowd were people of color, in plain dresses, though clean and starched. Straw hats, with a wisp of fresh flowers stuck in the band, shielded their faces from the towering sun. It was a town with many people, who held secrets like me, I was sure. Auntie lifted my spirit and taught me how important I was and how much I would be able to give to people, and most importantly to me—how I could begin to accept that I was worthy of love.

The bus lumbered to a halt, and we scurried alongside the others out the door. Auntie straightened her dress and adjusted her white cotton gloves as the bus pulled away, coughing a cloud of dark smoke around us. "I'll be…" She pursed her lips and backed away haughtily before she remembered I stood beside her. "Come, Callie."

And we ran, leaving the stench behind, and in a bird's flutter stood in front of Sosnik's ready-to-wear store for ladies. Auntie, who had never had the pleasure to dress a child of any age, pitched forward, pulling me with her. Bright-colored dresses, and ones of barely any color, hung from a rack. Tables were filled with folded blouses and skirts. A section at the back of the store, where modesty sat, were drawers of undies in specific shapes and sizes. But the smell of cloth dyes, akin to a decaying forest, began to fill my stomach and I bolted to the door, hiding from the window where no one inside could see me.

The fresh air found me, and I breathed in deeply and closed my eyes. A mist drifted through fields I had known, and I laid within it as it rolled over me, depositing its glistening dew. I wanted to stay there, but a familiar voice, distant, yet panicked like the sound of a mama bird scared for her young'un, called to me.

"Callie," the voice spoke urgently, then softly. "Callie, are you alright?"

I reluctantly opened my eyes to face the embarrassment of my actions. "I'm so sorry, Aunt Clarice. All the clothes and the smells. It was overwhelming."

The softness of her glove touched my arm. "Now, you be of no mind. I should have been more thoughtful, realizing this town is too much to take in, in such a short time. Please forgive me."

I knew in that moment, I loved her like my mama, and I threw my arms around her and cried tears like the mist I had stood in, each one releasing a bag of bitterness. She let me hold her until it was I who broke away, her handing me a hanky from her purse. "We can go home now," she said.

But I shook my head, knowing that this day would become a time we would remember, and I could not deny her this happiness. "No. I'm fine. I don't want us to leave."

With that assurance, she pulled out a puff of powder for both of us and dotted our noses as she spoke. "How about this? You stand here in front of the window. I'll bring clothes to you and hold them up. Then, you can decide which ones you like. It will be a fun game."

A smile crept across my face like warm syrup oozing from a maple tree, and at the end of the day, we carried home a parcel of bags, all meant for me.

My bedroom became a shelter, and I could lie down, drifting away from thoughts of the present. But Auntie, not allowing me a length of solitude, lightly tapped on my door and coaxed me to the front porch. A tray filled with cold lemonade and sugar cookies sat invitingly upon a painted wooden table between two rocking chairs. On the far side, a swing hung from the rafters that was wide enough for two people to wile away the afternoon. It was on one of those days, weeks now past, that I felt a healing change, both in mind and body, and my pillow began to remain dry from tears at night, though the loss and loneliness persistently dogged me. Neighbors dropped by, inquisitive about the new girl now living with them, and Auntie closeted me from their questions, her answering for me.

"She's a bit shy, you know."

Our shared glance lowered my eyes, and I often excused myself. Eventually, the questions stopped, unable to extract more information.

Uncle Tom cranked up his jalopy every morning and headed downtown to work, except on the weekend. He would joke when asked what he did for a living, and say, "Well I count other people's money for a living and bring home a little for myself."

Whoever would listen roared with laughter, and it couldn't please him more, the attention he got. Auntie and I often walked to the market, about six blocks away, and bought meat and vegetables and sometimes fruit. She loved picking each one up and smelling it to see if it was ripe. The proprietor wasn't necessarily pleased and lowered his chin, casting his brows over his disapproval. But she ignored him and went about her business, stopping to talk along the way to both strangers and friends, and the crowd along the way grew, chattering like a tribe of magpies. I became weary of the frenzied talk and wandered away, finding a quiet place to sit, watching people stroll and studying them. Some walked, shoulders high and squared, and their dress was cut along tailored lines, both men and women. Their demeanor was rushed and pointed. I drew in a breath and wished I could be running through the meadow or picking berries in that clearing in the woods. But I didn't linger on the wishes, for it was not to be.

Auntie and I continued to grow at ease with each other as we adapted to our new lives together, but not without occasional disagreements, regarding a pinch of sugar added to the kneaded dough, or an extra sliver of butter in the pies. Nevertheless, she certainly did not resist a second piece of either, and Uncle kept saying, "These sure taste extra special."

A snicker spewed between us, leaving Uncle with a quizzical pucker between his eyes. Each day greeted me with a pail of strong will, and I began to feel the curve in my back straighten, squaring my shoulders like the people in town, and every breath felt deeper and free. One quiet morning, before children made themselves known walking to school and motor cars were started, carrying their owners to work, a voice began humming a song as I swept the porch. It gathered the notes and sang with the birds. Soft steps approached from inside the house, and I turned to see Auntie standing there, the brightness on her face showing her approval. "I see that another morning bird has joined the others."

And I stopped and turned toward her, my face in mirroring affection, realizing the sound came from me.

Sundays were worship days and nothing, including a person's last breath, stopped a believer from entering the church's sanctuary. No amount of sickness, work, or excuse was tolerated by preacher, deacons, or congregation, and absence invited a presence of one or the other, knocking at your door. Uncle Tom and Aunt Clarice were never owed a visit of such nature, since they attended not only on Sunday morning, but also the night service, and Wednesday's prayer meeting. Papa grumbled when we girls went to church, but we were dressed and out the door before he had a chance to stop us. We didn't go on Wednesdays because of school the next day. It was the hymns that I liked the most, with Beulah, the pianist—stubby fingers, fat as pork belly—banging out those tunes. I always wondered if the sour notes came from her or the untuned piano. It didn't matter to me, as long as I could sing along with the others. I wistfully admitted that it had been a long time, though, since I graced those church doors, because of my circumstances.

I had been given me a long leeway since I arrived, undemanding that I attend with them, leaving me to decide when I was ready.

Gratitude continued to fill my ragged book of life, and one day I chose to walk with them, down three blocks, to the stark white gathering place, its steeple resting across the peaked roof and stained glass lining the sides of the building with images of Jesus and his disciples. The bell in the tower clanged, and worshippers began to lean into each other, talking above the noise. They wore their finest clothes, women with dresses and stockings where the seam lay straight against their calves, disappearing beneath the length of the hem. Hats adorned their heads, simple, with light netting. Men wore suits, some with vests, and ties around their necks, wrapped with knotted precision. Their hats, with respect, came off at the door. My attire, a pleated plaid skirt that brushed my calves, and a white cotton blouse with a length of sash that tied into a bow, reflected my new life.

"You're still young," Auntie said. "A hat is unnecessary. However, a new hairstyle—a bob, they're calling it now—would look adorable on you."

And I was open to her new ideas and her guidance, wearing this new style, a clip on the side, to keep the hair tamed.

As we approached the steps, most of the flock already cradled inside, my shoes became like set tar and my stomach clenched like a vise. Then, a warm hand slipped in mine and whispered in my ear, "You don't have to go in."

But I turned, lifting my eyes to hers, and drew in a deep breath, "Yes, I must go. It's part of the life I want."

The pattern was much like I remembered: folks greeting each other, a slap on the back, man to man, women complimenting one another on an item or color which they wore, or a quick piece of gossip, side glancing toward the person it was addressed to. My hands, gloved, still cold and clammy, reached out to meet each stranger's welcome. We all smiled graciously as Auntie introduced me to whomever approached. It was the sound of the piano that returned all to their seats. The choir took their places behind the preacher, him now standing with hands on each side of the pulpit, his shoulders thrust over it like he was holding it down, afraid it might rise before he got a wind in his voice.

"Now, y'all just settle down. The choir's worked hard this week, and it's going to be a blessing to ya. But first, Matt's going to pray and then make some announcements before he leads us in God's songs."

Matt, Auntie told me, was an all-around kindhearted man who was born with an incapability to say no to the preacher. His wife and children hardly saw him, due to his second dwelling place. But she remained steadfast in her support of the preacher and his demands. Guilt was always an enemy that bore itself like termites, eating away at a person's soul. And obedience was often a topic of preacher's sermons, keeping the sheep intact.

"Now, open your hymnals to page two-hundred nineteen," Matt began.

We all stood, hymnals in hand, and the music came, and my voice sang with it, soothing my soul. And during the months ahead, I sat each Sunday, the amens all around me, as I fanned the heat away like the others, listening to the preacher while beads of sweat rolled down his face, handkerchief in hand, dabbing them away as fast as they popped out on his forehead. His voice seemed to shake the chandelier hanging from the rafters, and deep breaths sucked in the air before he expelled words of damnation. And it was on one of those days when he pled for the lost, and the pianist played the third repeat of "Just As I Am," that I went forward, giving my life to Jesus. Though others came forward that day, dancing in the aisles and shouting, I sat on the front pew in silence, talking to God with thankfulness that He saw me, and I felt loved by Him. And I loved Him, too.

Although my days were filled with newfound happiness, the shadows of the evening crept through my open window, spiraling the lacy curtains into a mystical dance and whispering cries from my child. This tossed me about until the morning. I was so wrought from these frightful nights that I approached Auntie one day when we were alone, in a quiet moment, book in hand, our rockers still. Pointedly, I blurted, "Will I ever be able to see my son again?"

I had not spoken of him since they had taken me that fateful day, and I searched her face, but no grimace wrinkled her brow. "You would like to see him?" she asked, glancing from her book.

I nodded, the lump in my throat stubbornly lodged. "I would be happy to arrange that for you," she said. Her understanding curved the corners of her smile.

Within the month, she had arranged a visit with Dora and her husband. I overheard the request, and my ears burned like hot coals at Dora's apparent reluctance. "But it's just one time, Dora," Clarice encouraged.

"She knows you are his mother now," Clarice pushed. "Callie would be coming as his aunt…Very well, we will visit for an overnight only."

I stepped away quietly, hoping the screech of the wood floor would lay silent, and relief swept over me that I would be allowed to come, though the request was objectionable.

Aunt Clarice never mentioned the conversation with her sister, and I was grateful, because the both of us knew it would mean that we shared a sadness in the trip. Instead, with bags packed and Uncle Tom moseying along at his comfortable pace, we all sang church songs and songs like "Turkey in the Straw."

Turkey in the straw, turkey in the straw,
Went out to milk and I didn't know how,
I milked the goat instead of the cow.

We also sang,
She'll be coming round the mountain when she comes,
She'll be driving six white horses when she comes,
They'll all come out to meet her when she comes.

Their radio in the parlor had brought music to my ears, along with stories and news of interest, and I wiled away time, listening with them at night. Sometimes, I fell asleep when the tunes mutated into melancholy, and I awoke in my bed, not knowing the arm that guided me, until Auntie chuckled the next morning and said, "A man consuming an infinite amount of wine could not have staggered more than you."

She tousled my hair and sat me down to breakfast, kissing the top of my head. "Thank you, Aunt Clarice," I said. It was only one of many gestures I put in our mutual cookie jar.

* * *

We had long left the Piedmont's landscape, venturing higher into the mountain range with its snaky roads only wide enough for two motor cars to breathe the breath of the other in passing. I was glad that we were the ones hugging the side of the mountain instead of the far side, which lay stretched and open, birds below squawking to warn us of their protective nest below. But when a clearing came into view, the vistas lay like a sea of blue—the Blue Ridge, they were called by locals.

It was late afternoon when we arrived. The house stood simple, tucked underneath trees tall as God and with arms as wide, shading it like a bird's feathered wings. Beds of pine needles showered the lawn with a coat of brown, and the tires rolled over them, a brittle crunch underneath, sounding alarm as though watchdogs who announced intruders. The screen door whipped open, and Dora and Ebb with empty arms greeted us as though no harsh words had been spoken. Dora embraced me, and I knew right away without a glance toward Aunt Clarice that Ebb must've had a word or two with her. I could almost imagine.

"It's the Christian thing to do, Dora," he'd probably said. "She's no threat to us or our child. Let me remind you who's responsible for this child."

No matter what was said, Dora took me by my hand and directed me inside the house into a small room where pictures befitting a child hung on the wall. Curtains graced the windows. A soft blue, like the skies that had laid a trail before us. Embroidery of animals found in storybooks were stitched down the sides. A chair for rocking sat in a corner, padded, both seat and back with needlepoint in matching hues with birds and flowers. But on the other side of the room stood a crib, and I tiptoed to it, peering upon the small child which lay, thumb to mouth, sleeping, a suckle here and there when a sleep smile broadened his chubby cheeks.

I wanted to touch him, hold him, but I backed away, whispering to Aunt Dora, "He's beautiful."

She put an arm around me. "He looks like you. Why don't you wait here until he wakes? That way, you will be the first person he sees."

My eyes, unbelieving, nodded, and I sat in the rocker, waiting until a time I have no recall. Then, he awakened from his drowsy sleep, and I ventured to him, afraid. He flung his feet and hands, frenzied and without meaning. His disheveled mop of hair, and black ringlets of curls stacked like coal nuggets, split me into a chuckle. Then his smile burst open like daffodils blooming in the spring, and I picked him up, planting kisses on his warm, plump cheeks. Red like apples. I found toys in a bin and chose a few, circling us into the center of the rug. He had begun to crawl, and when he was pleased laughed like a squealing piglet, and I laughed with him. But laughter was short-lived with babies, as I had known, being around them most of my life. Tears came about like a sudden thunderstorm, and it was a matter of elimination to determine the cause.

Hunger claimed all of us, and we soon sat down at the table together, my child in a highchair beside Aunt Dora, squirming for that first taste of food. Uncle Ebb was a skilled craftsman and there was no doubt that he had carved his chair to his liking.

"Come, Callie. Feed Vern," Dora implored. I caught the tip of my chair, standing so quickly, and carried it, placing myself beside him. I absorbed him while the others blurred in my thoughts, with only the two of us sitting there. His eyes danced, reaching for me until his taunt belly was filled. Both aunties shooed me away from clearing the table and prodded me further, to my child. An impression caught in my troubled heart, scanning the house. A place unfamiliar to me, but home to him…and his Papa and Mama's thumb-print lay embedded in every corner. They gave him a family, safety, and love. Mama was the first person I ever loved, yet I had no choice but to let her go, and now, as the fading light turned pitch-black, I sat at the open window, my arms cradling another who would be torn from my heart.

The chant of a nightjar sang its song of whip-poor-wills, gathering a discord of musicians in accompaniment with crickets screeching like untuned fiddles and droning mosquitoes, fraught, with no escape.

"Beyond the canopy of trees, there is a sky sprinkled with stardust," I whispered in Vern's sleeping ear, "and I pray that God will blow a breath of it into your life."

In the morning, I would let him go to live a better life than I could give him, and maybe he would be sheltered from the silence of his beginning.

* * *

It was late summer, after the farmer's harvest, and the street markets were filled with produce. We opted to drive to the bare fields, where sharecroppers, sitting on the outlays of society and population, set up their open shed beside the road, where we purchased baskets of corn, beans, string, and pintos to broaden the farmer's profits from the profiteers. A bluster of dust kicked up, like the hind leg of our old mule back home, as we pulled alongside the road. But we brushed the dust away, eyeing the last of the plump red tomatoes, and went on to the others, loading the car with food bound for the canning jars. Auntie and I would spend the next days together, stringing and breaking the beans, shelling the brown ones, slicing corn kernels from the cob, and stewing tomatoes for tomato pie. The cans would sit on rows of shelves in the basement. I called it the cellar because that was what we called it back home.

It was during one of those days, that we sat amidst the stagnant heat, under cover of the awning on the back porch, humming sweet songs, between bouts of idle talk, that I approached Auntie with a request that had been churning like butter in my head.

"Aunt Clarice." My whisper emerged, raw and hoarse, tangled among nerves.

"Yes, Callie?" she said, her face never wavering from her chore.

"I've been thinking for some time about me getting a job."

She never missed the rhythm of a bean snap. "Oh, you have, have you?" It seemed as though she expected this announcement and had pondered already on her response. "Well, it looks like I have a niece that's growing up." She hesitated then and cast her eyes upon mine. "Are you sure you're up to it?"

I knew what she meant. She wondered if my mind had healed like my body. I had laid in bed, many nights before, the still of the night upon me, wondering the same. "Yes," I replied. "I'm ready."

It was then that a sly smile slipped over her lips. "Tom told me that when you're ready to ask, there'll be a job waiting for you."

Uncle Tom knew tobacco. Well, at least the numbers, which showed the factories' success. But I knew the product. I had worked it on our farm. I knew when the leaf's pale-yellow skin was ready to be plucked and hung in the barn to cure, and the smell of their nectar, when the leaves transformed like caterpillars into their brown, sticky sweetness. I was a quick learner. It was at that moment when a leap of excitement jumped into my heart, like the time newborn kittens were born behind a spot of hay. New life and hope began to grow in me.

It was on a crisp, cool day, a smattering of leaves already caught in the hands of a fall wind, that I rode to work with Uncle Tom. I chatted like a nervous Nellie until he pulled into a parking space and, in almost a whisper, said, "You're going to do well, and I will be down to check on you. If you need me for anything, here's the number to my office."

His voice was reassuring, but my heart still fluttered as I pried my hand from the door handle. He directed me to the foreman who had already spoken to me and tested my skills the week before. My taut smile was unmatched by the queasiness in my stomach as I took my place among the other women. They stood in formation on both sides of a long table, that fed not raw tobacco, but tobacco that had been chopped and blended between white portions of rolled paper.

"We were the collectors and sorters," I was told.

Right away, a woman of a sallow complexion, who stood to my shoulder, approached with hands like teapot handles posted on her hips. "You're a tall one," she said, glancing at the top of my head. "And I bet you're younger than you look." She eyed me with one squint.

I poked the restraint in my throat and followed with, "My mama always told me I was going to be taller than a beanstalk."

And with that, the woman howled with laughter, slapping me on the back. "Come on," she said. "Let's find you a spot on this here line, and we'll show you what to do. By the way, what's your name?"

"Callie," I replied, "and what's yours?"

She paused for a moment. "Why, it's Nellie! The girls call me nervous Nellie because I have to always have my feet moving like I'm dancing. Now, that wouldn't go over very well in the Baptist church downtown, would it?" She burst into a knee-slapping snort, and I chuckled a snort with her, remembering my nervousness shortly before. She became not only my boss but also my friend, who would guide me and teach me throughout the years that I worked there.

I stayed with my auntie and uncle for two years, saving my money and paying them a little along the way, even though they reluctantly accepted it. My need for independence grew as I did, and there came a day in the kitchen, when we had all sat down to partake in a piece of apple pie, that I stopped and took each of their hands in mine, and began a conversation which tiptoed like a mouse around a sleeping cat. I spoke of my enduring love for them and the grace in which they had accepted me, but that a desire flowed through me, and I knew I needed to be on my own, devoid of leanings. I felt strong when I began my rehearsed speech, but as each word was spoken, the air around me became brief and thin, and my lips moved in a twitch, causing the spill of tears down my cheeks. It was difficult to express my devotion to them without feeling like they'd see me as ungrateful. But in the time I had known them, their love of me never faltered, and they gingerly took me in their arms, holding me with assurance.

They were the ones who were grateful, they said, for our time together. That I had filled their home with something that had been foreign to them. A child, with an absence of love and nurturing, had come to them empty. And they were allowed to give love to this child and show her that she was worthy of their love. I felt a rush of comfort envelope me. Although Mama had loved me, along with all the other children, her affection was spent cooking and cleaning…and surviving. I now felt a new type of love that nurtured me beyond their presence.

* * *

The two-story boarding house sat at the top of the hill, and two blocks down, we walked to the bus stop. In the winter, the streets were slick with snow and ice, and the bus sashayed down the hill like a woman unfurled by her girdle.

Alberta and I questioned, standing there waiting, whether to snicker or run, not knowing if the sliding angle would smack us down. Albie, as I now called her, had worked on the "line" with me. As we became acquainted a friendship grew, eventually becoming roommates. An orphan, she had said. But she heard tell that her mama and papa had a passel of kids, and they were unable to feed another one. There was a sadness that flashed across her face when she said it, like a slip of the moon hiding behind a cloud. Her hair lay untamed, with golden streaks and a kiss of strawberries intermingled with uncut wheat. She often platted her untamed locks into two pigtails, and on occasion, persuaded me to iron her hair flat and straight on the ironing board. A smattering of freckles lay scattered like seeds for planting on her cheeks, and her smile lit up the room in which she entered. She radiated with enthusiasm, but everyone at work knew not to cross her. She had spunk. And I liked that. We got along well, and I began to speak up for myself at work. I asked for a raise after I had been there a year, and when it wasn't what they were paying the others, I asked for more…and got it.

We didn't attend the same church, and most of the time she shaded her eyes from the light on church day, pulling the covers tightly over her head as I dressed. But by the time I returned, after the last amen was said and the last nod from the women was received, I found her primped, with scarf in hand and a wave goodbye over her shoulder as her gentleman friend, Stevie, escorted her to his car.

A roadster, slick and black, like his hair. The afternoon took them to places she never mentioned, until one day, two men sat waiting in front of the house. I passed them with hardly a glance and strode up to my room.

Albie was beside herself, flitting from one garment to another. "How does this one look?" she asked, and before I could answer, "No, I like the one with the lace on the sleeves. Hurry. He brought a friend with him."

A rush of heat radiated up my neck. My cheeks warmed, and I placed my hands on them to cool my skin. "Albie, why would you do this to me? I'm not going!"

But she gathered my hands in hers, ignoring my complaints. "Callie, let go of whatever you're holding onto. Be happy!"

Words would not form an answer, but I allowed her to pull me to the front door, where the extra man waited. A nervous smile and timid, dark eyes glanced my way, with him summing up my reluctance as I stood before him. He tipped his hat and mentioned my pleasant appearance.

"I'm Calvin," he said, simply.

"I'm Callie," I returned.

"And this is Stevie," he continued. I nodded to him, but before I could speak, Albie and her beau raced to the car, a trailing scent of familiarity and affection following them, leaving us standing there.

"I guess we'd better get going, or they'll leave us behind," Calvin teased. A sigh took form and released itself from me as we reached the car. He took my hand, helped me into the rumble seat, and climbed in beside me, sitting on the edge of my skirt.

Our eyes briefly met when he realized the entrapment of the garment, his cheeks flushed like the tender petal of the first bloom on a rose. "Pardon me, ma'am."

I didn't know my eyes had softened at that moment, and an upturned smile spread across my face. No one had ever called me ma'am. The sound felt warm like I had just tasted freshly made bread, and respectful, like a person standing. An easiness came to my breath and the intoxication filled me like sap from a tree.

"You can call me Callie, Calvin." It had a ring to it, and he adjusted his demeanor in his seat, shifting his shoulders a smidge higher.

The car turned toward the open road. Albie and her beau, unable to split a pea between them, buzzed like June bugs, whispering words that held secrets only to them. I cast my face away, eyes closed, allowing a wind of contentment to caress me, setting aside for a moment any sense of mistrust. It was when the flickering of shade and light brushed across my eyes that I opened them to see that we were passing beneath a canopy of trees, cradling us like babies, and I shivered a little from the coolness. Calvin removed his coat and put it around my shoulders, careful not to linger on his touch. The road began to hug the mountainside, and we climbed higher, a steady stream of water seeping from the wall of earth, and it rolled across the road, the car slipping a little, just enough to give us a scare. But after a while, we reached a clearing atop the Blue Ridge, and Stevie steered the vehicle to a halt.

We walked to the furthest point, where the drop was deadly. The expanse opened the earth, exposing a lush valley of pleasantness, with a blue haze laying on the mountain ridges and a whiff of pure mountain air to clear my mind. This must be where God rested after His work was done, leaving his essence behind.

"It's beyond beautiful, isn't it?" Calvin had stepped beside me, and I felt my spine stiffen of his intrusion into my solitude.

"Yes," I said quietly, my gaze unchanged. "I'm glad I came."

Albie and I spread a quilt beneath a tall oak and laid out the lunch she had prepared. The day was so surprisingly enjoyable that an ant-like trail of guilt pained me a bit, of my reluctance to come. Stevie and Albie traded tall tales and questionable jokes between mouthfuls of chicken. My eyes were downcast shyly as I tried to cover my snicker, afraid to look at Calvin. But he caught me peeking at him out of the corner of his eye. They smiled not at Stevie, but to me, and I then realized that lighthearted chortle had grasped my heart, for the first time in my life.

Stevie was a person who doused himself with a cologne of laughter and feasted on the makings to draw attention to himself. He had a wicked mischievousness that was fetching and playful, yet I, in a quiet moment with Albie resting her head beneath the curve of his arm as he rested beneath the tree, witnessed a glance behind the curtain of his eyes, to see a young boy lonely and longing for affection. A dismal sadness that was willfully hidden to others. In a flicker, it was gone. I wondered if Albie could see that and feel his love for her. It would be difficult for him to let her see, for he was a puzzle, wanting people to see him in partiality. But she seemed to accept him and the way he presented himself.

Calvin and I hiked up to a ridge while the two slept, relieving us of the intimacy between them. Wildflowers had blossomed between the craggy rocks, their statement that beauty could rise among barrenness. I stopped to acknowledge them and brushed my fingertips lightly over their petals. He walked before me and extended his hand to help me over a wide trench, and I felt uneasy when I laid my hand in his. It was soft, free of callouses. I knew he wanted me to continue, my hand in his, but I let it fall and walked on, my thoughts in a wrangle of confusion. No man had touched me with this gentle kindness.

We walked farther than I anticipated, our conversation pointed and brief, of no fault of his, until the sound of an impatient horn announced our need to return. An attempt to scurry back to the car left us breathless, and taking a different path, I slipped and fell. Calvin rushed to my side, his eyes full of concern. I assured him there was no injury, but a scuffed knee disputed my word as a drop of blood oozed. He produced a clean white handkerchief and handed it to me. I dabbed at it, and this time I offered my hand to him, helping me to stand. I was uncomfortably grateful that I slipped and fell. It allowed me to touch him again and see if what I felt before was real. And when he pulled me up, I looked to him and smiled.

"Thank you, Calvin." That annoying horn sounded again, and we walked slowly, our hands beside us, content that there would be another day we would seek each other's company, and it would be easier somehow.

Calvin and I continued our friendship, my hand more willing to enclose upon his. We shared evenings of silent movies, seated in dark picture palaces with Albie and Stevie, and more lazy Sunday afternoons dipping our toes in cool mountain streams. Calvin showed me respect and never ventured beyond what I was willing to give. But it was on one of those nights, at the end of the evening, as a coy harvest moon posed on the horizon, that he turned to me and placed his hands gently on my shoulders. When he tilted my chin toward his, I didn't resist. I wanted to know what a gentle man's kiss felt like.

Still, fear planted itself between us, with its harsh bristled scour, reminding me of my tarnished flesh and bones. But he waited and looked into the shadow of my eyes for any hint of regret. Then, his lips lightly brushed mine. As the moon drew breath and broke ground from the earth's magnetic curve, our shadows stood in a silhouette of one. Then, I broke away and ran, not allowing him to see the tear that betrayed me, but turned and waved to him before I closed the door behind me.

"Good night!" he called.

"Good night," I whispered.

Auntie and Uncle remained cautious and protective of me, and when they met Calvin, there was no doubt that he had been quizzed, sizing up his character. Evidently, he passed their judgement, because they soon encouraged our supper gatherings around their table. Sometimes, Auntie would draw me into the kitchen while Uncle talked to Calvin in the parlor room. I strained to hear what they were saying, but she intervened with her own discussion of my intentions.

"Do you love him?" she queried.

It was after a long pause, my brows pinched to a baffled frown, that I realized I had never contemplated the idea. "I don't know," I finally admitted. "He's wonderfully kind and gentle. Considerate in every way I could want." But she raised a question which probed me for many nights thereafter. "I'm not sure I'll know love, if it ever comes to me. Or if I can allow myself to love a husband."

Auntie's eyes were wrought with concern, and she came to me, putting her arms around me. "Callie, as you can see with Calvin, he's a good man."

It was the words that were silent between us that hung in the air, like spoiled meat. *Papa.*

"You deserve to be happy," she said. "All men are not like your papa. See, I have married a man who gives me not just a home, but kindness and a pleasant life."

I let her words lay in my heart but could offer no assurance of a future with Calvin.

It was a time near Christmas when my heartstrings began to pine for home. By now, Calvin, too, had a car. Not as fancy as Stevie's, but more practical. And we ventured out on our own, occasionally. I had saved every penny I could and was able to buy enough winter clothing, with some left over for presents. Hazel and I had written to each other twice a month and told me that she read it to the other girls at night, in bed. She was courting a boy now and planned to get married before another year was up. Papa told her she better not get married, but he hadn't run the feller off so far.

Rachel and Lydia, she said, were as tight as ever, never letting each other out of their sight. The older boys were now out on their own, courting too. And Papa kept Lillian with a stomach full of baby, and an occasional bruised eye. I wrote back to her, offering my God-given ability to advise and told her to not let Papa tell her what to do and to not let him catch her alone. It made me want to go back even more. A score was to be settled with Papa and it might as well be at Christmas.

I pulled out the mason jar from under my bed and counted my money. There was enough for everything I needed, including the hired car and driver. Calvin and I were sipping on a soda down at the five and dime when I told him I was going home for Christmas, but he didn't let it hardly slip out of my mouth before he spoke up and said me hiring a transport was nonsense. He would take me, he said, and firmly spoke, "Not another word."

Ignoring him, I persisted. We reluctantly came to an agreement, that I would supply the petrol along the way.

Boldly, I wrote Papa and Lillian as to the date I would arrive, and to please tell my brothers and sisters. Then, the thought of it all gripped me like a vise, and my stomach retched me at no particular time of day until Albie threatened to call the doctor and dared ask me, with the rudeness of a bear slapping at fish, if I had a pumpkin in there.

I glowered at her and shook my head but would never confess to only a pecked kiss here and there with Calvin. "And what about yourself?" I retorted.

I expected a lift of her nose in the air, but she plopped down on her bed and burst out in a snorted chuckle. "I wish I was. Maybe Stevie would marry me then."

It was I who flew mad and leaped on top of her, my fists clenched by my sides. She lay paralyzed, like a trapped animal. "You don't have any notion of what it takes to have a baby and—"

I stopped and wondered if I had said it out loud before the darkness covered me with a blanket of emptiness. It was Albie's voice, on tenterhooks, that brought me back to light. She wiped my forehead as I lay on the floor, my head in her lap.

"You scared the bedazzle out of me, young lady! That face of yours paled like the face of a ghost." I tried to talk but she shushed me. It was better I didn't know if I had laid out my open wound to her. She didn't say, and no harsh words were ever spoken between us again.

A north wind shook the car like a baby with a rattle, making havoc for travelers. Calvin kept the car steady, and we crossed over the mountain and down to the valley before the sky spun its mixture of snow crystals, scattering them like a tipped pot of potpourri. It took a day of travel before Calvin lopped the car into the ruts of the front yard. The sun had dwindled away, unable to wait for me, allowing dusk to come and pour shadows over the land. Our dog, Copper, barked, making our presence known.

Then, the door held onto its hinges as a rush of warm bodies plowed through. Hazel was nose to nose with me, and Rachel and Lydia's heads were upon my chest, smothering me in a tight grip of solidarity. I tried to pull away, but they refused to release me until I nudged them with a poke to the ribs.

Calvin came from a large family, three sisters and two brothers all younger than him, so it was no surprise that a cackle of youngsters would intrude upon us. Lillian stood on the porch, hesitant, but carrying a pleasant and welcoming smile.

"I'm so happy to see you," she said. "You look well."

"It's good to see you, too," I said, stepping toward her, putting my arms around her.

She winced, gently pushing me away. Like many times before, she brushed it off. "It's only a little lumbago," Lillian said, trying to explain. "I'm feeling my age more lately." Her eyes were unable to meet mine, and her words were never challenged.

It was a welcome relief for us both when Calvin stepped up beside me.

"Lillian, this is my friend, Calvin," I said.

"Nice to meet you," Calvin said as he tipped his hat.

Lillian smiled graciously. "And this is Papa."

Papa stepped out from the porch's lingering shadows, his dark eyes peering above a trailing nutmeg beard, sprinkled with splinters of grey. He twisted a ringlet around his finger, looking past me toward Calvin, his eyes slitted in disapproval before he turned and walked back inside, without a word.

Thankfully, my sisters pulled at me, protesting my tardiness. A distraction from the weakness that tugged at my legs from seeing Papa again. Calvin returned to the car and opened a trunk of curiosity, where boxes wrapped with bright red bows were hidden. My sisters squealed with delight. Even Hazel, of an age to be married, was unable to contain her giddiness.

It pleased me, and as Calvin and I trailed behind, the girls in haste ran ahead to hold and feel a piece of Christmas in their hands, for as long as they could tolerate the unopened box.

"We'll stay as long as you want," Calvin said. His gentle voice would quiet a wailing child.

I stopped and looked at him, my heart filled with warmth and...I wasn't sure. But I couldn't think of that now, and simply told him, "You're a good man, Calvin. We will stay the night but leave first thing in the morning."

The eating table was filled with bowls of cured ham and gravy to be ladled on top of the creamed taters. Green beans, gathered from a canning jar in the cellar, were brimmed with a small slab of bacon mixed in, and Lillian's biscuits, brushed with a glaze of churned butter, sat predominately in the middle where there was equal opportunity to grab one or two. The girls perched in their seats like a clothesline of crows, bantering back and forth, vying for a first helping—except Papa. His absence was of no seeming importance to anyone.

"He got hungry," Lillian explained, "and ate quite early. He works hard and needs his rest."

An adequate explanation for the stranger who she had just met, before offering Calvin to pray for the food blessing. Calvin, a godly man, accepted graciously, and with an amen, we dove into the food, famished from our journey.

After the table was cleared and the dishes put away, Rachel and Lydia sat by the fireside, intently listening to a reading from the book Calvin had brought them. Hazel joined them and Lillian took my hand, directing me to the curtained bedroom, where the new babies lay sleeping. There were two girls, one of eleven months she called Josie, and the other, two years of age, named June. Both were already balled with a stouthearted fist. As I brushed my fingers through their dark hair, a pain of the heart cut through me, and I turned to the cot beneath the steps where I had born my own child. To smother the cry within my bruised soul, I grasped my mouth and closed my eyes with a steady breath, until my mind could clear and regain control.

When my eyes opened, Lillian stood with silent tears streaming down her cheeks, mouthing the words, "I'm sorry."

My heart turned like a raging storm, and a cruel vileness caused my fists to clench—not at her, but for each other, and I lashed out, "We can't be sorry anymore. We must survive him!"

Embarrassed by my outburst, I excused myself for the night, retreating to the attic bed, where I had slept before with my sisters. I missed Mama so much, but Hazel and Rachel were still here. People that I loved and could touch and feel. They both carried Mama with them in so many ways. Hazel, with her gentle spirit and humble brown eyes, and Rachel, whose cinder black hair, dark as a raven's back, matched Mama's. But it was their pure-hearted, infectious laugh, the same as hers, which had always drawn me to them, wanting to pull their face to my chest to feel the joy as well. That was the gift she left them, and it had been so long since I heard it until they joined me, tumbling into bed, and I put an itch to their feet, causing them to roll and holler and laugh.

I awoke to a house full of silence, the morning light a few hours away. Lanky arms and legs had thrown themselves over me throughout the night, keeping me from sleep, but I welcomed their touch. It reminded me of how much I missed them. I crept down the stairs, where a dance of firelight crossed Calvin's face. He was still sleeping on a tussle of blankets where Lillian had fashioned a bed for him in the corner. A wayward pair of unclaimed boots sat by the door, a cake of dirt still clinging to the sole. I slipped them on and grabbed a blanket, throwing it around me, and stepped onto the porch. A fresh breeze of pine scent renewed my senses and took my memories beyond my view to the earthy forest where the floor lay frozen beneath a covering of barren leaves. My eyes closed, and I could hear Mama calling us for supper. Hazel, Rachel, and I ran. We knew she would come for us, happily, and play with us for a while. It was the same game we always played, crouched behind a tree, hiding from her. Mama pretended not to know and began to search around all the trees but ours. Then, she would come and rest against our cover, muttering, "Now, I declare. Wonder where those girls ran off to? I sure do have a nice supper for them. Why, I even made a caramel pie. Guess the boys will just get extra helpings."

The same conclusion came on every occasion, with us screaming, "We're here! Don't give our brothers the pie, Mama."

Prevailing winter winds carried their voices away, and I opened my eyes again. The lamp of the moon provided a soft glow for direction as I ventured off the porch. The holly sapling Lillian had dug up on the edge of the woods and replanted in the yard had grown several more feet. In a few years it would be tall and strong enough for climbing, though treacherous with its barbed leaves. It wouldn't matter to the kids. They would learn to avoid them when the stickers grew past the stout arms from the trunk. I broke off a branch filled with hard round berries to take back with me. It would last a long time, and I would look at it and remember my time here. In doing so, I pricked a finger on the barb, dropping the branch. The blood oozed and dripped from my finger, renewing memories of the first time blood trailed from me.

My stomach began to ache, and grief tried to tap me on my shoulder, but I refused to wallow in it. My circumstances had provided me with a new life where I never lived in fear, nor felt my life out of my control. A faint light caught my eye, and I turned toward it. It came from the barn, and I knew who was there.

My pace, though unhurried, marched with a cape of valor toward the diffused strips of light which pushed through cracks of the old barn. A place where work was done, and wicked offenses were made. There had been no thought of leaving before seeing him alone. Pulling the door aside, my backbone wavered between courage and a crouch of fear as I looked for him. But suddenly he stepped out from a stall, pitchfork in hand, and rested it against a pole. His eyes were vacant and taunting as he said, "You've come back for more, have you?"

My strength deceived me, and I became ill prepared for the moment I had rehearsed so many times before. His breath, a frosty white vapor, and the chill that accompanied it felt like dirt scattering across my casket. His slow, deliberate step came closer, and the pounding of my heart ignited a jolt of fury that tore through my soul. I lunged for the pitchfork he had cast aside. Blind panic covered me with darkness.

"Git back," my voice spoke as a whisper still lodged in my throat.

"Now, little girl, you don't mean to treat your papa like that."

I gripped the weapon tighter and thrust it toward him. "Git back!" I bellowed. "I'm not your little girl anymore! You will never touch me again!"

The darkness in his eyes left him and resided in me. As he backed away from me, he tripped and fell backwards, helpless on the floor of strewn hay. I had no favor of forgiveness to him, no will to stop myself. Rage clothed me with fury, and I stood over him, the sharp tips touching the breadth of his chest. It was a vision of me he had never seen before, his face stricken with fear. The power of life and death lay in my hands.

Bitterness on my tongue spit from me, "You took something from me I can never get back, but I will not let it destroy the rest of my life."

Tossing the pitchfork aside, I left him there in the stench of the animals and walked out into the break of dawn, claiming my own destiny. I now realized why I had to come.

Our trip back over the mountain, though cold and blustery, was brightened by the sun, chasing the clouds away. Burdened tree limbs now dripped with melting snow and ice, and like children, we stopped to break off an ice cycle and catch a drip of water on our tongues. Coming upon a spryly stream, we cupped our hands and slurped up a good portion to quench our thirst. A spontaneous moment of joy, it was.

"You seem different somehow, Callie," Calvin said as we walked back to the car.

"How so?" I questioned, not even aware of my demeanor.

"Happier! More relaxed," he said. So that was the feeling my heart was singing. I couldn't pinpoint it. But I would not tell him the reason.

We had left the girls with full hearts, grateful for our presence, and hugs tucked in our pockets for dreary days with promises of more frequent visits. It would be a month before I could bring myself to tell him that I was going back home.

Albie got her Christmas wish when Stevie asked her to marry him. In the spring, they were to marry, but she was persistent, and they married the next month. Just five days before the wedding, we had to release three inches from the waist of her wedding dress. No questions asked.

Calvin stood beside me during the wedding, but with a realm of sadness in his eyes since I told him of my plans to return home the week before the event. He accepted the revelation with little surprise. "After I saw you with your family, I knew time wasn't on my side," he said. "Their love for you fills your needs. They look to you and your strength to protect them." He took a deep breath and continued quietly, "It is good that you go. There must be no question that I will miss you."

He left it said at that, avoiding any more words of affection to me. I was grateful.

When Albie and Stevie married, Aunt Clarice and Uncle Tom welcomed me back into their home. Calvin and I decided it was too hard to continue our friendship the way it stood, so we parted warmly, and our last embrace on the porch was wistful and not without tears. I knew he would find another whose heart would not be divided as mine. It was on a Saturday afternoon, when the winter had left and buds of new growth on trees began to grow that I saw him in a cafe, downtown with a lady friend over lunch. They sat near the window, and their conversation appeared warm and inviting. I must have caught his eye as I began to pass, for he looked up at me and smiled, and I returned his favor with affection. That was the last time I saw him, but a year later, Auntie relayed to me that he had married her. It released me of my guilt from my abrupt dismissal.

My money-filled mason jar grew ample in the time I had moved back with Auntie and Uncle. Even though I continued to pay them, it was not as much as the cost of my rooming house. "Just for food and a little water for laundry," was all they asked. I had told them of my plans to return home, but not a word was to be sent there until I had saved enough money to leave.

Hazel continued to write, and her letters spurred me forward on my journey, especially in her last letter.

Dear Callie,

The farm is beginning to bloom again, and we have started plowing sections for corn seeds and tobacco leaves, and of course, the garden. It's still my favorite time of year. When the honeysuckles bloom, I want to pick it and put it next to my bed. It would be like I was laying in the meadow when I woke. But then I wouldn't be able to walk to it and feel it and smell it. For it wouldn't last long, so sometimes I just go to the meadow and let the sun cover me with the warmth and the fragrance of the vine's sweetness.

Peter wrote to me that he's in Georgia now, but he never said what he was doing for work. He said he had to leave because he couldn't stand to see Papa be so mean. We still haven't heard from Baxter. I know you're sorry to hear that. Stanley got a room in Elizabethton and is working for a clothing store there. He was telling me about a factory called Bemberg, and they were looking for help. He said they're going to be making fabric of some sort. I thought about filling out an application, but as you know I still plan to get married soon. Stanley got into a little trouble last week. Now, don't you worry, he's okay now. At least I think he is. His name ended up in the newspaper. It was no fault of his own, mind you. May as well tell you what happened since you're not coming back for a long time.

He started dating this girl over in Elizabethton. We hadn't met her yet because the courting hadn't been going on very long. He seemed to be happy. One night, he went to pick her up in his car, knocked on her door like a gentleman is supposed to do, and this man jumps out from behind a bush and beats Stanley up. Stanley didn't rightly know what was happening. When he started bleeding, he saw that the stranger had a straight razor in his hand. Well, his face got slashed, and Stanley tried to defend himself, but two of his fingers got sliced off. Turns out, that man was a former jealous boyfriend of his love. It might have near scared him to death, but we're just glad he's alive. I thought it best that I tell you before someone else wrote to you. I sure do miss you but know you've got your own courting going on over there.

Love,

Hazel

For two weeks, the latches on my eyes refused to shut, and I made the decision that I couldn't wait any longer. I wrote to Stanley, telling him I was aware of his injuries and would be there the next week, hoping he could provide a cot for me to sleep on. I gave him no time or opportunity to protest with a reply. Uncle arranged a driver for me. I turned in my resignation and packed my traveling bags. The last bittersweet embrace of Auntie and Uncle shuttered me with a silent sob.

"Now, you go on and do what you need to do," Auntie demanded. "God has let you be here with us, and for that we are grateful. A blessing you have been, and we are so fortunate that we have had the opportunity to see you turn into a fine young woman. Now, go and remember that when you're trying to find the answers for your life, ask yourself, who is whispering in your ear, and follow the right voice."

Uncle bent down, and I threw my arms around him, then turned, unable to look back, and climbed inside the waiting car. My aching heart was punctured and bleeding again, but I had learned in my short life that hearts and souls could be mended, like stitching up an open wound, and they would heal.

By the time we had reached the plains of the Piedmont, before we had traveled to the base of the mountain, I rolled down the window and let the breeze blow through my hair. I could not yet smell the honeysuckles, but at least I was going home.

The sun was lowering, and clutches of light slipped through the shadows, unveiling themselves between corners of storefronts in Lizzytown, a nickname branded to her long ago. The motor car shimmed across the railroad track, causing me to bounce from my seat, grabbing at whatever was available to hold on to. The same railroad that brought Lillian and Lydia to Papa. The same covered bridge still stood where they were married. A sleepy little town that yawned and rolled back over, never wanting to wake. Reaching over the seat, I handed the driver Stanley's address.

"Take me to 301 South Watauga Avenue."

He knew where it was. It was within a few blocks from the main street, on the upward side of a small hill where a grand house sat with broad white columns, posed like warriors in protection of who might reside inside. Bricks of burnt clay dressed it with a cloak of dignity, and white shutters adorned the windows as though a dressing of jewelry. Grand as it seemed, with closer review, flakes of loose paint clung to the bolsters, and the shutters hung precariously, graying from the weathering of many seasons.

I paid the driver and carried my bags up the steps. Rows of tin letter boxes were attached beside the front door, some with mail still to be gathered. Patterns of stained glass shared on a half door of wood blurred reflections within. I turned the tarnished knob and stepped inside. A parlor on the left reeked of cigar smoke, as a bevy of men compared their day's undertakings.

"Pardon me," I said, stepping in only to the point where they had to lean forward to see who might be there. "Could any of you gentlemen tell me where Stanley Cordle could be found?"

No one spoke, until a man with a growth of beard seeded with specks of sawdust, indistinguishable whether from color or powder, sat back in his chair with an air of authority. "Who are you? A reporter? We don't want any of the likes of you here. Stanley's already told the police what happened."

I set my bag down, the burrs on my spine pricking at my frayed nerves. "You are assuming a lot, sir! I am his sister! I don't have time for your nonsense. If y'all can't tell me, I'll find him myself." And with that announcement, and no hesitation, I turned on my heel and began calling out, "Stanley! Stanley!" The words echoed up the stairwell before the men could stop me.

The now less confident man came running after me. "Young lady. You can't go around disturbing these folks like this." His breath was deep, and he sighed, relenting. "He's on the third floor, at the end of the hall on the right. I'll carry your bags if you don't mind."

With a nod of my head and a wily glance his way, he followed behind me. "You know, this boarding house is for men only," he said.

His attempt at conversation was shallow and I was uninterested. "I'm aware," I said simply.

By the time we had reached the third floor, he had whipped out his handkerchief, wiping the sweat off his brow. I knocked lightly on the door before I called out Stanley's name to the silence. I tried the knob. It released and I pushed the door open. A small room with a plain iron bed against the far wall and a table, blistered by the sun with spots of dried water from the water pitcher, filled the sparse dwelling. He was lying on the bed, clothed and soaked like laundry on wash day; only this was a pool of fever.

"Get me the doctor! Quick!"

Stanley's prison of delirium lasted a week, leaving him with a feebleness which required the help of a stronger person than myself. As fate would have it, the same man, Macy Malone, who had previously offered only annoyance, became my cohort, friend, and protector in this house of men. He was the one I could call on during the middle of the night to help me with Stanley. And I overheard him telling the others to keep their distance from "the little lady."

He brought our breakfast to us in the morning and sat with Stanley when I needed to leave for a few hours on the weekend. The landlord made an exception for me staying. They most likely preferred the room to still be let, rather than have an absence of money. I dug into my savings to pay.

"I'll return the favor, sis, when I get on my feet again," Stanley assured me.

"Nonsense, we're family," I told him, reaching for his hand.

By the second week, Stanley was able to return to work, and I had found a boarding room for myself. My money was almost gone from the added expenses, and by now I was fretting that my blanket of security was thread worn and bare.

During the time I cared for my brother, when he sat napping near a window, which filtered a warm afternoon sun, I moseyed down to the parlor, making myself invisible over a cup of tea and pretended not to hear the conversations from the men. And yet, I leaned on every word.

"Yeah, those northerners thought they could come down here and hire us to work for nothing. They knew we were poor and couldn't turn down what they were offering. Pennies! That's what they're giving us! And it stinks to high heaven around here since they've come. Why, I never thought that making fabric could smell so bad. There's talk of a worker's strike, and we should look into that."

I bristled from their thoughts of rebellion at the factory, hindering my prospects. They complained, but rightly, as well. The pay was a penitence to the number of working hours they put in. Having no choice, I was becoming desperate as my money dwindled and would take anything they offered.

The line snaked around the building, with people of the same needs as me. I had put on my best Sunday dress, the navy one with white polka dots and a white Peter Pan collar, and seam straight stockings, with comfortable shoes. It was mid-morning by the time I sat down for my interview. Balancing myself on the edge of the chair, I straightened as stiff as a poker in attempt to muster up confidence in my backbone.

"I'm a hard worker," I told the man and handed him my references.

To my surprise, I was hired on the spot and started the next day. Bobbin operator, he had said.

"Just show up, and someone will teach you what to do."

Although I had no inkling of what it meant, I accepted gratefully.

Now past noon, my stomach rolled with hunger. I caught the downtown bus, stopping by Stanley's workplace, a haberdashery, hoping he had not eaten and would join me to celebrate. As I opened the door, a bell overhead jingled, announcing my entrance. Stanley glanced up from the customer, nodding to my presence. Suits of modest color—midnight blues, beige, and black mourning suits—lined the wall on one side of the store. A pin stripe suit, bold and daring, displayed in the window caught the eye of two young gentlemen as they passed. They laughed and poked at each other, most likely imagining how spiffy they would look on a Sunday morn, hoping to catch the eye from a girl, unspoken for. A page of memory with my former beau clutched at me, until I heard my name called.

"Callie." Stanley motioned for me to come to him. The customer was paying for his purchase, a new hat cradled in a protective box.

As I strolled to the counter, the gentlemen turned to me, and the spirit of his smile quickened my heart, disarming me. "I'd like you to meet James. James Sullivan."

A man, only slightly shorter than my height, faced me with a steady gaze. His hair, mussed from the arrangement of different hat attire, lay tossed. I saw it was of a color, like chinquapins, as his fingers, worn with sun and soil, swept through his receding hairline. It appeared he was of an age in his thirties, and I could not determine from his manner of clothing if he was a businessman or a farmer.

"It's a pleasure to meet you, Callie," James said. "Stanley has spoken about you many times, and I feel like I already know you."

He wore a fragrance of humility and ease. In any other circumstance, offense at his familiarity would blister my skin. But I found myself, lips parted, wordless in response. It annoyed me, but I finally found my voice: "Sometimes, my brother speaks even when the conversation is already finished."

Stanley ignored my slight and discourtesy, turning back to James. "Hope to see you soon, James. And looking forward to seeing you on Sunday, in that new hat."

James tossed a hand goodbye to Stanley, and with a tip of the old hat he had worn in, to me he whispered, "Ma'am."

I wandered toward the window as he was driving away, still pondering on the flush of warmth which he had created.

"How can I help you?" Stanley asked. The edge of his sharp tongue cut through the air. I had almost forgotten why I came, and rushed to him, in my excitement.

"I have a job, Stanley! Down at the factory. They hired me today. Let's go to lunch. My treat."

He hesitated, then breath escaped him in a resolution of my misconduct, not denying me my moment of pleasure. "Come, sis. No one deserves this more than you."

Now that Stanley was able to drive again, we visited with the young'uns and Lillian regularly. But Lydia had left.

"Where is she?" I asked.

"She moved out right after you left at Christmas," Lillian said. "Got a job taking care of the Henrys' baby boy, so Mrs. Polly could work outside the home. She lives with them now and seems happy. I go by a few times a week and visit with her when the baby's asleep and take her some pie or cookies. I miss her sorely, but knew it was for the best."

Words suddenly disappeared, and we sat in silence, gazing toward the mountains.

Hazel would be married in a few weeks, and Rachel would soon follow behind her with Johnny Atkins, a fellow she had her eye on since fourth grade. He drove a produce truck, and the company let him and the other workers take home the "unsellable." Lillian said it was a blessing to have a little extra food occasionally. Rachel worked at the hosiery mill and would bring home some "irregulars," as she called them. Now, we had stockings to wear to church on Sundays.

Lydia apparently foresaw that the older ones would be gone soon, leaving her there as the oldest girl. I went to her as soon as I found out she had left, and we sat on the Henrys' front porch, dangling our legs over the edge, talking. She appeared older than her years, now, with a twinge of loneliness and well-being, mixed together with conviction.

"They're so good to me," Lydia told me. "They treat me like I'm part of their family. And that little boy of theirs, well, he's a charmer, alright. Just now trying to sit up. I clean for them too and do the laundry. Much of the same as I had done at home, so nothing was really new to me. Just getting used to their ways. I'm happy here, Callie, and I'm never going back. Only wish I could bring Mama with me." A sorrow welled up in her eyes, pulling her chin down.

"Now, don't you worry about your mama. She knows how to handle Ben," I lied.

We wrapped our arms around each other, and I kissed her on the forehead before I walked back home, knowing I would see her again soon.

Papa always made himself absent from me when we came until he had to sit down at the dinner table with all of us. I chatted with the babies and Lillian, ignoring his presence. It was he, now, who sat nose to plate, shoveling food in his mouth so he could leave quickly. Stanley still shot the breeze with him out in the field or upside the barn. I worked hard to not let that put distance between us, and never asked what they spoke about.

Stanley was good to us, often times taking my sisters, of which I considered Lydia now also one, and me for long rides down back country roads I had never travelled. He found a swimming hole up in the holler, and we all waded in the shallows, holding our dresses above our knees. None of us girls could swim, so we stood close to each other in case one of us slipped. Stanley could swim, though. And we all felt safe.

It was on one of those hot, sultry Sunday afternoons, as the brimming sun slipped through the tree limbs and danced on the water, that we gathered flat stones and skipped them in a game of competition, and another car came out of nowhere and parked alongside Stanley's. I could only see the front end, for the swimming hole lay low, with a winding shaded trail leading down to it.

The man stood at the edge, removed his hat, and wiped his brow. The sun at his back, I was unable to make out who he was, although the shadow of him was somehow familiar. Stanley waved to him, motioning for him to come and join us. The girls distracted me, and I turned my focus back to them. Their toes curled in the mud, and they gathered a bit in their hands.

"Look, Callie, we're making mud pies."

"You girls are too old for that nonsense," I reprimanded them.

Just as I said that, taking a step toward them, I lost my balance and slipped in the slimy mud. My mortified humiliation rose from the water with me, flapping my arms like a duck on the pond. Shrieks became hollow bowls of laughter at my expense. When the girls were able to control their amusement, they helped me to my feet, one of them grabbing the blanket we had laid out to cover my nakedness from clothes that now clung to me, like a veil of sheer curtains, allowing no hinderance of what could be seen beyond. Stanley had gone to meet the man, not seeing my spectacle. But still, I fumed at my circumstances, just coming short of blaming the girls for my predicament.

I wanted to leave, but sat down, not willing to deny the others their afternoon pleasure. The men returned, their footsteps approached behind me, and their exchanges welcoming to each other like brothers reuniting. Stanley called out to me, starting the introductions before we came face to face.

"Callie, I believe you've already met my friend."

Turning to look up at him, I did indeed remember. "James, I believe." I full well knew his name.

James nodded and smiled with no hint of acknowledging my soaked appearance. I cared not how I looked, but pulled the blanket around me a little tighter, casting my watch on the girls until the men walked away. They strolled along the embankment as Stanley puffed on a cigar, while James slapped him on the back. His fetching laughter was pleasant and appealing, like Uncle Tom's was when he goosed Aunt Clarice unexpectedly, slipping up behind her in the kitchen. I wondered what the conversation entailed, finding myself unable to withdraw my line of vision from them, until a blood curdling scream snapped me back to sensibility.

I could never say how Stanley reached her before I could stand, only that I found James beside me, comforting me, as Stanley calmed Rachel and the others. Rachel, in her haste, had ventured near a half-sun-baked rock where a rat snake was curled, napping in the warmth of the day's mellow decline.

"She'll be alright," James said. "Just a little fright over a snake. It's probably more scared than she is."

I just nodded my head, still peering over toward the calamity.

"My family lives just over the ridge from your folks," James said. My head gave a jerk at that revelation. "Yeah, my papa retired and bought the farm over there, last year. The old Lowrie place. Papa got sick shortly after, so I came back to take care of him and Mama. My apologies, ma'am. I meant no attempt to bore you with details."

I became more curious and softened my voice. "No, not at all. What did your papa do before he retired?"

His eyes widened, and his smile curled up mischievously. "Why, my papa was a preacher man. So, I was at church most of the time growing up. Now I'm a farmer and live a farmer's life, so I don't always get to church every Sunday if the cows are ornery and decide to birth their calves on that particular day. When I can go, I put that brand new hat on that I bought from your brother and situate it just right."

I found myself laughing along with him and began to sense the ease that comes when you feel you've known someone for a lifetime, even though you just started.

We all left the swimming hole that day, each with a different experience of life and a muddled state of mind. Rachel's confidence was ripped like strips of dough, ready to be laid on a pan of humble pie, and the other girls grew quiet on the ride back home, pondering on the possibilities of a rattler or copperhead lying there instead of the innocent one. It wasn't long before they recovered and bragged and shared the great tale of Rachel looking upon the face of death, bravely. Her confidence returned, and she preferred to remember in great detail their story, instead of her own. We all said goodbye to James that day in a pleasing manner. I, surprisingly, found for me, it was of minimal effort to afford him that courtesy.

Work was demanding, and murmurs of another walkout grew like weeds among the gatherings of lint and dust balls that swagger in the air. They whispered in every ear, as a bottle of whiskey would promise pleasure to a drunk. I kept my own opinions to myself, hoping I wouldn't be forced to join the revolt if there was another. Us women were well aware that the men were paid more, and their other grievances were well justified, but fighting with the bosses didn't seem to get us any relief.

The other strikes were quashed after violence came to the forefront. I heard that two union officials were kidnapped and toted out of town to the state line, with threats to never come back. But they did return, more determined than ever, which riled up the workers even more, causing hundreds of men to step out on the picket line. During that same time, two houses were dynamited, and two barns burned. That's what brought the national guard to town. There were armed guards on the roof, but eventually Anna Wainscot, a worker who was both mother and leader, became a mediator and was able to get some calm and order to the situation, as well as a little compensation. Mostly that they would rehire the men and women who caused the ruckus, and not hold any grudges.

That didn't last, though, and most of them weren't rehired. Now, the workers who were left mostly complained and showed up every day for the grueling routine, washed in sweat and stench at the end of the day. Even a slight breeze put the delicate thread at risk, so the windows were shuttered.

My body odor was no better than the rest, and my feet ached from standing all day in front of the bobbins. About a hundred of them spun their web into cloth, and each one served up a tension and personality all its own. I was responsible for their care. If one thread broke, they all broke, ending their cycle. It was challenging and tedious, with little room for error.

Since the factory had received a more extensive demand for the rayon material, my coworkers and I had worked six days a week for the last month. Exhaustion sat beside me on Sundays, not in a pew, but on the porch of the boarding house which I lived. On any given Lord's Day, that's where I could be found, feeling the guilt that's bred into you, of your absence.

One particular Sunday, a familiar car pulled alongside the curb. It was James. I sat up to get a closer look. He still had his "goin' to preaching" clothes on, as well as his spiffy hat. Standing beside the car, he brushed down the dust on his trousers, tidying himself. I was amused already at his meticulous appearance and wondered if the cattle were groomed accordingly. That shameless snicker crept into my mouth before he reached the bottom step, fortunately avoiding my misshapen humor.

"Good afternoon, Miss Callie." His fingers now rummaged around the brim of his fedora, holding it in front of his pinstripe suit, which fit his strapping frame to a T. I had never noticed the dimple in his cheek when he cocked his smile to the side, until now. Or realizing that halfcocked smile was meant just for me.

I sat back in the rocker, casually, my paddle fan cooling me from the afternoon heat. "Hello, James. What brings you over in this neck of the woods?"

He took out his handkerchief, wiping the sweat off his brow. "Well, I thought maybe you and me could take a ride today. Haven't seen you over at church on Sunday lately. Got a little concerned. Haven't seen Stanley either, but I hear he's warming up to another girl. Hope he doesn't get caught up in another trap."

His soft-spoken words spread out like warm butter on newly baked bread, piping hot from the oven. Unaware, I fanned a little faster, attempting to cool the blush off my cheeks.

I am unable to pinpoint on that day which part of it or action that took place welded my heart to his. Or even if it was the first day I saw him in the store, speaking to my brother. All I know is, it took both of my hands to support me standing, because of the weakness I felt, not from any physical ailment, but a condition of the heart, which now possessed me.

He seemed quite taken aback that I accepted his offer, and once he recovered, he approached the car swiftly and opened my door. We headed toward the mountains, where winding roads led to cool breezes and water seeped from rocks alongside. He watched closely for a cluster of rocks, which offered a steady stream of water for drinking. We cupped our hands and caught the cold water, sipping and slurping it into our mouths. The sounds that give way to that type of drinking. And we laughed at each other as a drop clung to the tip of our noses. The day ended too quickly, leaving me to want more.

"It's been a lovely day, Callie. I was wondering if we might do it again sometime."

For some reason, I wanted to lay my hand against his cheek, but held it tight within the confines of my dress, and instead said, "I would like that very much."

He tipped his hat and walked to the car, but turned just before he got in to say, "How about next Sunday?"

I didn't want to appear too eager, though the fringe of my emotions were uncooperative. "Next Sunday, it is." Those words flew out of my mouth like a pair of starlings in flight. And he smiled, waving to me.

The car soon turned at a distance which I could no longer see before I retreated to my room. A drought of air stilled the curtains, even with the open window. I turned on the bedside fan, placing my face in front of the whir, and closed my eyes, reliving every moment of the afternoon and the peacefulness that covered me with his presence. Drawing my bath, I reached for the bar of soap and reclined in the warm water. It was then that the pleasant memory left me alone to argue with the voices in my head. A sprout of uncertainty grew and reminded me that one memory would outlast the others, causing me to wonder if I would be able to overcome the insult to my body. I splashed a handful of water on my face before a brim of tears fell.

We continued to court, with him picking me up for Sunday preaching and afternoon rides, and picnics shared with my sisters and their promised beaus. But not before I had been presented to his ailing parents, whose eyes caught each other's in concern of their son and our intentions. Surely, they knew of his honor and commitment to them. Never was there a time when I came empty-handed. And in time, they accepted me.

It was the weekend of Thanksgiving when we sat at Papa and Lillian's table, James beside me, that after the supper table was emptied of its feast, he had asked me to take a walk to settle our food. I willingly accepted. Before long, I found us at the brink of a treeless ridge. A light wind competed with a mellow sun when James faced me and took both my hands in his. I thought he was going to kiss me, but he stood there for some time before he smacked his lips and cleared his throat. Then I became riddled with anxiety, thinking he was trying to find the right words to leave me. And a tear hung in his eye, like the last raindrop from a brief shower, as he began to speak.

"Callie," he cleared his throat again, "I'm not really good at saying things like this, and I don't quite know how to begin."

I tried to pull my hands away from his, to run, not wanting to hear what he said.

"Please don't leave," he said. "I've slept poorly all week, wondering what to say, and all I can do is just say it."

My heart could take no more, and it began to weaken and betray me. "Just tell me," I mourned.

He shifted his feet and searched my face. "Callie, from the first time I saw you, I knew that you were special. It didn't take long for me to fall in love with you. I pray you feel the same, and if you don't, do you think you could come to love me?"

He caught me as my knees buckled, and I held tight to his arms, looking to him and letting his words feed my understanding. "James, you silly man. I'm not certain when I started loving you, but you're like a flow of endless satin ribbon to my senses."

And with no other prompting, he lowered his head to meet mine, taking my face in his hands, and tenderly pressed his lips against mine. "Callie, you know I don't have much, but I'll give you all I can. I would be obliged if you would marry me."

It was no longer than the time it took for him to brush a wisp of hair from my face when I whispered to him, "You grasped my heart the first time I saw you smile. I like the way I feel when I'm with you, and even when we are apart, I long to see you again. Never did I expect to love anyone the way I love you. I will marry you, James."

We walked on a cloud off the ridge that day, returning with a light hearty step and a blush in our face. Lillian noticed and inquired about our appearance, but we brushed it off to the cause of a blustery day, with a burn of wind. I wanted to hold our secret in our hearts for a while.

James drove me back to Lizzytown, and we stood just beyond the porch light before I retired to my room. His goodnight kiss, now sprinkled with a taste of passion, lingered, as we did in each other's arms with no words left to say. I laid awake that night, my fingertips resting on my lips, remembering him. After I finally fell into a fitful sleep, I awoke, the covers disheveled, and my body worn to a frazzle. Drawing fresh water to the bowl, I covered my face with it, hoping to wake me and give me clear thought.

My day at work was fraught with breakdowns from tired machinery, which refused to produce, and irritable foremen who had presumably fought with their wives over the weekend. Sleep still shunned me at night, until the dreams appeared and tortured me with their possibilities. By the end of the week, I was no longer able to deny what I must do. It was the coming Saturday, before the Sunday I was to see James again, that I went to Stanley and asked him to take me to the farm. His store closed at noon and without questions he took me there and parked the car at Papa's.

I strode off toward James's farm, searching for him urgently. Unable to see him in the field, I headed to the barn, where the moaning of a heifer sounded in discomfort. He would be attending to her. My pace slowed and a weight of despair cloaked me in a heavy robe, as I approached and stood quietly behind him. He was gingerly placing both hands inside her, turning the head, while pulling the calf out, breaking both creature's agony from birth. Now the calf stood beside its mother, and I continued to watch as he directed the calf to her tit to suckle. He talked to her as if the calf were his child.

It was a moment uninterrupted of which I would always remember, of my own child's birth. The pain was no less for me, and the memory was too vivid. I started to back away, hoping he wouldn't see me. A letter sent would have been perhaps more appropriate for the both of us. I would leave it with Hazel to forward to him. But a bucket, hung and misplaced on a post, rattled my hasty departure, and he stood up, pleasingly bewildered at my presence.

"Callie, what a wonderful surprise. We have a new calf. I almost lost both of them, but they're doing fine now." I stood with no expression of feelings and without words. "What's wrong, Callie? Has something happened? Is someone sick?"

I shook my head. "No. No. No one is sick. I had to come. To see you. To tell you."

Panic still sat in his eyes, not believing me, and he stepped closer to me till I motioned for him to stop. I bit my lip to stop it from quivering until I tasted blood. It was as bitter as the words I was about to say.

"James, I need to tell you something. Something important. I know it's going to hurt you, but it would hurt you more if you found out from someone else." He started to speak, but I put up my hand again. "I-I had a child. A boy. When I was thirteen." He stood there, the words still impenetrable, but I continued, "The child's father. You know him."

I wished I could say no more, but I would not attempt to deceive this good and honorable man. "It's Papa's child," I said. "He took me after Mama died and wouldn't quit."

James stared at me, blank-faced, uttering no words. A slip of disappointment began to grow in his eyes, and I could stand there no more. I turned and ran and ran to the woods that were my solace, embracing them wantonly until I reached the face of the cave, where I, with no light, felt my way inside as though returning to my mother's womb. It was there I stayed until my composure returned, and a voice called out to me. I walked out of the woods to Stanley's impatience.

"Where were you?" he asked.

I brushed passed him, ignoring his question. "Please. Let's go!" I demanded.

Though Stanley attempted a conversation at one point, we rode back to Lizzytown in silence. After a brief word of thanks to him, he left. Unable to tolerate the solitude of my room, I walked to the park and sat on a far bench, away from polite greetings. A harried squirrel, gathering nuts for the winter, scurried up a tree with no concern of me. And no patrons of the park were present as dusk rolled in, bringing with it an imminent winter chill. Tears ran down my face, and I continued to wipe them away, not knowing when their end would come. The salt and the wind chafed my cheeks, burning like smoldering embers. Soon, the first depth of darkness came, and I pulled my coat around me before weariness laid me on the bench. It was when my body shivered and played games with my mind that I thought I heard someone call my name. Then, a flash of light danced from side to side, coming toward me. My name was called again before I succumbed to the sullen night.

"Callie! Come! We must go!" Stanley pulled me up, anchoring his arm around me, and I leaned against him. "I knew there was something wrong when I left. You just weren't yourself. What's wrong, Callie? This ain't like you."

I tried to speak, but my teeth chattered, rendering me without apologies. "Don't try to talk," he said. "We'll speak later. Right now, I have to get you warmed up.

Stanley walked me to my room and tucked me under the covers, leaving abruptly. I had caused him anger against me and felt sorely about it. But I heard his voice, and another, just beyond my door. He bid the person goodbye, and his footsteps trailed off in the distance before the sound of the front door closed. I stirred beneath the quandary of blankets and quilts, feeling their warmth on my body, which stopped the shivering. Then a knock came to my door.

"Who is it?" I called.

The person on the other side hesitated. "It's James, Callie. May I come in?"

The sound of his voice was like a treasured relative from long past that suddenly appeared, wanting something you couldn't give. Along with it, he brought sad news. My heart couldn't take his stumbled words of rejection, and yet I did not want to wait another day before we could formally end our arrangement.

"Come in, James."

The door slowly opened, and he came to the side of my bed, dropping to his knees. He took my hand in his and wept. "I have been beside myself with worry for you. You gave me no chance to respond to your revelation. I tried to find you. Ran to the woods and called for you. Then I saw you and Stanley leave before I could reach the car. I came here shortly after, looking for you, and when I couldn't find you, I went to Stanley. He was aware of the time you liked to sit in the park alone. That's when he found you." His words sat on the surface of my understanding, waiting for more. "Callie, my dear, I love you, and nothing can change my mind about you. My disappointment is that you have suffered more than anyone I know, at no fault of your own. There is no blame on you, but your papa... My anger toward him is fueled from the hot coals of hell, and God forgive me, I want to throw him into that fiery pit."

I had never seen such rage in his soft-spoken eyes. "He will not be the end of us. I still want to marry you. And I can promise you I will protect you and love you. Say you will marry me."

James gave me no time for thought, but instead leaned over and kissed me, and I found my arms around him, returning his affection. There was no doubt now that James was the man who carried his heart as he lived, noble and kind, no compromise of his standards.

Only a few weeks later, we stood in front of his preacher father, along with his mother, my sisters, and Lillian, that he married us. It was the happiest day of my life.

Lydia

When Callie left, I was still but a child. We, my sisters and I, came home from school the afternoon of the same day we had relatives come and visit, only to find they had left, taking Callie and her baby with them.

I remember vividly that no one, absolutely no one, talked that night at the supper table. It was like a hole had opened up and swallowed Callie, and every time we tried to ask a question, a slap up the side of our head was threatened by Papa. Rachel stubbornly persisted, as a glint of fire flashed from the cold darkness in her eyes.

"Where's Callie?" she demanded. "And where's her baby?" She spit it out like bitters in her mouth.

Papa stared at her for a moment, his eyes hollow and unflinching, before he almost caught her with a brush from his hand. She ducked the wallop and pushed away from the table, her stool scraping across the floor like the sound of a match charging a flint of anger. Hazel and I, choked with a swell of apprehension that we might receive the tail end of his ire, didn't ask to be excused, and followed after her. There was no comfort for any of us, although Hazel attempted to pull us into a cuddle under each of her arms as we piled into bed.

"Now, girls, Callie and her child are where they're supposed to be," Hazel said. "So don't y'all fret, you hear. And don't be causing Lillian any trouble. She's going to need us more than ever."

I wondered how much Hazel knew and wasn't telling us. And I would later ponder how a moment from time past is remembered, though no particular thought was given to it, at the moment. Like the time I saw Callie and Hazel, sitting on a close hillside huddled together, apparently sharing a whispered wind of secrets, like Rachel and I often did. As the sun shone behind them, a silhouette of their foreheads touched, and praying hands clasped as one. Callie appeared overwrought. Then, they embraced, and when they parted, Hazel took her hand and brushed Callie's cheeks the way Mama brushed her feather duster across a delicate piece of glass. That must have been when Callie entrusted her with a heart that had been broken, where no needle or thread could mend.

It was not until the following week when our neighbor, Mrs. Stout, a sturdy woman with broad hands and a dark trickle of hairs on her upper lip, came to visit. She and her husband lived down the road a ways, far from the sight of our house. He was a man of few words, who often stood, thumbs in suspenders, as though he was keeping a wayward wind from blowing him out of his pants. Although he was as scraggly as a twig, between his weather-worn face lay a smile, as warm as the sun bursting through the window on a summer morn.

Now, in the country, most folks have a nickname. Some are said out loud, and some aren't, depending on if it's a compliment or poking fun of you. Like John Oliver, for instance, who ran a grocery near the church. They called him "that ole miser" behind his back because he would short people on the poundage of corn meal. They'd say, "Didn't you short me, John?" He denied it and didn't care. Just as long as they paid him. And if you ran up a bill of more than two dollars, he wouldn't sell a piece of floor dirt to you until he was paid. But we all needed him, and he knew it. Still came to church on Sundays with his wife. Bless his heart.

Or Henry Marshall, who they called Big Ears, because he had the biggest cornfield in the county, and always managed to give part of it away to poor people when their crop didn't fare as well. Sometimes we were the recipients of his good deeds. He knew it was meant to be a good name, because the only big ears he had were ears of corn in the field.

But Mrs. Stout. Well, my mama never called anyone a bad name, and she spoke the truth when she saw Mrs. Stout walking up our road. "She's only coming here to see what she can find out," Mama mumbled. "That gossip!"

She shooed me out the back door, as Mrs. Stout was coming in the front. I snuck back in, though, and overheard Mama tell her that Callie had gone off with Papa's sister to Winston, for work purposes. No mention of the baby.

Callie's secret was now a ghost within the walls of our home. We had suspected as such where she was, but the confirmation eased our minds, and we wondered at night after the lamp light was darkened what her life was like now. We imagined her in a bed of her own, with her baby beside her. If her kin folk could afford a car to travel in, we conjured up a royal house filled with pantries of food and closets filled with clothes and real dolls. We cried ourselves to sleep on many an occasion, wanting to be with her. Even Hazel was heard whimpering at night when she thought we were asleep.

It was during that summer that Papa told Hazel she wouldn't be allowed to return to school. "After all," he said, "no one needs to go past sixth grade."

Lillian needed more help with the three young'uns, he told her. She knew it was coming. Hazel never talked back to anyone. Her nature was as gentle as an afternoon breeze that caught your hair and cupped it caressingly around your face. Rachel and I became closer, her ever my protector, and in the fall, we walked together, swinging our arms and skipping our way to school. Hazel would stand on the porch, a wave on her hand and as sad a face as I had ever seen. One of Mama's babies weighted on her hip. It would be our turn one day to stand in her place, when she found a boy to marry. I was twelve years old when I left home. Two years after I swore. Yes, for the first time in my life, God forgive me. I swore that I would never speak to Papa again. Never mind the reason. I just wouldn't.

I may have said before how I loved going to church. Rachel and I would sneak and ask Mama if we could go behind Papa's back and were out the door and running before he had a chance to stop us. In Sunday school, our teacher, Mrs. Bonnie, would read us a story from the Bible and then explain how we could apply that to our lives. Like Esther or Ruth, for instance, and how we should make ourselves become ladies of humbleness and obedience. Rachel 'bout near broke my ribs, poking me on that one. There was no denying that she had a problem with obedience. I got into trouble because I yelped out loud and had to cover with a fib, right there in God's house.

"I caught a cramp in my leg," I told Mrs. Bonnie and gave Rachel a mean look I didn't know lived in me. As a matter of fact, I never let her forget the time she bout made me go to hell, for lying in church.

Overall, we made friends with other kids, especially on Sunday night when we played Bible games and sang. Twice a year, we stood up in front of the church on Sunday morning and showed everyone what we had learnt. After Rachel informed me that my voice screeched like our back porch door screen, I hid behind her and moved my lips, pretending.

"Jesus wants me for a sunbeam," we sang. I loved that song, and no one knew I wasn't making a sound. One Sunday, a ray of light came through one of the stained-glass windows, piercing my sight and nearly blinding me. I was convinced that God had caught up with my deceit. I couldn't seem to stay out of trouble with God. At least, I thought, I'm getting His attention, so He must love me a fierce amount.

Even though I thought worse of myself, other people seemed to see me differently, in a kind way. I was always hugging people and felt at ease at church. They could see the joy in my heart. If there was a home gathering or church lunch on the grounds, Mama would make some of her specialties for me to take. I would, after helping to uncover the dishes, stand to the side and listen to the compliments of Mama's contribution.

"My, my!" they would say. "Those rolls are something else. Melt in your mouth. How does she do it?"

I didn't say a word, for the preacher had just issued a warning from the pulpit about bragging, and I didn't need any more reprimands from God.

It was the week before the last day of school, and at the beginning of summer, when I walked home from school and neared our house. Mama was sitting on the porch with Mrs. Polly Henry, a new mother of an almost two-year-old son, who lived with her husband near the school grounds. On occasion, when we had recess, I could hear the baby cry. In a rare instance of an empty lap, Mama bounced him on her foot, causing him to erupt in a hiccup of laughter.

"Lydia, Mrs. Polly and Joseph came for a visit with us this afternoon."

I nodded to her. "Hi, Mrs. Polly. It's good to see you again."

She and her husband, Dennis, were pillars of the church and community. She always wore cinched-waisted dresses with tiny pleats, molding her figure in the middle. It didn't seem as though she was eating more than a bird's snare. But her face was kind and soft like she had bathed it in cow's cream. And her eyes carried the beauty inside her as she touched Mama's hand and squeezed it before she stood and walked away.

"Please, just give it some thought, Lillian," she said.

Mama, holding a brief smile, nodded and told her she would let her know in a week.

"Know what, Mama?" I sat down beside her. "What's wrong?"

Her shoulders slumped and she turned to me. "Mrs. Polly wants you to come and live with them. To care of their child, while she takes a job outside the home. I told her no." Before I could utter a sound, she put her hand in mine and said, "You're too young. It's better if Rachel or Hazel go."

I leapt to my feet, my mind in a whirlwind of confusion, trying to focus on what she said. Numb with disappointment, I challenged her. "Mama, I want to go. I have to go. Please let me."

My knees grew weak and crumbled at her feet as a rush of tears wet the lap of her dress. It was the first time I had cried in two years. My tears became sobs, then wails of grief and pain, grabbing me like a stitch caught in my side. Mama let me stay there and cry out what needed to be. And when I had finished, she lifted my chin to say, "I didn't know it would mean so much to you."

Mama never cried, not because she didn't want to, but because she never had time. Now, her swollen eyes brimmed and spilled over, silently. I reached for her, our arms wrapped like vines, clinging to old wood posts.

"Don't cry, Mama. I'll stay with you," I said.

But she whispered in my ear, like the sound that comes from a foggy dream, "No, you must live as you want. And I must allow you. It is well with my soul." I felt a rumble run through her, from the struggle of give and take and letting me go. She wiped my tears away. "It's time that you know."

Then, her voice became choked and halting as she told me about the man she had truly loved. He was a gentle man, unlike Ben, and I was a piece of her and him. As she remembered, her eyes widened playfully, and a soft smile washed over her face like a soothing rain. I wanted to know more about the man who had shared her love, and if he loved me, too.

"Of course he did," Mama said.

"Where is he? Why did he leave us?" I was fraught with questions that Mama was unwilling to answer.

Instead, she told me that sometimes we are left with a journey, unplanned and forsaken, full of doubts and regrets, which cannot be changed. I should look forward to my life ahead. Marry a good man and have the children I deserve.

She continued, "I may not have Hugh in my life, but I have you. And every time I look at the blue in your sweet eyes, I see the same blue in his, and know that both of you are here." Her hand glided down the side of my face. A brief kiss she planted on my cheek. Then, her brown soulful eyes bore through my own, and the net of wrinkles in her face softened when a slip of contentment found its way to our hearts. She would never know how relieved I was to know that the man I was told to call Papa was not mine.

It was on a Saturday morning when I kissed everyone goodbye. Mama had kept a tight lip from the family on the offering of Mrs. Henry. She had walked to their house, telling her that I could be there the following Saturday.

"That would be a good day to start," she had said. "I'll be able to show her how we do things around here. Joseph is finicky about some foods I try to get him to eat. And sometimes he's a bear about settling down for a nap."

Mama took her a fried apple pie to thank her for entrusting me with her child.

On Saturday mornings, before the sun had eased above the bow of the horizon, Ben would leave for town and join the other farmers that came to sell their produce. It was an all-day event, and sometimes we rode along with him. A chance for us to be social and learn about the happenings around us. This morning was no different as far as he was concerned, except for Mama making an excuse of the need for the girls to stay behind to help her with the washing and such. Ben was at the barn hitching up our mule when he let out a bucket full of curse words that I'm sure echoed across the valley and into the ears of our neighbors. Mama paced back and forth when she heard him and wrung her hands, unable to keep herself from peering out the back door.

"He has to go today," she mumbled. Fear gripped her, shaking her violently, and she bolted toward the barn to see what the matter was. I was afraid for her and me. If he found out I was leaving, he'd beat her for letting me go, and me for trying.

In a short manner of time, he was commanding a "giddy up" from ole Jack and headed out on the dusty road, with Mama waving goodbye in a smile of well wishes, until he was out of sight.

"Git me a swig of water, child," she said as she plopped down on a porch chair. I ran and pumped her a glass of water. She gulped it down in half a minute and let her eyes close as she reached for my hand, the trembles in hers still present.

"It's alright," Mama said. "He's gone, and we're going to get you out of here. Now, I'm going to fix breakfast for y'all. So, go get your sisters and little brothers and help them get dressed. He won't be back till the sun starts to set over the hill."

I did as I was told, and when Mama set the table, she prayed a thankful prayer of the quiet and peace that God had provided this day, and the love we had spread to each other throughout the years. However today was a day to free and loosen each other. I snuck a look at Hazel and Rachel, who were staring at each other, shrugging their shoulders.

"Pass the gravy, please," I said after the amen, not meeting their gaze.

Mama began, "Mrs. Henry has asked me if I can spare Lydia to help her with housework, and her child. I told her that I could."

Everyone at the table who was old enough to know the meaning put their fork down and tried to chew what was left in their mouth. Except me. I never looked up and shoveled more in, as fast as I could, so there was no room for my mouth to form words. Almost choked myself to death. We all knew the sacrifice she was making. Ben would near kill her when he found out what she had done.

But Mama continued, "Now, Hazel. Rachel. You know I don't have any say-so about what y'all do. So, I'm taking Lydia to the Henrys' this morning. It's not like she's so far away. It's only a mile. And y'all see each other at church. And of course, Lydia is welcome to come back and have a meal with us whenever she wants." Silence hovered in the room, and I was still afraid to look at my sisters. A tear gave me away, and I brought up my face to theirs. They pushed their chairs back and came and embraced me in their loving way. We all cried a little, knowing that life just took a turn down the road again for all of us.

I packed a sack bag with the few treasures that I had accumulated over the years. A marble that I found in the school yard, which, after three weeks in the lost and found, no one claimed. A flat rock I had kept. One of many which Rachel and I used to skip across the pond. She always beat me with three skips to my two. And my corn shuck doll that Mama had given me. Though tattered and broken, I kept it in an old rag, occasionally unwrapping it and mending her as needed.

We walked together, our hearts heavy for each other, until we reached the edge of Mrs. Henry's yard. When she placed a parcel of sweets in my hands, I laid my head on her chest and felt the steady beat of her heart. "We're going to be alright," she whispered, gently pushing me from her. "Now, neither one of us is going to mess our face. Just know I love you."

Before I could respond, she handed me her garment bag, stuffed with a new dress she had made for me, as well as my other sparse belongings, turned, and walked away. My words lodged in my throat. "I love you, too, Mama."

Whether they were carried to her, I do not know. For she never looked back.

I tapped lightly on the door, and Mrs. Henry welcomed me in. "Let me show you to your room, and the rest of the house as well."

She put her arm around my shoulders and began to guide me down the hallway when Mr. Henry, soundly absorbed in the newspaper print, lowered it to speak to me, "We're certainly glad you could help us out, Lydia. I'm sure you'll find Joseph to be pleasant."

I turned back to meet his smile, which left me at ease. "I'm sure I will, Mr. Henry. Thank you for having me."

The house was smaller than ours, it seemed, but with polished floors and finished, smooth walls. No upstairs. There were three actual bedrooms with doors for privacy and they had indoor plumbing with running water to the kitchen sink. There was still an outhouse, but Mr. Henry was in the process of adding on, for an indoor toilet room and tub for bathing. I could see that it was about finished, with only linoleum to be laid out on the floor and curtain shades to be added to the window.

There was a lot of watching and learning for me to do before they left on Monday. I was afraid to ask too many questions, for fear that they might change their minds and send me back home. As it turned out, by the time she finished showing me around, I was invited to the kitchen table where she placed a note pad in front of me.

"Read this," she said. "You'll find everything you need in here."

She was thorough, and when I finished, she was sitting across from me, dipping one of Mama's cookies in her cup of coffee. Her eyes shone brightly with a seed of trust as she pushed the plate of sweets toward me, along with a glass of cold milk.

"If I didn't think you could do this, Lydia, I wouldn't have asked your mama. A kind, gentle spirit cannot go unnoticed." My shoulders relaxed a little, as I sat back in the chair. The glass of milk tasted like a poultice of honey and sugar, flowing through my body, patching my inner wounds and soothing my soul.

For the rest of the day, she stepped back and allowed me to take her child and follow the notebook. And on Sunday, we all went to church together. She picked out Joseph's clothes, and I dressed him while she prepared herself. Lunch meal would be simple, I was told. The cellar was stocked with many a glass jar of food, for just popping open and heating. And fried chicken and gravy was quick. Meat was bought at the market in town twice a week by Mr. Henry, along with a little cured ham. But on Sunday afternoon, before the evening service, I warmed up the leftovers and cleaned up the kitchen, so she could spend more time with her son. Mr. Henry proved to be a man who lived his convictions every day of the week. Not just on Sunday. He was a proud father, who encouraged Joseph to show off his new yet unsteady step-ping skills to the church folk, after service. However, I discovered that same day, he would not, under any circumstances, change a diaper that was filled with pee or poo.

On Monday, they told me goodbye after a peck on the head to their sleep-ing Joseph. "Just a reminder, Lydia," Mrs. Henry said. "Don't hesitate to call either one of us if you have any questions or concerns. And Mrs. Walston, just below us, will come by sometime today to see if you need anything."

I didn't mind her repeating anything she needed to say. We both wel-comed reassurances.

Joseph was a good baby, although Mrs. Polly was right about him being finicky with food. I finally got him to eat everything and put down for a morning nap. Then, I went to their garden and plucked a few weeds, hoeing around the edges too. A few peas remained, and I picked them, along with a couple of squash. I had just brought them in when I heard a pounding on the front door. It wasn't a neighborly knock. But one of desperation and boldness and command. Hesitantly, I tiptoed down the hallway to a side window where I could peer around.

"Open up! You damn bitch! You're coming back home with me!"

It was Ben. He had come to take me back. I was so frightened that I lost control of my water, unaware at the time that it had run into my shoe. I reached for the telephone, my head clouded with a sack of dust, but then realized Mr. and Mrs. Henry would not be able to reach me in time. I surely would be dismissed from the home when they were told I had placed their son in a dangerous position, though his anger was toward me. I went to Joseph's room, checking to see if he had awakened. He was still asleep. Then, a shadow passed by the window, mumbling and growling as it looped to the back. It suddenly occurred to me that I had, in my haste, left the back door open. My heart in a tizzy, I raced to the kitchen, slammed it shut and locked it, just before he reached the steps. With him still cursing and hollering, and me still praying and making promises, I wondered if my prayer would reach God before Ben's reached the devil.

It was at that moment when another voice, at first vague and looming in the distance, became demanding of attention. Then it grew frantic like a hen confronting the fox in the hen house, daring the intruder to touch her eggs and chicks. I slowly pulled back the edge of the curtain to see Mrs. Walston from the house below. A fine upstanding church lady who had recently lost her husband in one breath of a heart attack. And her son, Herbert, postured with a shotgun cradled across his arms. She was a marching up that hill madder than a porcupine that had lost its quills.

"You leave that girl alone!" she shouted, wagging her finger as she went. "Get out of here!"

But he held his ground. No one had ever spoken like that to him, let alone a woman. "This here is none of your business, Rosa Belle," Ben said. His voice, thick with authority, was now calm as the furrows on his brows deepened and a smirk lifted the edges of his mouth. I felt a sickly wave of disappointment when he started toward her.

It was the first movement of the piece which lay in her son's possession and his finger resting on the trigger that halted Ben's approach. With squared shoulders and hands planted firmly on her hips, Mrs. Walston belted out, "Like I said, you better high tail it out of here right now, and don't you ever step foot on their property, or mine, again! I have five more boys down there to make sure you don't."

She was surely still mad at God and anybody else who gave her an ounce of aggravation for taking her husband away.

Ben eyed her coldly before he spit out his chaw of tobacco and wiped the sleeve on his shirt to catch the last drip of juice from his mouth. He glowered at both of them, like an animal that was forced to give up its kill. But then he turned and walked away, taking with him a rolling thunder of vile oaths and curses. Her boy followed closely behind Ben, making sure that he didn't lose his way back home. My knees remained weak to carry me, and my body still shuddered when I came out and met her on the porch. She came right over and threw her arms around me.

"Now, you don't have to be of any concern about him coming back," Mrs. Walston said. "And I don't think it necessary to mention this to Polly and Dennis. So, go wipe off your face and take care of that baby. And don't worry about supper tonight. I'll send one of my boys up later with some food."

I nodded my head and stumbled out gratitude to her as I ran to a crying Joseph.

It was early afternoon, after Joseph had fiddled with his lunch and I had put him in his crib for his second nap of the day, when I took a moment to settle into a chair near the window, book in hand. But the words ran together, and I kept reading the same passages over and over again, unable to focus. A light sleep took me, for what amount of time I was unaware, until I was startled awake. It was merely a rap of announcement at the door. Still, the hairs on my arms stood straight up, like a brawling cat. The knock came again, louder and more urgent.

"It's me, Lydia. Herb."

Trying to separate dreams from reality, I straightened my dress and pinched a little color into my cheeks before I tucked my hair behind my ears to greet him in a more orderly fashion. Just the same, I peeked through the window for a presence of mind. Sure enough, he was standing there, basket in hand, a plaid cloth covering the contents. He shuffled his feet, looking up and down and out to the yard, impatient to leave. With dread, I opened the door, my body slathered with a jar of awkwardness. The attempt to pinch color into my cheeks was without necessity, because they were now torched with a flame of fire.

He must have noticed my discomfort and shifted his impatience to tender-hearted concern. "Mama wanted you to have this. There's enough for supper and leftovers for tomorrow."

We had just always seemed to know each other. His family was at church a lot more than mine. It was well known that they had been blessed with a couple of preachers in their family, from generations back. I kept pushing down, like soured milk on my stomach, the thought that they were better than us. Although, right now, it was hard to put a singe on that thought. My words began to come out in pieces, like they were mushed together.

"Th-thank you, Herb."

We stood there for a lifetime, it seemed, before another word was spoken, or even caught a look at each other. A fever of shyness gripped both of us. "Well, I better be getting back down to the house," he finally said. "We're patching up the barn where the horse reared up and knocked a hole in the wall."

"Oh, I'm sorry. Was your horse hurt?" I asked.

He mustered up a wry smile and said, "No, but the person standing on the other side was blistered with a plank, upside his behind." That set me into a giggle, which amused him.

Then, he turned and walked down the steps, me still in a grin, when I asked him, "Which one of your brothers got blistered?"

He looked back. A broad and mischievous smile now covered his face, and a twinkle in his dark brown eyes stood above it. "It was me," he declared.

And before I had a chance to show him a snicker, he turned and walked away. His hair, black as a raven's wing, was caught in a light breeze and tossed like shedded feathers at midnight. Why hadn't I noticed before that he had grown a spurt or two above my head, even though we were the same age? His jawline had become chiseled like carved stone, and his shoulders, broad and squared. I caught myself in a deep breath before I stepped back in the house and shut the door. And before he might catch me staring at him.

No word had gotten out, it seemed, of my unfortunate circumstances that day. Mr. and Mrs. Henry came home that night, tired from their workday, ready to eat, without question, the meal before them. It was not uncommon for Mrs. Walston to offer a meal during the week. Mrs. Henry would return the favor, though, baking up apple pies and purchasing store-bought jams and jellies. Sometimes, she would send me to deliver them, but most often she would take Joseph with her and visit, leaving me to my own enjoyment. Ben never came around again. At church, Rachel and Hazel would seek me out, asking me what my new life was like. I had nothing except good news for them, but there was never enough time to catch up. During church service, I would try to discreetly search out the pew where Herb's family sat. Sometimes, he would catch me looking, like a minnow on a hook, and other times I caught him sneaking a peek. At first, when caught, we popped our heads around so fast, one might think the Holy Spirit had burst through the church doors, smacking us upside the head with reprimand. But eventually, we just smiled at each other with an understanding nod.

A year had passed before we actually spoke in a private way again. He and I both knew it would have been improper for him to approach the house without Mr. and Mrs. Henry at home. I would see him occasionally, though, in the field, gathering hay, or hear him with a hammer, banging away on some ill-gotten piece of wood that had become misdirected. He had been absent from church one Sunday, along with his mother, which was most unusual.

Mrs. Henry walked down to their house, and in no time at all, came back on mission to her kitchen, in preparation of a meal in great proportions. "He has pneumonia," she told me.

"Who?" I asked.

"It's Herbert," she said. "He looks real puny. I'm worried about him. I've called for the doctor under Mrs. Walston's protest because I know she has no money to pay the doctor. But we'll help her. Dennis and I have the money."

We cooked all afternoon, as Mr. Henry took charge of Joseph. When the cooking was completed and the food packed in baskets, we trotted them down to Mrs. Walston's house. She welcomed us in, and Mrs. Henry, after putting the baskets on the counter, embraced her, then pulled away to allow Mrs. Walston to catch the hem of her apron where the tears would be hidden in the cloth.

I tarried behind them, wondering which room Herb was in. Mrs. Walston caught me straining my neck to see. "He's the second door on the right, as you go down the hallway."

The flush in my cheeks exposed my embarrassment that she had noticed, but I thanked her and moseyed around the corner with a light, cautious step until I reached his room. I saw him lying there, hair ruffled like a six-year-old, eyes closed and hands clasped on his stomach.

I turned to leave, not willing to disturb him, when a racking cough woke him. "Lydia?" he spoke. He shuffled around in bed and straightened his pillows.

I looked back over my shoulder and returned to his beside. "Hi, Herb." My words came out in a whisper, and I fidgeted with a small posey of wild flowers, which I held behind my back. "I heard you were sick and brought you some flowers."

A spark of life gleamed in his eyes as I laid them on a side table. "Maybe your mama would have a jar to put them in," I said. He continued to cough and tried to speak, so I interjected, "Don't talk. You're going to get better real soon. The doctor's on his way to see you. If you'd like, I can come and read to you on the weekends, providing your mama don't mind."

I don't know if he heard me, because his eyes closed again, and I slipped out of his room, carrying with me a sadness in my heart. It brought me back to my little sister who had, years ago, died from pneumonia. I prayed really hard that night for him. It was another two weeks after the doctor had come, and more meals dropped off at the front door, that I heard he was up and walking a bit. He never summoned me to read to him, and I never mentioned it again.

I lived with the Mr. and Mrs. Henry until Joseph started school. By this time, Callie had moved back and married James. They set up housekeeping in a farmhouse just around the bend from Mama. A block of trees hindered the view, but you could hear the goings on, which were none too pleasant at times. Mama had been faithful to come and visit with me over the years, usually bringing one or two of her young'uns so I could get to know them. With permission from Mrs. Henry, I arranged the times so Joseph could play with them.

Rachel and Hazel still lived with Mama and Ben, but they now had an engagement of work in town which kept them busy. And they had found boys who were courting them with intent to marry, in spite of their papa. We still met up at church on Sundays and hung out after church, usually where a seam in the mountain rock ran a stream of water down to a small pool, and we dangled our feet in the icy water, talking the afternoon away. That's where all the kids hung out. Including Herb. We remained friendly since his illness, sometimes finding him sitting next to me, picking at me in a teasing way. But we were too young to be attached to each other, and too busy trying to make a living for any courting.

My family was aware of my need for a job. Rachel was the one who, mid-week, had walked to the Henry house, presenting me with a form to fill out. "I'll come back tomorrow for it, and don't forget to have the Henrys write you a letter of character," she said, and I assured her I would. "You'll have a job, Lydia. Maybe next week."

Her confidence and enthusiasm were steeped like strong coffee. Soon, I had no place to live. Callie, however, sent word for me to come visit her and James. I arrived on their doorstep that Saturday afternoon and she sat me down in her kitchen with a dish of her blackberry cobbler and a scoop of homemade ice cream, which James had hand-churned that morning. She was a no-nonsense type of person and got right down to business.

"Lydia, James and I want you to come and live with us." She wouldn't even allow me a twinge of refusal. "You come whenever they can spare you. It'll probably be the day before Joseph starts school. Have your bags packed, and we'll be expecting you."

Once Callie had made a decision, there was no changing her mind. I simply nodded in agreement and showed up at their house, bags in hand, after a last reminiscence in the room where I slept, an embrace to Mrs. Polly, a last kiss to Joseph, and a handshake offered to Mr. Henry. He declined the courtesy, his voice trembling as he smothered my ear to his chest. Unable to speak, he swallowed hard. I could feel and hear it, like a pebble thrown in a deep hole, and the sound it makes when it hits the bottom. Then, he released me and pulled out his pocket kerchief, dabbing at his eyes.

"I'll be back to see you, Mr. Henry," I said. "I'll never forget you."

The poem I had written the week before was posted in an envelope and left on my nightstand for them to find after I was gone.

Oh, Sadness flee from me, and let me see, Where joy therein lies.
Come, Joy, and fill my heart and my desires, Within the tree of life.
Lydia

James and Callie were sitting on the porch when I arrived. Sweet lemonade and an extra glass sat on the small table, waiting for me. James, being ten, maybe twelve years older than Callie, could not fit in my mind of a likeness being a brother, or a Papa. I would probably say he was a combination of both. Nevertheless, he was a pleasure to be around. A harsh word or deed did not dwell in his body. He was the opposite of what I had often heard—that a preacher's son was wilder than a coon dog after his prey. Instead, he was a man devoted to his God first, then his Mama and Papa. Guess that made him a good husband to Callie, and a good friend to me.

I started work on a Monday at the Big Jack Company, sewing shapes from fabric into wearables, like overalls and dungarees. We started work at five in the morning, 'cause the heat fired up by midday. The workers called it a sweat factory, which was true, but I was just happy to have work, so I tried to ignore the moist stickiness that formed in a droplet and rolled aimlessly down my back.

Seemed like the longer people worked there, the more complaints festered in them. I didn't want to risk being fired, so I kept my opinions to myself. The rooms were large and dusty, with rows of sewing machines, each one occupied, clattering above any attempt at conversation. Outside, women were standing in line, waiting and hoping for an empty one to come available. We had to make production, which meant sewing faster and producing as many pieces as we could. Almost every day, a shrill scream floated above the noise where someone had mistakenly placed a finger too close to the sewing needle and had the unfortunate misery of having someone to remove it. It was hard work. After their back was bent and twisted, a crick wrenched in the neck as well, and the pain ran all the way down your spine, numbing the other cheeks, which never saw sunlight or were cooled by fresh air, I began to see how the others, bound to this way of life, could easily complain.

Callie had also found new work at the hosiery mill, making stockings for women who could afford them. Since we worked in the same town now, and others in our community worked nearby, we shared a ride, paying the driver appropriately. On Fridays, though, James came to town, stopping at the market before toting us home. Occasionally Callie would bring me a pair of "irregulars," she called them, though I never found a slight in any of them. Slipping those nylons over my toes and pulling them up my legs, careful to get the back seam straight, felt like a glaze of cool water poured over me. Callie brought cotton gloves home so we wouldn't nick them and taught me the art of the slow walk upward, attaching each one to the garter that would hold them up. We only wore them on Sundays to the church meeting, and without doubt, I was feeling prissy the first time I wore them. Maybe a little too much, because Callie caught my eye eventually, with a stare that would shake the bones of a skeleton.

Hilda became my best friend outside of my sisters. Our sewing machines faced each other, and though there were signs posted, "No Talking," we managed to get to know each other on our break, and lunch time. She liked to talk as much as I did, so there were never any lapses in conversation. In the afternoon, the giggles would set in, if we even for a moment looked across from each other. We were silly, and silly felt good. It wasn't long before we planned a shopping day together. Strolling down State Street, window shopping is mostly what we did, until on a particular Saturday, she spotted a garment of which she had a yearning for.

"Oh, it's beautiful Lydia, and I will get a lot of wear out of it," Hilda said. She apparently was trying to reassure herself. "I bet there's one in the store that you would like as well."

My lips pursed together. "I don't know, Hilda, if I can afford one."

But she persisted that we simply try them on. I felt no harm in that suggestion, at the time. We asked the proprietor if he would mind taking it out of the window, of which he was most willing to oblige. "It looks so good on you," I told her. The brownish red fur hugged her tiny frame like a package wrapped for Christmas, and it cast light on her long pile of curly, auburn hair. It was made for her.

"Maybe there's another," she said. But I shook my head, unwilling to budge, until her eyes shown past me in surprise, grabbing my arm and turning me.

The proprietor, walking from storage, carried the most fetching coat I had ever seen. He slipped my arms into the sleeves, the black fur warming and soothing like a mellow fire and tranquil water. And with the coat, he said, comes a matching fur hat and hand muff. I yielded to the moment, delighting in the luxury, before I forced myself to remove the coat.

"I couldn't possibly," I said.

"And how about you, young lady?" He drew his attention to Hilda.

She looked at the price tag, shaking her head. "As much as I would love to have it, it's unaffordable." She, too, removed her coat, and shrugged. Wistfully, we thanked him, reaching the door, before he called out to us.

"I have layaway, ladies. A dollar down and a dollar a week until it's paid for."

Our mouths gaped in disbelief, and we shrieked with delight, pulling out our first dollar from our purse. It became a ritual each week, when the whistle sounded and we leapt from our chairs, trotting down to the fashion store. A year later, our treasure was coddled around us, and our friendship was sewn tightly like the seams we stitched together.

The knack of living settled into a normalcy, of such. A routine of working, worshipping. and gardening for the winter. Rachel and Hazel often visited on weekends, tagging along with them their boyfriends. I liked Hazel's friend, Bobby Edens. He had a nature of warmth and friendliness, making everyone around him at ease. The love they had for each other was evident, in the manner of their flirtations. He was tall and slender like her, sporting the same kind of thick, curly brown hair that proved untamed. I would imagine their children would be of the same circumstance as theirs. He held a free laugh and spirit, which filled the rest of us with hearty laughter. She was now sporting a promise ring on her left hand, simple in design, as she wanted.

Rachel, though, brought home Johnny Atkins. The same boy she had noticed in school. But now, he was a man who liked to flip a stubby cigarette with one finger and crush the light out of it with the tip of his boot, like he was settling an argument with his fists. Short and stocky with brooding dark eyes sat deep, he held onto grudges and resentments. I couldn't understand what Rachel saw in him, except that he was what they called a "charmer," devoting all his attention to her. She had lost her reasoning and had fallen into his grasp. It was not I who would snuff out the new light in her eyes. Because she, too, sported a promise ring. Though made of twine, she showed no concern.

"I wanted to wait until we get married before I got a real ring," she said, trying to convince us. Putting an arm around her, he shook her like he was jostling with an old school buddy.

"Yep, she insisted on that, or I would have gotten her the biggest diamond ring you've ever seen."

Strange, how I remember James's old hall clock struck at that moment, and thought back to Peter in the Bible, when the crow sounded. But Callie and I kept a frozen smile on our face, not taking our eyes off of him, for fear of Rachel reading us like a page in a book.

It was the ever-presence of mind, Callie, who announced the evening was finished. "Y'all know it's late, and we have jobs we need to keep, so ske-daddle out of here right now."

There was no room for discussion, and we all said our quick goodbyes before they were shooed out the front door. It was when they were out of earshot that Callie said, "She'll not marry that man. I'm going to have a good sitting down talk with her on Sunday."

But Saturday came before Sunday, and she married him by elopement. Callie had no say so. I caught her on the back porch, Sunday, after the sun went down, sitting on the stoop and crying the silent tears that no one is supposed to be aware of. I sat down beside her, me now the strong one, and she, the one who showed no pain, crumbled in my arms. I just let her cry, saying nothing, because if I did the spell would be broken and she would retreat, hiding her hurt again, afraid to show weakness.

When she had finished her cry, she simply got up and left me there, as though nothing had happened. That moment was never mentioned again, but it was a memory I carried with me all my life of the time I could be there for her.

It was Easter Sunday, as I recall, when I started back to church. A nasty cold had kept me home for several weeks. I woke up that morning with the sun streaming through the window, warming my face as though it were summer already. I was excited that Mama was bringing the young'uns to church and to Callie's thereafter. Callie, James, and I gathered the eggs from the hen house days ago, saving them to boil and color so we could hide them in the yard, only to sit and watch the smile on their faces and hear the shrill laughter from them of their discovery.

Although humbleness, meekness, and maintaining a lack of vanity was preached pretty near every Sunday, on Easter, every attending woman presented herself without remorse in hats of color, with netting wrapped and tucked in the hat. Occasionally, a sprig of plastic flowers was poked on the side. Chiffon gloves with tulle and lace, adorned their hands. Dresses, newly sewn or bought, saved for the special day, were worn with new stockings. Shoes, though scuffed and worn, were freshly polished and buffed. I was no exception. Mama had offered to make me a fresh dress, but her pile of requests from the children were more than she could manage, and I wanted her to have time to sew a new dress of her own. One bitter cold day, during my lunch time, I walked to the fabric store and purchased material, a pale green and yellow, Mama's favorite colors. Within the fabric, tiny flowers lay like a meadow in full bloom.

There was a sale bin near the checkout, with assortments of matching lace that she could add to the hat, already in her wardrobe. She was thrilled when I gave it to her, and when she stitched the last piece, it fit her perfectly. She stepped a little prouder and smiled for a moment, escaping the reality of her life. James picked her and the children up, and all of us squeezed into his car, careful not to put a wrinkle in our Easter best.

It had become the one day of the year where people who ordinarily were absent arrived without notice or excuse from the previous Easter. Our Sunday school teacher promised us that she would dismiss us early so that we could secure a pew for our family, knowing they would be squeezed with once-a-year backsliders, trying to claim our self-designated seat for their own. She was of the same mind as well. James liked to sit halfway back, which was fine with me. Callie, Mama, and I sat with a child between us to avoid any disturbances that might draw the ire of the preacher man. People began to gather in, filling the sanctuary, the buzz of voices excited for the promises of spring, visit from relatives come from afar, and the reminder of the main purpose of the day.

I, too, was caught up in the pleasantries, chatting and laughing to the nearest people beside me. It was the feeling of familiarity that passed in the aisle which sought my attention, as he, who commonly sat in the balcony, far away from the preacher's pounding, embraced his mother, Rosa, who always sat with her sister on the second row from the front. It was his way of letting her know he had not skipped out on this particular day. Some time had passed since we had seen each other. He was fortunate to continue his schooling, and attached himself to upper school friends, and even had a part-time job sweeping floors at the mill. He had grown at least two more inches, making him about six feet tall. Somehow, he had acquired a suit, dark blue, plain with no adornment, and a long tie, knitted with brown thread. His frame remained lanky, but no bit of slouch sat down on his shoulders. He stood confident. I couldn't keep my eyes off of him, and when he left his mama and started back to his hiding place, he saw me. It was so odd of him and out of character that he stared at me. I quickly turned my head away, pretending I hadn't noticed. I felt his presence and the slow in his pace as he passed me, his eyes boring into the back of my head.

Not only was it Resurrection Day for our Lord, but also a revival and renewal for the women after the misery of winter, and maybe even going as far to say a little sin of defiance from being ignored for the work they had done in the church, without any action of expressing appreciation. Now, the preacher had no recourse, but to acknowledge the ladies in their finery from the pulpit.

"Why, y'all lookin' mighty fine today," he said.

I always thought he was hoping for an invite to partake of homemade goodies in the following weeks upon his visitation. By the size of the protrusion over his belt, I would expect he had never turned down even one.

When the kids start squirming and whining in hunger, and when the men's stomachs growled for the fried chicken waiting for them back home, that's when the preacher draws out his last chastisement to the congregation, and the choir sings "Just As I Am" until someone comes forward, confessing their sin. Luckily, a boy of about ten years of age had witnessed this expectation many times before, coming forward to meet the preacher, before the first stanza was finished. He lickety split it out of there, as soon as he confessed that he was sorry for aiming his sling shot at a rabbit he intended to kill. Now, we all knew a rabbit had been on near everyone's table at one time or another. The preacher was satisfied and praised the boy for being so honest, before he dismissed us.

Everyone tried to stifle the long sigh we held inside, but we soon returned to the fellowship of each other, shaking hands and offering well wishes. I couldn't help but glance up to the balcony. Herb was still there, watching me as though I had sprung up like a flower he had never noticed. Then a smile crept over his face, warm and inviting. I returned the gesture until Callie called me by name.

Churchgoers never left the church yard without lingering and sharing stories of births and deaths, and growth of their children. Today was no exception, renewing acquaintances from relatives and friends who had come from long distances. I had not noticed his approach, nor had my sisters fore-warned me, when I sensed him standing beside me.

"Hello, Lydia," he said. He appeared noticeably uncomfortable. But I was glad he was near enough that I could smell the after shave, which caused me to breathe deeper.

"Hi, Herb. It's good to see you."

He spoke to the rest of my family, sharing the trivial talk that unbridles the conversation, until the real point is taken.

"May I speak to you a moment?" he asked.

Without a glance toward my family, and the possible implication of a snicker from my sisters, I directed the whole of myself to him. "Of course," I replied, and he guided me to a quiet space, underneath the broadening old tree where others before me had leaned against, pondering the boy who was pursing them, a blush of awkwardness on their face as I felt on mine.

"You sure do look pretty today, Lydia." He tinkered with the change in his pockets.

"Why, thank you, Herb." The compliment left me with a skip in my heart.

"Haven't seen you around lately," he continued.

"No. I've been sick. And of course, working a lot of overtime. Then, Mama brings the kids down to Callie's sometimes on Saturday."

He now rearranged the pebbles on the ground with the tip of his shoe. I had forgotten how shy he was. "Lydia, I-I was wondering if you'd like to go with me up to the springs today. You could bring Rachel and Hazel if you want."

Years ago, I had dreamed of this day and imagined what it would feel like to kiss him, but my heart began to race, and a fit of nerves came over me. "I-I can't today. Family day."

He nodded his head and said, "I understand."

Then, he turned and started to walk away, when I found my voice again. I called after him, "I can go next Sunday, if you like."

That broad smile flashed across his face again, and his eyes widened like a door opening from a dark room, where a candle sat lit on a table. "I would like that," he said.

Herb and I started courtin' regularly after that day, and I was giddy with his attention.

Even Herb could not remove the great heartache when I thought of Mama, especially as I lay in bed after the lights were silenced and blinded me to the night. Her cries and wails could be heard as we sat about the porch in the late afternoon. Though, as Callie reminded me, we were helpless with her entrapment, it did not ease my pent-up anger.

It was on a particularly sultry day, the air thick with humidity, that I was sitting on the porch and heard her agony again. I could no longer tolerate her misery and, yielding a kitchen knife, started up the road, blind with fury.

A scream came, calling James from the barn, and a mixture of voices, both man and woman, commanded me breathlessly, "Stop, Lydia!"

I stopped, waiting for them.

"You can't go. You can't ruin your life, too," Callie said.

I turned on my heel. "He's going to kill her," I sobbed.

There was no comfort they could provide for me, but I fell into their arms, my face wrought with tears, confessing my plea to God that day: "Either take him, or take me."

Lillian

It was an ordinary Sunday afternoon, the sweltering sun now lowering to a whisper, announcing the end of the day. Twilight began its trek, which usually offered a respite to the heat that leached itself to brow and clothing. But not tonight. And of no importance to Ben. He had filled his day with his usual frivolities, leaving early that morning wearing the pressed suit Lillian had ironed for him. The same day Lillian and the children dressed for church. No tip of his hat, wave of his hand, or backward glance he gave them, but instead, he pursed his lips to a whistle and gaily stepped away with anticipation. It was a reoccurrence every Lord's morning. Lillian didn't know of his exact destination. Only what she was told. Relatives, he had said. But she and their children were never asked to join him. And that was of no importance to Lillian.

Sundays were like a breath of fresh air and a blessing of worship for her. She loved to sing the old hymns and ran her fingers over the page as she sang, like a blind person reading Braille. But it was the women's Sunday school class where she chatted with farm women like herself, whose weathered and stained hands lay confined in knitted gloves, the colors of threads woven into design, giving the ladies a sense of elegance for a few hours. They sat huddled in the tiny room just off the sanctuary before the teacher began, chattering like magpies. And in the fall, after the harvest, they compared the quantity of their bounty. A word thrown about, for no God-loving Christian woman would "brag" about the number of jars they had canned. Beans, both green and brown, beets now treading in crimson water, and plastic pickles, of which Lillian refused to share her secret with their transparency and sweetness. She was not alone in her reluctance. Each woman would "take it to the grave," as they often proclaimed, rather than give up their treasured ingredients. Fall had not arrived yet. Instead, the heat of summer still hung in the air, and the ladies passed a fan to each other, exchanging the stale air from one side of the room to the other.

The women had been warm and welcoming to Lillian, although they hid their pity like veils shading eyes on a funeral hat. Ben, with his hand still strong and belt nimble, still thrashed her, when his ill temper took hold of his soul. It was his heavy hand to her face, which left her hidden on certain days of worship, rather than face the parishioners. Instead, she shuffled the children off to their friends, who were waiting their presence.

On those Sundays, her solitary retreat took her to where she could never be, to other people's stories of romance and history, as she languished over each book, her eyes occasionally trailing beyond the windowpane in melancholy. Absentmindedly, she brushed silver wisps of hair from her face with acceptance of her approaching age, and the fate of her life. Small comforts she had found over the years, and memories of the one she had loved. They were the moments where Ben had no control over her. When given the chance, she walked past the farmland, to a meadow, and laid down among the field of wildflowers. Hugh beside her. And they spoke to each other until her eyes opened, separating them from the fantasy of their existence.

Ben

Now, Ben returned from the long walk over three ridges where the woman was, who had no husband and was willing to take him in, if only for an afternoon. The dusty path clung to his shoes. He removed his coat to cool the reek from beneath his armpits and rolled up his sleeves. His steps slowed and his breathing became labored, trudging through the sea of humidity. He stopped for a moment and pulled out his handkerchief, already stained with traces of tobacco, to wipe his brow. The far distant light of a lantern glowed from a window in his home, an assurance his journey was near an end. Maybe next Sunday, he would stay. But then again, probably not. He would ride ole Jack next time.

Still sporting a hollow-hearted grin, he failed to notice that twilight had been consumed by a gathering of dark, rolling clouds. A flicker of lightning renewed his attention. He stopped and wiped the sweat from his brow again, welcoming the oncoming shower. Then, without warning, a strong gust of wind roared through the trees, rustling leaves along the path, and the branches began to bow in submission. It drew in its breath again and blew out a violent cloak of rain, filled with pellets of hail. The fury was weighted with glass-like spears of lightening, which spread throughout the sky in clusters of tangled webs, and rumbles of savage thunder followed. Ben sought refuge under a nearby tree.

Impatient with his detainment, he cursed at the storm, "Get the hell out of here! I've had enough of your belly aching." He had no one else to shout to, not having ever believed in God.

The bolt of lightning struck swiftly and precisely to the tree under which he was standing. It tossed Ben to the ground, with dust and dirt mixed with rainwater, forming a dressing of mud around him. He spit the muck aside, wiping the remainder on his sleeve, and staggered to stand. As suddenly as the storm came, so did it leave, settling to a mere wisp of a breeze like the last swipe from a dragon's tail. He looked around, dazed, and tried to get his bearings.

It was then that a silhouette moved from behind a distant oak tree. Its approach began slowly, seamlessly, toward him. "Who's there?" he called out. But only silence loomed between them. Even the night owl held its voice. There hadn't been anything in Ben's life that he was afraid of, and there was no reason for his heart to begin to beat wildly, with a dizzying sense of anxiety.

Fear. A feeling he had never felt before snuck upon him and trapped him in its snare. The blurry silhouette continued, and Ben called out again, his voice a little weaker, "Who's there? Make yourself known."

Again, no utter of greeting was heard. Only a slow, calculated advance of determination could be felt. Ben stood, unable to move, as though the roots from the injured tree had seemed to creep around him, binding his feet. Trailing around his body and wrapping his arms to his sides, entrapped. The striking rhythm in his head pounded like a hammer to nail. Louder it came. His own heartbeat.

Then, the sky spit out its last brief flash of lightning, and the silhouette became human, though the night's shadows shielded the distinction of it being man or woman. Not more than ten feet in front of him, the clouds suddenly parted, and a full moon appeared, casting its light against the shadows. He heard the cock. A shotgun was raised and leveled at him. The holder of the gun removed their hood, wanting him to see and feel the same fear he had created. Ben was no longer afraid, because he saw.

"You!" Ben laughed, mockingly. A smug twitch began to curl his lips, and an icy calm came over him. "You always had a yellow streak down your back. You're not going to shoot me," he laughed.

Ben, unflinching, walked closer, and the holder of the gun began to back away, their arms suddenly heavy and trembling. "Get away from me," they called out.

Ben ignored the command, having put the intruder in their place, as he had done before. But the tortured soul, the holder of his life and death, spit out words like cinders, now enflamed in a furnace of fire.

"You destroyed our lives. You don't deserve to live a day longer!" the voice screamed.

"We'll see who lives another day," Ben vowed. And the man who possessed the devil's tongue and bathed in his likeness lunged forward, his face suddenly contorted, grasping for the barrel. They struggled, and both of them fell.

A gunshot echoed and sounded to the ears of those in nearby houses. Lillian jumped from her chair, grabbed her lantern, stood on the porch, and called out to her husband who was unusually late.

"Ben? Ben?"

But Ben laid on the ground in a mire of scat that was his own. The figure standing over him turned and ran, leaving a trail of footprints behind.

Callie

I had slept in a patch of restlessness, mulling over what Lydia had said earlier that evening. She never denied hating Papa.

"Why don't you hate him for what he did to you?" she exploded.

I had no answer for her, except that I, weary from years of sadness which crawled into my bed at night and haunted my dreams, gave way to my waking hours of which I had more control over putting Papa aside, and loving James.

Instead, I said, "Just pray for him."

Lydia screamed, "Pray for him? Why would I pray for him? We sit out on your porch nearly every night, and I have to listen to him whooping up on my mama!"

"There's nothing you can do, Lydia," we all repeatedly told her. Still, our hearts hurt for her. She went to bed this night with tears of rage still inside her like I had never seen before.

After I turned the lamplight off, James pulled me into his arms. "Callie, she'll be okay in the morning. Don't worry."

James always had a calming effect on me and eased my mind. I said, "I'll try, James. Good night."

During the time when drowsiness releases itself to the deep pockets where dreams are made, lightning flashes and rolls of thunder moved its way across our land. The sound of rain pouring down the bedroom window aroused my sleepy state, and I lay quietly, thinking that the cistern would be full, and the cows would have troughs of water to drink. Crops would flourish once again, and I would fully awaken to a yard of green grass waiting for bare toes to walk through. Then, the storm dwindled to the occasional patter of rain-drops seeping through cracks in the gutters, and inside, the house remained still until I heard a whimper coming from the back porch.

I grabbed my robe and slipped out of bed. James was sound asleep. The moonlight seeped through the windows, laying its footprint inside in a mimic to my own. I brushed the kitchen curtain aside. Lydia, her shoulders caved and head in her hands, sat on the porch step, soaking wet and in a lurch of tears. The sound of the door opening startled her, and she leapt from the steps and started to run.

"Lydia! Stop!" I called out.

She turned and ran back to me, crumpling in my arms. Her arms and clothing were covered in mud, as well as a smear on her face.

"Come," I said. No questions were asked until I had wiped down her shivering body and wrapped a blanket around her. "Do you want some hot cocoa?"

She simply shook her head. I sat down beside her and held both of her hands in mine, until the whimper that caught in her chest and the heartbeat that pulsed in her neck quietened.

"Did you go to your mama's house?" I asked.

Pulling her chin up to face me, she said, "I couldn't live another day wait-ing for the next time he would beat her. And I wanted to kill him." I put my finger to my lips and shushed her, afraid that James would wake. Lydia's voice softened to a whisper, and she continued, "But I turned around to come back and slipped on the hillside."

I didn't know whether to believe her or not.

That was the last words she said before there came a knock on the door. I looked out to find Lillian standing there, frantically pacing back and forth. When I opened the door and she tried to speak, words would not form. Lydia ran to her and comforted her, and we brought her to the kitchen table until she could catch her breath. She helped her hold the cup to her mouth, as Lillian gulped the water down, trying to find her voice.

"Ben! It's Ben!" Lillian said at last.

Without hesitation, I ran to our bedroom and shook James awake. "James, I need you. It's Papa. He's been hurt."

James staggered out of bed, pulled on the same clothes he had shed just a few hours before, and rushed to the kitchen. "Lillian, tell me what happened," James demanded.

"You have to come now! We can't wait! He's dying," she moaned.

"Dying!?" I interrupted.

"Yes," Lilian said. "I think he's been shot."

The words lay in my mind, jumbled into nonsense. "Shot? Where is he?" I pleaded.

"In the middle of the road, not far from our house. I was waiting for him to come home, and I heard a gun go off." Lillian stopped a moment to catch her breath. "So I ran and found him lying on the ground. He just groans. Can't get a clear word from him. It was right after the storm hit."

Throwing a searing glance at Lydia, I found her eyes downcast, afraid to look at me, knowing I would later question the truth of her whereabouts. "I'll get my coat. Lydia! You stay here!"

I never gave her a chance to look up before I bolted to throw some clothes on. James started the car, and Lillian and I climbed in beside him as we drove into the night where Papa lay past three bends in the road from our house.

"There," Lillian called out, pointing to him as we turned the corner. Papa laid still.

The headlights cast a dim light on his body. He was sprawled face-first into the mud. James went over to him and bent down, turning him to his back. His arms flopped over, limp like a rag doll. James laid his hand on his chest. Then, he stood up, his gaze past the headlights to Lillian and me waiting in the car. His face was somber, shaking his head. I burst into tears. Lillian did too.

Papa was dead.

"Please take me home now," Lillian insisted. A case of fidgetiness came over her, which was most unlike her character. Her tears had dried quickly, and her jaw set. The children might wake, she had insisted. That seemed like an excuse, because the older children were responsible for the younger ones mostly. I hadn't noticed until now that fresh bruises and scratch marks were on her hands and arms. But country women were often covered with scratches and scars from working outside. In passing thought, I wondered where Papa's gun was stored and if it was still there, in his house. And if the barrel was still warm.

The car had hardly stopped before she jumped out and ran, not asking nary a question as to how Papa was going to be taken care of.

James took me back to our home, my head filled with a confusion of questions. What lay ahead for me, I didn't know. I had to confront Lydia. Find out the truth. If she would tell me.

James cleared my head for a moment. "Callie, I'm going to find a cover for him at the barn until I can get into town and get the coroner out here. I'll wake the undertaker too. I've got to take care of this before daylight." As an afterthought, he spoke softly, "I'm going to have to bring the constable out as well."

I nodded, unable to choke down the worry and pain that numbed me. My head began to throb as I watched him drive away. It was when a shadow passed by an upper bedroom window that I noticed Lydia had retired to her room. I would not allow her to crawl quietly into her bed tonight. Yet, a faintness of exhaustion, both of the mind and the heart, pulled me down, and I sat on the same stoop where I had found her in her misery.

Now, stars shown, dancing within the midnight sky, far away from the full moon. And a gentle breeze blew in, cooling my face. I succumbed to the darkness and laid my head down on the hard slats of wood that formed the porch, too weary to approach Lydia. My eyes became heavy, and I felt myself falling into that bed of relief.

It was the jolt of noise coming from the woodshed that brought me to my feet. Probably our new stray cat, of which we had not yet named, who enjoyed the chase of a varmint, sometimes with success, and sometimes leaving the remains of an uneaten carcass. It was a chore I could not face in the morning. Broom and dustpan in hand, lamplight in the other, I opened the door and caught a shadow of movement behind stacks of wood, far larger than the frame of a small animal. I steadied myself in the doorway, ready to run, when I noticed a shotgun leaning on a close stack. The smell of fresh gun powder still lingered. The weapon was not one of James's.

I grabbed it and aimed it, not knowing if a shell had been reloaded after they shot Papa.

"Who's there?" I shouted. No one spoke. More forcibly, I demanded, "Who's there?"

And out of the shadows rose a figure, which caused time to be stilled, and memories returned of buried heartache. And yet, now he stood before me, fearful and defeated, his head hung low, shoulders limp in despair. I lay the gun aside and rushed to him, my arms smothering him. Both of us cried for each other. Baxter had come home.

My only thought was to hold my brother, whom I had not seen or heard from since he was forced to leave on that fateful day, from Papa's grasp. We held tight and hugged longer until I wanted to see his face. Aged beyond his years, his deep brown eyes held a cavern of sorrows.

He dropped his arms from around me and stepped back, pulling at his hair. "God forgive me! I killed him!"

I staggered backwards, catching myself before I fell.

"Callie, I'm sorry. No! I'm not sorry he's dead. I'm just sorry I'm the one who had to do it."

The spin in my head and the smell of gunpowder returned. Papa had put painful scars in many of our hearts. But killing him! I couldn't condone that. Yet, there was no thought of mine to turn Baxter in. I would not be responsible for his suffering in a jail for the rest of his life.

"You have to leave now!" I said. "Does anyone know you're here?"

He shook his head, no.

"Stay here," I said. "I'm going to fix you some food and get you some dry clothes before you get along on your way." I turned to walk away and stopped.

He started to cry again, and I went back to him, holding him for a moment. Then I ran to the house, looking up to Lydia's bedroom. She had turned out the light. Both of us were grateful that a confrontation had been postponed.

After wrapping up the baked bread I had made the day before, slicing off a slab of ham and gathering two hard boiled eggs from the icebox, I pumped a canning jar of water from the cistern and ravaged through James's old clothes to find some he wouldn't miss. It didn't fall on my shoulders, one iota of guilt, that I was helping a killer escape. He wasn't a killer in my eyes. He was the brother who had sacrificed himself for me.

"Where do you live?" I asked when I returned.

He slid his fingers over the rim of his hat. "I live in Ohio. I have a wife who's good to me, and a child on the way. I told her I was going to visit family before the baby was born."

"You were never here," I said, stopping him. And I slipped a pouch of money in his hand and bid him God's speed, knowing it would be years before we saw each other again.

It was before daybreak that James came home, his sap of strength laid on him like felled trees covering the earth. Unable to sleep, I made a fresh pot of coffee, and we sat at the table, me waiting for him to talk. Beneath his eyes were crescents of shadows from his long, sleepless night.

"Callie, I've never seen anything like it. The coroner and the constable hadn't either. They were looking for blood that would have come from a gun. But there was none to be found. It appeared to them that he had been the target of a lightning strike and suffered a stroke in the end. There was no evidence of harm that someone would have caused. But what was confusing to them was the footprints near him, encircling Ben, and then trailing away. Maybe, they said, someone walked by after the fact and was scared to report his circumstances."

Fortunately, I had stood and walked to the sink with my back to him, washing my coffee cup, so he didn't see the relief in my face.

"Nevertheless, the undertaker took his body, and everything is settled," James finished.

Baxter had not killed Papa. I would write to him later and mail him the obituary, and a copy of the death certificate, showing the true nature of Papa's death.

James went off to bed. A few hours of sleep would be enough to get him through the day until night came again. It was when I sat and thought about the enormity of the tragedy which had occurred that I remembered Baxter's gun that I left in the woodshed. Still in my nightgown, I slipped it under my garment and walked to the outhouse.

I dropped it in a deep pool of stink where it belonged.

Lydia

He was dead! I shed no tears!

The undertaker brought him to the house, as was the custom. But I didn't go. I couldn't. Not even for Mama. Callie went, and a few of his relatives came. But no one else.

They all knew who he was, but no one ever stood up to him. No one in our small community. People minded their own business. We were probably not the only ones who suffered. There must have been others.

He was buried on a Tuesday, and I moved back in with Mama the next day. At nighttime, his presence lingered for a while. But eventually, the house became ours. And laughter returned, bringing with it a joy which we embraced.

A year later, I married Herb and followed him when he joined the service. Mama got a job working in the school cafeteria. I had never seen her so happy. And I was grateful.

Patricia,
Lydia's Daughter

1981

I gripped the steering wheel and drove faster down the country road. The same way Mama did when I was a child. The dip and lift would take my breath away, and we'd laugh, "Go back. Do it again."

Every time I came to visit, it still gave me a thrill. Now, I rolled down the window, drinking in the fragrant honeysuckle that clung to the fences. They were blooming, and the bees would be darting around the flowers gathering their meal. I stopped alongside the road and plucked a flower off the vine, pulling out the stem and tasting the goodness, as I had done when I was a child.

Mama was waiting for me on the porch in her favorite chair, as she had done so many times before. I honked and waved to her, pulling into the driveway. Struggling to stand, the feebleness now gripped her. We embraced warmly and kissed each other's cheek before we sat down.

"How are you doing, Mama?" I asked.

"Oh, as good as could be expected," was her typical reply. "Let me get us some lemonade," she continued.

I patted her hand. "I'll get us some. Do you have sweets?"

She grinned and nodded, us both knowing how she loved a sweet of most any kind.

"I'll have a little oatmeal pie, if you don't mind. Get one for yourself, too!" she shouted as I reached the kitchen.

We sat there, rocking and talking and nibbling on treats until the afternoon hours were wiled away. We laughed and snickered about old stories that had been retold many times. She knew it was late and I had to go. But it was then that she laid her hand, now spotted with age, upon mine.

"Can you stay just a little longer?" she asked.

"Of course," I told her. I took her hand then and held it.

"I have wanted to tell you before now, but I could never seem to let the words come out. It's time, and I want you to know." Her eyes brimmed with tears, and I slid my chair closer to her.

"I'm listening, Mama. Whenever you're ready."

She began, her voice hesitant and trembling.

"It's strange, the things a person remembers, when pain holds them in a vise and won't let go. I remember it was a day when no cloud could be found. I was ten years old. The sound of fresh laundry flapped on the line, and a light breeze lifted them, like sails on ships. I could smell bread, the kind of smell that closes your eyes, forcing you to take a deep breath, to take in more. I could see it in my mind. Just out of the oven, waiting for us, at the evening meal. It was a perfect day. The cornstalks were high above my head, and the field stretched out and beyond like a lazy old man in need of a nap. The silk tassels glistened in the sun, and a whiff of wind swept through them like a brush combing their hair. I knew our cellar would be full of canned corn and the remains would fetch good money at the market.

"It's strange the things a person doesn't remember, or doesn't want to remember, on their journey through life. Like where my sisters were that day. Was Mama cooking in the kitchen? Were the older boys gone for good? Thoughts that hang onto you like that day our dog Copper decided to run into the cornfield, chasing whatever was his pleasure, and I ran after him, fearful that he would tackle another copperhead and wouldn't be so fortunate. But he outran me, and I called out his name. He didn't come. I grew frantic that he was hurt and ran blindly, trying to find him. He was my friend. A friend you could trust.

"Somehow, I didn't notice that he was suddenly standing there, behind me. I felt his presence, turned, and gasped, stumbling. I tried to speak, but a stutter bit my tongue. 'I-I-I was looking for C-Copper.' I hoped he wouldn't hear my heart pounding and see the tremble in my knees. My head jerked from side to side, looking for Copper, my protector. Where's Copper? I couldn't see him. I'm alone. I could no longer feign my panic. The beating would be hard and swift, so I had to prepare myself to take the blows. Then, it would be over, and I could run, crying to Mama. Or maybe I could just run now and avoid punishment.

"So, I did! I turned to run, but within one step, his arm scooped me up, while the other hand clasped over my mouth before I could scream. My flailing arms and legs could reach no substance to fight back. As suddenly as he grabbed me, and as powerfully, he threw me to the ground in a bed of dust and hardened earth. I wondered, where's Copper? He could protect me. After all, he was the snake killer.

"Even the blackbirds fled that day. I saw them go. And there was a stillness, an absence of the air I breathed, an awareness of emotions that I had never felt before. Trapped! Terrified! And helpless! My heels dug into the dirt in a useless attempt to distance myself from him. But his booted foot clamped down on my stomach. He said, 'Don't move.' His steely, calm voice laid me frozen. Waiting. He knelt down, and I could smell the tobacco in his mouth and could see the brown spit on the corners of his lips. I closed my eyes and turned my head as though to ward off his presence. The grit and dirt on his hand gave me no buffering from the force that slammed across my face. 'Open your eyes, little girl, so you can see me.'

"Obediently, I opened my eyes to Papa, sobbing with tears that were wet and stinging, but never forgotten. He let loose of me for a second, and I turned on my hands and knees, crawling, clawing away from him, willing the dirt to cover me, hide me. My hands were numb to the shreds of skin and the trail of blood from my skinned knees. Then, his hand gripped my ankle, and he pulled me back over the blood and dirt, filling my mouth with a vile pungency that was suffocating me. He picked me up and threw me on my back. I felt consciousness fading. The smell of rancid, putrid sweat gave away to inescapable nausea.

"Someone was screaming. I realized it was my soul. Deep, deep inside, he had reached a part of me I didn't know existed. The pain. Oh, God! The pain! I can't bear the pain. I retched vomit of blood and dirt, then faded again into darkness. When I awakened, he bent down and whispered with an eerie calmness, 'I will throw your mother down the sinkhole if you say anything.' And he left.

"I don't know how long I lay there in the cornfield before trying to move, trying to live. I hear my name being called, and it's Mama. Panic sets in because I realize she must not see me in the cornfield. She'll know, and he'll kill her. I try to run. The pain stops me. I can't run. I can barely walk. I cling to one of the cornstalks, willing it to hold me up. Both the cornstalk and my legs fail me, and I fall to the ground, crying. My mind wants to die, but my soul urges me to live. I pray and run, clutching my stomach, stopping only to vomit again before I reach the barn.

"The hayloft had always been a happy place where my sisters and I played and hid among the hay bales. Now, it was my fort. A place where I could see if anyone was coming. I could burrow myself under the hay where he wouldn't find me. My mind felt numb and confused. I couldn't stay here. Mama would be worried about me. I climbed back down the ladder. Desperate to rid myself of the filth on my body, I plunged myself into the water trough. The place where the cow and the mule dipped their heads for a drink of cool water. I didn't care. Water wasn't enough.

"Our mule's grooming brush hung close by. I dipped it into the water and forced the bristles over my body. I tried to wash everything that just happened away. Bone-weary, I laid my head back on the rim of the trough. Slowly, I descended underneath the water, allowing life to flee. Deliberately and consciously, I prayed that it would be quick, knowing it could not be any more painful. But death would not take me. I sat up, coughing and sputtering, attempting to rid my lungs of the taste of blood, dirt, and water. I wiped the hair and water from my eyes and looked down to see Copper sitting at a distance, fearful of my anger for leaving me alone. I was angry. I took the grooming brush and hit the water over and over and over, daring him to come near me. He bolted, and I cried after him, begging and pleading for him to come back.

"Exhaustion gave way to sleep, and when I woke up, Copper was licking my hand. I grabbed him, hugged him, and cried. All was forgiven.

"I lied to my mother that day. I told her that I fell out of the barn and hit the water trough. That was why I was so bruised and wet. She believed me and comforted me. She scolded me a bit, too. And to her surprise, I accepted the scolding tears flowing down my cheeks until her arms held me tight. She said, 'I just don't want to lose you, Lydia. I love you, child. You are the light that keeps me happy.' I rested my head on her chest, and she rocked me back and forth until my sobs turned to whimpers and whimpers turned to silence. I had never lied to her before. It was mine and Copper's secret for the rest of my life."

Patricia

They were gone now. And I travelled the road one last time. Past the house where Mama lived. Past the porch where I took her in my arms that day, consoling her in her pain. Staying through the night. Holding her hand as she lay in a moaning sleep. Wanting to soothe the ache and the scar that had lain on her heart throughout her lifetime.

As I rested the car to a stop, at the top of the hill a farmhouse sat on a low knoll below, long deserted and bound for demolition the next day. It was Grandma Lillian's house. A pathway of weeds lay among the gravel, but I maneuvered past them, settling the car at the front door. It was as barren as the ghosts which kept it upright. I cast my eyes over the untilled land, now covered with ragweed. Briar patches were choked with wandering vines, their thorny stems bent in defeat. Crows and blackbirds, having eaten their fill of berries in the spring, left the scavengers to pick at the rest. The barn where I had played as a child had been dismantled and salvaged for other purposes. And the house that I had only known with pleasant recollection sat postured with splinters of stories which troubled me.

I walked to the edge of the lower field, where the giant holly tree towered and still stood strong, trying to mimic the nearest oak. Soon, red berries would appear, just as they would when family used to come and break branches to put on their mantles at Christmas. Beyond the tree lay a field where wild strawberries had grown. I squatted and searched under aged leaves, hoping to find one that had avoided both the heat of the sun and the wandering creature. But there were none. The season of bloom and fruit had passed. Grandma Lillian and I often sat on the porch stoop, eating from the same berry field, the plucked fruit floating in a pool of cream while we talked and laughed.

I shook the memory aside and walked to the front door, testing the knob. In an attempt to keep outsiders away, the door had been locked. It didn't deter me. I reached into my pocket and pulled out a skeleton key, which as any country person knows, will fit the keyhole of almost any farmhouse in the community. It turned, and I pushed the door open. A field mouse frantically skittered this way and that way in a state of confusion, seeing my presence.

We were both startled, but I managed to call out to him, "Don't worry. It's only me."

He paid no attention, having already found a hiding place through a well-established hole in the wall. I continued to talk to him. The sound of my voice gave me credence that I should be there. "You'll need to pack your bags, because your home is going to be gone tomorrow."

It sounded so final, and I regretted my sarcasm. "You're so silly, talking to such a creature like he's human," I scolded myself. Nevertheless, I put my nonsense aside and scanned the room.

Cobwebs of neglect were weaved in the corners of the ceiling. The floor beneath me creaked and groaned as I tiptoed over it. The broken seals around the window frames allowed the wind to whistle its mournful tune. The curtain was still hanging over the doorway to her bedroom. I pushed it away and walked into the room where Grandma had often sat, reading and sewing. Her bed had been in a far corner. Bible on the nightstand. Now all that remained were images in my mind.

I turned and walked up the steps, which led to the attic. Pushing the ceiling door open, another mouse on a mission ran straight away, perhaps to warn the others. As I looked around the dusty room, I remembered every piece of furniture which had been cast aside: a flour bin filled with tattered quilts, a highchair marked with teeth bites, and wood stains from past feedings.

One small window opened to a view of the mountain, and lying on the sill was a brick. Perhaps the one Mama had told me about. The one that had warmed her feet at night, now lying there with no one left to know of its purpose. I took it and put it in my pocket, easing back down the steps and into another room where a couch and chairs had resided, where the chatter of aunts, uncles, and cousins, and the cries of babies could be heard. I saw a bounty of food laid out on the table and children playing in the yard. I saw opened boxes with gifts inside, and ribbons and bows scattered all around at Christmas. The same at Easter, with colored eggs hidden in the grass, new bonnets on the girls, starched shirts, and scratchy bow ties for the boys. The sound of laughter. The stories of grown-ups telling tall tales. Things that we store in our mind's memory box, for safekeeping.

I turned the key, locked the door, and walked to the far hillside. The afternoon sun warmed my back as I sat, peering toward the homestead. A house which had harbored both good and evil. I closed my eyes, and my mind wrenched with the indecision of which I should choose to remember.

Suddenly, a flicker of movement touched my hair, presumably a misguided bee, in search of food. I swatted it away. But a voice touched my soul and whispered, *Remember them all…Tell the stories.*

I opened my eyes, and a kaleidoscope of butterflies surrounded me. Monarchs and swallowtails and skippers. Their presence was a mural of moving colors.

Then, they turned and flew away, leaving only three hovering near me. One came closer and sat briefly on my shoulder. I lifted my hand slowly, and it lit and lingered on my fingertips, raising its head to me, and I caught sight of her eyes. Blue as the heavens. The same blue eyes that held me as a baby, wiped my nose, and cleaned my bruised knees. The same eyes that danced and laughed with me throughout my life.

I spoke to her, "You are free now. One day, I will come to be with you."

She flew away, joining the others at their home, where immortal happiness and peace exist.

Ecclesiastes 3:3

…and a time to heal.

Epilogue

While the content of this book and the lives of these three amazing women may, at times, be difficult to read, putting words to paper knowing these events happened to three women I loved and in turn, loved me, was sometimes piercing.

However, their stories are much more than the pain, loss, and tragedy they experienced. It's about love, forgiveness, gratitude, resolution, and their faith.

Grandmother Lillian was one of the most kind, humble, and gentle women I have ever known. Her life was filled with God, the Bible, and Church. As I grew up, she lived "just over the hill," alone, in the only place I had ever known her to live. I was a frequent visitor and could savor the aroma of homemade apple pies made in her cast iron skillet and sample the rolls that everyone snatched up during holidays. When it was time to make butter, she stood in the kitchen and hand-churned the milk until yellow curdles were swooped up in her hand to form the customary ball. At the end of our day, she would drag in a large metal tub from the smokehouse, fill it with warm water, and prepare a soothing bath for me. As I grew older, she worked in the elementary school cafeteria, walking with contentment and pride, knowing she could support herself. At night, beside the dim light of her chair, she always had a book to read. She passed away at age 88, surrounded by her children and grandchildren.

Callie was like a second mother to me. She and her husband, Jim, lived just beyond my grandmother Lillian's house. Although kind and loving to me, she was fiercely independent, spoke her mind, and walked with her head held high and shoulders back. She worked in a hosiery mill and lived on a farm with Jim, who tended the fields and had a mail route. They had no children of their own but taught Sunday School for the youth, who were often treated to Jim's hand-churned ice cream at summer socials. There was no doubt she loved Jim, and he loved her. They had a long, contented marriage, and when he passed 22 years before her death at age 95, she never stopped missing him.

My mother, Lydia, was filled with love and affection. She was kind and generous, giving to others. Her faith propelled her forward. She laughed often, finding humor and joy in the presence of life. She married Herb, and they lived a quiet, happy life with my brother and me. She made the choice every day to relive the best moments from her past so that she could live her best life in the present. At the age of 93, she passed on, leaving her own legacy to benefit others.

Acknowledgments

My heartfelt love and appreciation go to my husband, Alan, who patiently listened as I read him the day's writings and in return, gave me boundless encouragement. He would ask me to carry my voice during the readings with the most pronounced drawl that a southern mountain woman could ever utter, hanging on every word. You made me feel like a seasoned writer, Alan. Thank you for staying long enough to hear the ending. I miss you, and I'm grateful for my life with you.

To my brother, Steve, with his persnickety persistence, who prodded and poked me along for years to "finish the story." How fortunate I am to have you for a brother. Thank you!

To my children, Bryan (Angel) and Dionne, who are my joy and give me acceptance, even when life's adventures took me on foreign mission trips and beyond their comfort zone. My life would be incomplete without you. I love you!

Sandy, thank you for holding me up when I fall. I could not have written the story without your support and guidance. Carol, you gave me courage to move forward, and our lives melded together. Julia, even though the miles between us are of a great distance, I feel your heart beside me. You are the three women who have mentored me and hung on for my next adventure. Your friendships have carried me through life's ups and downs, laughter and tears, and bonds of endearment. Little did we know where life would take us. You have been wonderfully unexpected, and it is your river of endless love and positivity that fills my heart with admiration for you.

To my grandchildren, Brett, Tyler, and Hannah; my nieces, Amanda, Lisa, and Teresa; and my nephew, Paul, who walked down memory lane with me. Thank you for your remembrances and input.

To my bonus family, Greg, Heather, Grant, Hannah, Haley, Seth, Rachel, Shan, Bob, Brayden, Halle, and Ethan. What a blessing you are to embrace me with your love. Thank you!

To Xavia, thank you for giving me shelter.

To Jane Hodge, who, during twelfth-grade English class and the dispensing of a term paper, laid on my desk a message which read, "You should write." I never forgot your words, and I finally did it! Thank you!

To Tara Sizemore, Draco Bailey, and Allison Chudina for putting each piece of this production in place and wrapping it up with a beautiful bow. Thank you!

Janie Jessee, thank you for taking a chance on this first-time author and seeing the vision I had for telling this story with the purpose of reaching out to survivors who may be encouraged to ride on the wings of their own butterfly and soar to a newly-enriched life.